BROUGHT TO HEEL

'Legs apart,' came the crisp command.

The splayed nude whimpered. *Crack*. Bostick spanked the upturned cheeks savagely, swiping her flattened palm dominantly down across their proffered swell. The spank elicited a shrill squeal of outrage from the writhing nude across the table.

'I said get your legs apart, bitch,' the spanker warned the spanked.

Her reddening cheeks wobbled as the thief sullenly obeyed, inching her thighs apart. 'Please don't –'

'Too late for that now.' Bostick snapped on a pair of rubber gloves and pulled the nude's cheeks apart.

By the same author:

THE ACADEMY
CONDUCT UNBECOMING
CANDY IN CAPTIVITY
SUSIE IN SERVITUDE
THE MISTRESS OF STERNWOOD GRANGE
TAKING PAINS TO PLEASE

BROUGHT TO HEEL

Arabella Knight

This book is a work of fiction.
In real life, make sure you practise safe sex.

First published in 2000 by
Nexus
Thames Wharf Studios
Rainville Road
London W6 9HA

www.nexus-books.co.uk

Typeset by TW Typesetting, Plymouth, Devon

Printed and bound by
Cox & Wyman Ltd, Reading, Berks

ISBN 0 352 33508 4

Contents

1	Hard Court	1
2	Sticky Fingers	24
3	Rough Shoot	47
4	Stocking Filler	71
5	The Mousetrap	96
6	*Sachertorte*	122
7	A Penalty to Pay	145
8	Night School	161
9	Party Line	183
10	Low Fidelity	204
11	Double Yellow	224

1

Hard Court

The young blonde rose up on to the toes of her white pumps. Her ponytail swished as she jerked her head back.

'Keep your head down,' he rasped, tightening his controlling grip at her wrists.

She staggered slightly, collapsing the swell of her pert buttocks into his groin. The short, pleated tennis skirt flared and rode up over her hips, exposing white-pantied cheeks to the firm length of his erection. He pressed his lean, athletic body into her lithe warmth. The blonde squealed as his stiff shaft raked her softness. Her pumps squeaked as she trod the polished gym floor, grinding her buttocks into his crotch.

Pinning her left hand down against her golden thigh, he grasped her right wrist and thrust the captive arm upwards.

'See? That is where your arm should be for the forearm smash. Elbow straight.'

In the deep mirror before them, the young blonde's brown eyes opened wide. She gazed into her own reflection, noting with a sudden surge of pride her full breasts bulging within the bondage of her tight T-shirt. Beneath its stretch of taut cotton, the dark nipples showed boldly, their alert peaks betraying her arousal. Once more, the ponytail swished enticingly.

He snapped at it with a flash of white teeth. He captured it and sucked hard at the fragrant blonde toque.

'Good. Next week,' the warm breath at her neck murmured, 'I will be teaching you how to improve your service.'

The blonde closed her brown eyes – but the image of his thighs straddling her bottom, which she had glimpsed in the glass, continued to burn brightly. His supple, golden-haired thighs, trapping and squeezing her soft buttocks as his hot shaft nuzzled her cleft. She thrilled to the controlling hands at her wrists – wrists now pinioned to her thighs. She blinked and swallowed silently. The restraining hands at her own were causing her panties to grow damp at her pussy.

Would he? The whisper in the locker room was that this was the moment when Gunter made his move. She jerked her rump back into the club's new German tennis coach. He growled softly, hammering his hard thighs into her in instant response.

Yes. He was making his move. The ponytailed blonde shivered expectantly. Gunter was young, fit and evenly muscled. *Vorsprung durch technik*, as the girls in the tennis club showers giggled. His eyes were ice blue. They had a piercing, pitiless glint. His mouth was constantly fixed in a cruel curve. And he was holding her now like a fox taking a hen – ruthlessly. Between the blonde's clamped thighs, her cotton panties grew heavy with the soak of her wet warmth.

Gunter lowered his face down between her shoulders and sniffed. His ice-blue eyes narrowed as his nostrils flared. He sniffed deeply, catching the sensual harmony of her orange water, her sweat and the feral whiff of her arousal.

'*Ja*,' he muttered savagely, tonguing her flesh. 'I must improve your service.' His English was impeccable, but the Teutonic vowels gave his voice an erotic charge. She shuddered, fleetingly remembering black-and-white B-movie fantasies: the flash of the monocle, the crack of the riding crop in a leather-gloved hand. The German officer interrogating the captured French resistance girl, before using her for his brutal pleasure.

His lips at the nape of her neck broke into her reverie. 'Your lesson is over now. Almost.'

Amazed at her own honest lust, she jerked her buttocks urgently.

2

'There is, perhaps, one thing I can do for you.'

Drawing her wrists together up over her head, he pinioned them single-handedly against the glass. She whimpered her willingness – a willingness he had already taken for granted – eager for the tennis coach to commence with the special tuition. Spreading her feet apart, he thumbed her cotton panties down, dragging them over the rounded swell of her peach-cheeks to a tight stretch between her upper thighs. He gazed down, savouring his handiwork and approving of the band of cotton supporting the gently wobbling buttocks. The blonde ponytail swished as she squirmed, anxious for her panties to go lower and reveal the wet plum of her pubis.

A ringing crack echoed around the training gym as his right hand, palm flattened, swept down across her right cheek; he spanked the defenceless globe fiercely. At the glass above her bowed head, her captive hands starfished in a reflex of sudden pain, her fingers splaying wide as she scrabbled at the slippery sheen.

After quelling her with a second spank, Gunter knuckled the blonde's sticky cleft dominantly. He hissed pleasurably as he sensed her sphincter shrivel in fear, then flower in eager anticipation. Slowly, deliberately, he worked his knuckled fist deeper between her passive cheeks, forcing the satin flesh-globes painfully apart. She wiggled her hips, then kissed his dominant hand with her hot anus. A third harsh crack broke the silence as he tamed her impatience with yet another harsh spank. The ponytail swished as she jerked in her pain. She bowed her head, mewing softly – not in protest but in pleasure.

Then he entered her. Swiftly and assuredly. First she felt his thumb-tip, then the teasing length of his probing index finger. Working his finger rhythmically, he gradually widened the tiny pouting crater of her anus until it opened like a rosebud. He slid the straightened finger in full length. Pumping slowly, dominantly, he easily mastered the resistance of her tightened muscles. Lubricating her with her own wetness, Gunter prepared the blonde for his shaft.

Guiding the glistening glans up against the inner curve of her spanked cheek, he lodged the tingling knout at her hole. The young blonde collapsed into the full-length mirror, crushing her nipples painfully into their own reflection and smearing the image of her contorted features with a sticky pink lipstick smudge. He entered her ruthlessly, up on tiptoe as he speared between her heavy cheeks, and pumped savagely. At the glass, her lips whispered silent obscenities, leaving pink lipstick arabesques which were instantly clouded by her hot, panting breath. One hand still pinning her wrists up above her head and the other hand spanking her punished cheek soundly, the German tennis coach thrust into his captive pupil furiously. Accustomed to fast play and a sudden finish, Gunter's arrogance was almost contemptuous.

The blonde shrieked and started to come, hammering her belly into the glass and squashing her bunched breasts painfully. He rode her with increasing fury, his muscled thighs taut and glistening. Then, with a dismissive grunt, he orgasmed. Withdrawing instantly, he squirted over her spanked cheeks, silvering their crimson with his hot seed.

Released from Gunter's cruel grip, the young blonde slid down across the surface of the deep mirror, both her pink lipstick and her wet slit signing her utter submission to him in ragged smears as she sank to her knees. His ice-blue eyes read her spidery confession in the glass. *Ja.* He nodded. The pupil had learned her lesson. Gunter wiped his wet cock in her blonde hair as, stretched tightly beneath the deliciously plump swell of her punished buttocks, her cotton panties caught the slow drip of his semen creaming from her cleft.

Gunter grinned, his parted lips revealing wolfish white teeth. As his hand stretched up for the cold tap in the shower and twisted it on, his teeth clenched and his grin become a snarl. *Ja.* So good, the ice-cold water that cleansed away his sweat and hers. Gunter took a shower after every sporting engagement. For the German, fastidious as he was vain, it was not a necessity but a ritual.

The freezing sluice raked his upturned face and firm, lean body, rinsing away the suds of his expensive pine gel from his nakedness. He spread his legs wide and, cupping his balls, offered them up to the pleasurable pain of the stinging shower.

It was good here at the English tennis club. Here, deep in moneyed Hampshire. The English had their little jokes at his expense – but Gunter was having the last laugh. A little under a mile away, there was excellent fly-fishing on a stretch of the River Test. In the car park of the exclusive tennis club, beneath the whispering beech trees, BMWs glinted alongside snub-nosed Audis. Gunter grinned again, taking pride in the sleek German machines occupying the asphalt.

Stepping out of the shower, he towelled himself vigorously, leaving the tiny golden hairs on his legs erect. *Ja.* It was good here at the club. Coaching the young women. And no men. No pale, flabby Englishmen to bother him. They were too busy in the City each day, and too tired at the weekends for anything but a drink too many in the private club bar. But their young, lonely wives . . . *Ja.* Gunter grinned.

Tossing his towel aside, he strode, naked, across to the small fridge by his locker. Opening it, he took out a fresh pair of blue boxer shorts and pulled them on. So good, the crisp, cold cotton at his aching balls. He fingered and snapped the elastic waistband pleasurably. Turning to his locker, he extracted a small golden trophy. The Challenge Cup. He had bought it for thirty marks in a Dresden flea market and had had his own name enscribed at the base. With an impressive CV and the deception of winning a Challenge Cup, he had been appointed tennis coach here at the club. The English were so trusting: with their jobs, with their young wives.

Returning to the small fridge, he selected a chilled Pilsner, snapped it open and filled the Challenge Cup. Sipping slowly, he savoured the bite of hops. When he'd finished off the golden cupful, he poured out another and scooped up his black leather appointment book. His finger turned the pages for the week ahead, his delicate touch as assured as when at a bra strap or inside the tightness of a nylon stocking-top.

Tuesday. Penelope at eleven. Yes. He would be having Penelope from eleven until twelve-fifteen. Her husband was in pharmaceuticals – frequently overseas. Gunter sipped his drink. Penelope, the neglected brunette, liked it down on all fours on the polished wooden floor of the gym. Always hot and eager for her tennis coach, she would start to strip straight away. Gunter would order her to redress, replacing her bra and panties. By the time he took his teeth to her, she was whimpering for him. Her breasts would tumble and bounce as he bit away her bra, and he took a dark delight in humiliating her by waiting until she was soaking wet before removing her panties, catching her spindling stickiness with his tongue-tip before bringing his hungry mouth to her hot slit.

Gunter closed his eyes. Penelope. Playing with her breasts as he took her furiously from behind. She loved that, she had whispered hoarsely the first time. Loved having her naked breasts pleasure-punished as he rode her. Almost as a concession, Gunter would reach around her captive nakedness and encircle her, cupping and squeezing their soft warmth – snarling as her thick nipples kissed his wet palms – before emptying himself inside her. As he came, pumping and squirting his sweet release, he would remember to ravish the bare bosom savagely. That is how Penelope loved it. As she came, with that haunting, stuttering cry of hers like a curlew in the rain, she would quickly gather his hands up to her mouth and kiss the palms that had been so brutal at her bosom.

Gunter finished off the lager and poured out another cupful. With a 330 cl bottle, he could fill his Challenge Cup nearly four times. It was a small trophy, but it had landed him a big prize. Tuesday. Penelope. He smoothed the page down with a firm fingertip. Squeezing her breasts as he took her, on all fours, brutally from behind. Gazing at his drink, he studied the beading of condensation. Like little pearls of his semen sparkling on her inner thighs. He thumbed the dull gold slowly as he flicked over the page.

Thursday. He tapped the page. Amanda. At four-thirty. She drove a black VW Passat. Gunter closed his eyes.

6

Amanda. A big-buttocked young beauty in her mid-twenties. More horsey than sporty – until word reached her of the special tuition on offer at the tennis club. He was in software, frequently selling in Frankfurt. Gunter grinned, relishing the irony. Amanda's husband sweating in some trade fair while Gunter sweated on his big-bottomed wife. With her husband away, Amanda was at a loose end. And always wet and willing. Amanda was receiving coaching to improve her forearm smash – Gunter was improving his. She adored being disciplined before making love. Demanded it, in that shy, eager whisper as she struggled out of her panties to bare her bottom for his cane. Gunter was happy to oblige. He liked ordering her around in their private corner of the secluded gym. Ordering her to bend over. *Ja.* Like the naughty schoolgirl. *Bend over and touch your toes.*

Discipline. She had brought the length of whippy yellow cane on her third visit – plucking it out of a bed of sweet peas after a sudden summer shower. Gunter had been able to smell the fresh earth. He kept it in his locker. It had a little white label tied to the tip on which she had scribbled 'For Amanda's naughty bottom'. Gunter remembered her trembling hand. He found the English a curious people. So correct – yet still eager for correction.

He finished his lager and slowly poured out another golden cupful. Bend over. Amanda would bubble at her slit but obey instantly. Gunter liked that. Prompt obedience. His twitching shaft would nod approvingly. Then he would flex the cane. He did this every Thursday, a little after four-thirty. At tea-time, as the English called the hour. Gripping the cane firmly, he would stand directly behind her bending, bare buttocks and trace the tip of the yellow cane up along the inside of her thighs until it paused, quivering, to tap-tap at her wet pubis. Sometimes her fearful fingers splayed across her cheeks protectively but Gunter flicked them away with the cane, baring her buttocks before visiting them with the pain of his cane. With her upturned bottom perfectly poised and presented for punishment, Gunter would silently tread the two and a half steps necessary to bring him into position. Raising the cane up, he would pause for a moment, inspecting and approving of the clenched cheeks dimpled by fleeting spasms of expectant fear and dread.

The cane made such a delicious swishing sound – like the fat tyres of an S-class Mercedes cruising the autobahn in the rain. And Amanda's responsive hiss of exquisite agony was equally pleasing to his ear. After five slicing strokes across her broad, bulging buttocks, Gunter would pause to watch the thin, pink cane stripes deepen and darken into crimson weals. Amanda's fingers would be busy at her pussy, working her wet flesh-lips frantically as her bottom blazed. *Swish, slice.* Another couple of slow, deliberate strokes. Another pause. In the snatch of silence, Gunter strained to hear the soft, liquid lapping sounds of the whipped girl's wet fingers scrabbling in her warmth.

Teetering off balance, the punished nude often stumbled, buckling at her knees. Gunter's alert cane steadied and stilled her instantly, back into the punishment position for her remaining pain. Administering another four strokes briskly – four crisp cane kisses across her beautiful buttocks – Gunter would depress the whippy wood down at the nape of her neck, forcing her to kneel. Bringing the cane to her lips was their intimate signal: she would lick the bamboo feverishly then come, her moans melting into sweet groans. As her hips pounded into the polished wooden floor, and her striped cheeks writhed, Gunter gazed down at the outstretched nude, contemplating her as pain fuelled her pleasure. If she climaxed too quickly, remaining hungry for more, he would kneel and lash the proffered bottom until she squealed her second – then her third – orgasm.

Amanda. After six minutes, Gunter would rise up from his knees and stand, straddling her hot buttocks. By placing his rubber-soled pump neatly along the cleft between her cheeks, and treading firmly, he could coax another paroxysm from her tightly squeezed thighs. Then he would command her to slew around and kneel up before him – and accept his stiff length into her mouth.

Suck. His German accent was harsh. Almost as harsh as the imperious command. Still molten at her slit, Amanda worked her mouth busily to please her cruel chastiser. *Suck*. Wide-eyed and fearful of the raised cane – dreading the swipe across her outer thigh – the kneeling nude pleasured her punisher.

Gunter's throat tightened as he remembered – and anticipated – his sessions with Amanda. The young Englishwoman with the desire to be disciplined. The superbly buttocked, neglected *hausfrau* who bared her cheeks like a naughty schoolgirl for his cane. The naughty Amanda. The ice-cold lager from the Challenge Cup loosened his muscles as he swallowed. Gunter closed his eyes – just as Amanda closed hers when she swallowed.

His forefinger delicately flipped over the page of his diary. Then another page. Saturday. He traced the name of his next appointment. Susie. *Ja*. Susie at noon.

On Saturday morning he would rise, eat cold smoked meats with rye bread and then read the poet Pushkin until noon. Susie was so proud of her volley shots. And her breasts. They were so ripe, so pliant. She wore a sensible sports bra to control them in the stern embrace of strengthened cotton cups when leaping around out on the grass court. Inside, after her gruelling game, she would surrender her bare bosom to Gunter, her bra abandoned on the floor. He would crush her heavy breasts with his racket, bunching up the glistening orbs with the netted strings. They would bounce enticingly. Swinging the racket around to spank her, Gunter would propel her into the shower.

Emerging, pink and eager, Susie would skip across to him, her arms behind her back, her breasts proud and thrusting. Though naked, they did not remain unadorned. Gunter saw to that. He liked to take a pair of blue-and-white sweat bands and force them on to her breasts, fitting the soft, stretchy fabric to each swollen mound of warmth, leaving them bulging painfully and quite helpless before his gaze. He always forced Susie into wearing dark bronze tights. Through the dark sheen at her pubic mound, he

9

would thumb her matted coils. The poet Pushkin left Gunter slightly melancholy. He thumbed the pubic hair tenderly, as a vixen licks her blind cub.

Whimpering softly, Susie would become impatient. Gunter would order her to kneel, joining her down on the polished wooden floor and quickly guiding his fierce erection up between her gently bobbling breasts. Cupping and squeezing them dominantly, he would use the deep cleavage to cushion and comfort the length of his hot shaft. Rocking gently, Gunter would then pleasure himself at leisure within the warmth of her satin-soft flesh – coming violently, his spurting release splattering her neck, chin and left shoulder. Up on his feet almost instantly, Gunter would dry the wet snout of his cock in her hair. Susie would palm her breasts, working his semen into their shining, rubbery flesh.

A curt nod from the tennis coach would have Susie on her back, thighs wide, waiting for him. Crushing his chest into her wet, bulging breasts, and pinning her outstretched hands down into the floor, he would enter her. Wriggling beneath him, her slippery breasts maddening him, Susie would pantomime a pretence of coquettish defiance. Gunter mastered her easily, every Saturday, a little after noon, punishing her with brutally deep thrusts for her brief show of rebellion. Later, he would bury his mouth between her thighs, replacing the memory of his cold meat breakfast with the sweet salt of her juicy flesh. *Ja*. Susie. Slippery-breasted Susie. Every Saturday. At noon.

He was on his twelfth press-up and the trickle of stinging sweat forced him to close his eyes. Utterly naked, in the seclusion of his training gym, Gunter eased himself down, elbows angled. He pressed his sac gently on to the polished wooden floor, dragging his balls deliciously across its sheen. Straightening his arms abruptly, he powered his nakedness up. His thickening shaft nodded as it rose.

A soft sound broke the spell of the surrounding silence. Gunter opened his eyes and blinked away the stinging sweat that blinded him. Head bowed, he was amazed to see eight white toe-caps of four pairs of pumps breaking into the periphery of his circle of vision. Soft perfumes suffused the air – violets and damask roses, their understated elegance redolent of money, manners and middle age. His wilder, younger women sweetened their nakedness with more strident scents. Gunter's sixth sense signalled danger.

His sixth sense had not deceived him.

As if in response to a silent command, the right pump of each encircling pair rose up from the polished wood and swept towards his naked body, instantly prostrating him beneath their collective, pinioning tread. One at each trapped hand, one planted at the nape of his neck, the fourth crushing down the swell of his subjugated rump.

Gunter tried to twist his face to glimpse his tormentors, but each white pump was planted very firmly – the one at his neck the firmest of all.

'So,' the plummy tones of suburbia purred, 'we have heard that you fancy yourself as number one seed hereabouts, Gunter.'

The German relaxed. Nothing to fear, his arrogance assured him. Just a few more neglected wives seeking his special tuition. He grinned. Soon his little black appointment book would be full.

The voice spoke again. Gunter froze as he caught the darker note of menace. 'Number one seed. Or so our daughters-in-law have confessed.'

Gunter's mind raced, calculating his situation. These matrons had somehow discovered the truth of his special coaching sessions with their sons' wives. Suddenly, his heart weighed as heavy as a stone. Were they merely the advance guard? Would the door burst open, filling the gym with vengeful husbands? Angry Englishmen swinging baseball bats? No, Gunter thought. Not baseball bats. That would not be cricket. But he shrank at the thought of a cricket stump being rammed up his anus.

No. That was not how things were done in Hampshire. Gunter relaxed, letting his arrogance sweep away his fears. A quick grin revealed his white teeth. These women were here to demand more of the same. Straining, he was just able to glimpse into the mirror. Reflected in the glass, he saw his captors: four stern beauties immaculately attired for tennis. Voluptuous and powerfully thighed women. Like Jaguar Mark II saloons. Sleek and in mint condition. Beautifully upholstered. *Ja*. And plenty under the bonnet when the right pair of hands nursed them into top and opened them up. Gunter felt a surge of anticipation, certain in the knowledge that soon he would be going to relish taking them for a spin.

The rich, plummy voice broke into his reverie. 'Get him up against that mirror. I gather that he has become accustomed to using it in his sessions.'

Strong, capable hands clutched his hair, wrists – one slipped in between his thighs and captured his balls cruelly – and dragged him towards the full-length mirror. Kneeling before it, he squirmed as his erection was trapped against the cold surface of the glass. Glancing into his own reflection, Gunter saw his mouth pursed in its usual sardonic smile. Then he studied his captors more closely. Four cock-thickening specimens in the full flowering of their early forties. English roses in the high summer of their splendour, aching to be plucked. The pride of the Shires, ripely bosomed, heavily buttocked and superbly thighed. He half recognised them – not as grass court players but as club members who frequented the bar. *Ja*. He knew the type. Turning up for gin and tonics in trim vests, spotless pumps, and teasingly short pleated skirts: perched on the red velvet bar stools, their tanned thighs openly displayed. 'Welcome, ladies –' he started to announce.

'Silence,' a luscious-limbed brunette barked. 'Gag him, Jane. We don't want the other members to hear our Hun howl.'

Jane, a strawberry-blonde with eyes of wild honey, bent down over his kneeling figure to apply an efficient gag of sweat bands to his protesting mouth. Gunter caught the intoxicating perfume of her body lotion as her deft hands silenced him. He felt the full weight of her breasts against his nakedness as she checked – then further tightened – the gag. At the glass, his trapped shaft throbbed.

'Thank you, Jane. As I said, we don't want to disturb the other members when our Hun here starts to howl. Howl,' the stern brunette continued, answering the mute question framed by Gunter's widening eyes, 'during his punishment.'

They were here for punishment. His punishment, not their pleasure. Gunter swallowed and struggled to rise up on one knee. The brunette's pump shot out, the ribbed sole flattening his buttocks and splaying them painfully apart, pinning him into the glass.

'We don't play lawn tennis, Gunter. Not our game at all. All that grunting and sweating. Younger women seem to like it. We prefer to play hard court.'

An image of red clay flashed before Gunter's eyes. The court was in session. His punishers were encircling him. Would his bare bottom be as red after they had administered justice? As red, and as hot, as the sun-baked clay?

'We have already found you guilty. Our daughters-in-law confessed all – eventually. No,' the grim tones of the brunette continued, 'I'm afraid we are not here today to play. Our purpose is your punishment. Jane. He is all yours.'

The strawberry-blonde returned from Gunter's locker brandishing the bamboo cane reserved for Amanda's bare bottom. He shivered at the squeak of her approaching pumpsteps, and shivered again as, in the glass, he saw her swish the whippy wood.

'We have discovered all your little secrets, Gunter. Every last one,' the strawberry-blonde whispered, tapping his buttocks with her bamboo. 'How else would I know of the existence of this cane, hmm? Amanda is my son's wife. It was a painful interview, but she answered all my questions.'

Sensing his absolute doom, Gunter closed his eyes.

'Hold his arms out. Up above his head. Just like he holds Emily against the glass.'

Gunter remembered the ponytailed nude splayed against the mirror. Now, he realised, it was to be his turn. He struggled, but was overpowered; the hands that had

13

dragged him to the glass moments before now stretched his arms up against it.

'Hold him,' the strawberry-blonde commanded.

The controlling grip at his wrists tightened. Kneeling, his face pressed into its own frightened reflection, he waited bare-buttocked for the burning bamboo.

Like a July thunderstorm cloudbursting from the sky, the rain of pain lashed down, searing his defenceless cheeks with vicious strokes. Jane, biting her soft lower lip in an effort of concentration, plied the thin cane with cunning cruelty, frequently flexing her supple wrist to sweep the whippy wood upwards and inwards to stripe the lower curves of his rounded cheeks. Cursing into his gag, Gunter swallowed his screams.

The strawberry-blonde paused briefly. Once to pluck her damp vest from her breasts. Again, after seven more cutting strokes, to finger her panties from her hot cleft. The cane left his whipped cheeks ablaze and seething. The original pale ivory of his buttocks had now completely disappeared beneath an irregular pattern of red and purpling cane stripes.

Swiftly dropping down on to one knee directly behind her victim, Jane brought her face close to Gunter's bottom; he flinched as he felt her wet tongue flicker across the buttocks she had severely beaten. The gag at his mouth did not quite smother his scream as she sank her teeth into him as if he were an apple. She bit softly but painfully, tugging away a fleshfold between her white teeth. Then, without warning, she inserted the tip of the cane into his sticky sphincter. Clapping her palms around the bamboo, she rubbed her hands slowly, rolling it and inching it a heartbeat at a time into his tight warmth. Gunter squeezed his thighs together and came, spurting spasmodically into the glass, spurting and splashing his painful release up high so that it clouded the reflection of his contorted features.

As the others gazed down upon Gunter in his abject humiliation and smiled, Jane prised him away from the mirror and, slowly lowering her face down to the glass, licked his wet smear. Gunter closed his eyes, his face ablaze with both suffering and shame.

'Excellent,' the dominant brunette pronounced. 'Thank you, Jane. A good opener. And now, Angela, it shall be your round. Your turn to punish our cocksure coach. How do you want him?'

'At my mercy,' the statuesque matron whispered excitedly, peeling off her tennis outfit until she stood proudly naked. 'Bind his hands behind his back, would you? I won't be long.'

Ignoring Gunter's semen-soaked belly – and his imploring eyes – the three women fulfilled Angela's instructions, presenting their victim kneeling, bound and gagged to her when she returned, dragging a chair with one hand and bearing the Challenge Cup aloft in the other.

'Undo his gag, please,' Angela requested, deftly positioning the chair before settling her heavy buttocks down on to its leather seat. 'I'll have him seated on my lap.'

His thigh grazed her flourishing, dark pubic bush as Gunter was guided down. He flinched as his whipped cheeks sank on to her supporting thighs. Behind his back, his bound hands writhed as Angela nudged the golden cup towards his cock. Jane yanked the gag away. Gunter gasped aloud.

'A Challenge Cup,' Angela murmured, forcing it over the end of his shaft. 'You didn't win it, of course. We've checked. Silly Gunter,' she admonished, as if impatient with a squirming schoolboy. 'You can't hide anything from us. We know all your little secrets. Understand?'

Leaving the golden cup covering his shining glans, she insinuated her hand between his thighs and toyed with his balls, palming them as she weighed his sac with brutal tenderness. Gunter wriggled. Her palm closed into a fist; Gunter whimpered, becoming passive and submissive in her thrall.

'I have a challenge for you, coach. I want you to fill this cup.' She shook it, bullying his shaft within the golden shell. 'Fill it, or suffer.' She whispered the punishment for failure into his ear. Gunter paled. His ice-blue eyes now dimmed as fear flooded their former contemptuous stare.

Angela cradled him – carefully keeping the Challenge Cup positioned to catch and capture his ejaculations – and began to dominantly breastfeed him. After burying his upturned face beneath both of her heavy breasts for a full six minutes, she forced the swollen warmth of her right bosom into his mouth, smothering him ruthlessly. His eyes bulged as she filled his mouth, widening his accepting lips painfully apart. Easing the breast out, she adjusted it so that his lips formed a sucking circle at her engorged nipple. He struggled, rallying to escape. Angela tweaked his balls, breaking his resistance. Gunter sucked obediently, now utterly helpless at her breast. He sucked hard, guzzling at the dominant flesh. His shaft, the veins now visible, throbbed and jerked in response, the heat of his angry glans dimming the encircling gold. Angela cupped her breast and squeezed it, commanding her captive to suckle harder. Glancing down at his twitching length, she sensed that his climax was imminent.

She gave the golden trophy a cruel half-twist. Gunter cried out into her breast as the cold gold raked his glistening snout. As his buttocks clenched at her supporting thighs and his hips jerked – signalling his imminent orgasm – Angela steadied the Challenge Cup and buried his upturned face in her bosom. Spluttering, Gunter groaned and came; the squirt was long and loud, the thin jet splashing noisily against the gleaming gold.

'Good little boy,' Angela enthused, hug-shaking his helpless nakedness. With her left hand, she caught the last few sticky semen beads with the rim of the trophy. 'Well done, Gunter. I knew you had it in you. After all –' her tone darkened '– I've seen it when examining Penelope's soiled knickers.'

Bound and helpless, Gunter sank his face down into her deep cleavage. Her breasts cushioned his perspiring features with their swollen, satin warmth. Angela had broken him. Broken his Teutonic pride and arrogance. Like a cruel Prussian princess in a dark, medieval castle, she enjoyed supreme sovereignty over his submissive serfdom.

'Kneel,' came her curt command.

Slumping to his knees, head bowed abjectly, he obeyed. Peeling her heavy buttocks away from the chair's leather seat, Angela rose. She passed the small, golden cup to Jane.

'Be careful not to spill a drop. I want a full cup out of him.'

Jane took the cup and nodded. Kneeling down behind Gunter, she nestled her breasts and pubis into him. Snaking her hand around his left thigh, she positioned the Challenge Cup at his penis.

Angela moved slowly and gracefully. As she stood, naked, before the kneeling German, she planted her feet apart. Her ripe bosom wobbled as she brought her large, dark bush into his face. Gripping his bowed head and taloning the golden hair dominantly, she crushed his mouth to her labia. Up on tiptoe – causing her buttocks to joggle – she drew his lips to hers. Gunter gasped as his mouth tasted her wet slit.

'Your serve,' she snarled.

Gunter closed his eyes and worked his lips and tongue busily. Soon, his face was shining with both his exertion and her wet pleasure. As his length thickened and engorged, Jane deftly angled the golden cup to catch his shooting seed. Angela remained passive as the tennis coach lapped frantically at her wet heat. Gazing down sternly at her kneeling slave, she murmured the occasional threat of encouragement – detailing explicitly the impending punishment if he failed to meet her challenge. His tongue drove deeper into her, the thick, wet muscle arching and curving to lick and lap her sensitive flesh.

A ripple – a frisson of arousal – across her proudly nippled bosom acknowledged Angela's rapidly approaching climax. The other women watched, their eyes wide with expectant excitement. Angela's buttocks tightened, her deep cleft becoming a fierce crease as the heavy cheeks clenched. Arching her head back, and tumbling her hair down in a wanton cascade, she ground her pubis into his face with increasing urgency. Then she hammered her hips and, clutching his trapped head tightly, she orgasmed aloud. Seconds later, the thin hiss and liquid splatter in the cup betrayed Gunter's ejaculation.

'Again,' Angela commanded, tilting the German's agonised face up by his chin and staring dominantly down into his frightened eyes. 'Twice more should almost do it,' she added, glancing into the cup Jane was cradling carefully. 'Fill the cup, coach, or else you'll be calling for new balls.'

Babs, at forty-six the oldest of the four vengeful matrons, shook Gunter awake. Those who called Babs Rubenesque were being both tactful and kind. She was a proud owner of 38DD breasts. They slapped the German's face as she bent over him. He had been dozing fitfully – whimpering in his troubled dreams – upon the polished wooden floor while the four mothers-in-law had showered, sipped Chablis from clear plastic cups and munched potted shrimps.

After her shower, Babs had towelled and talcumed her ample flesh and had smoothed on a pair of pale tan tights with her strong, capable hands. As Gunter slept on, their talk had been that normal to any circle of middle-aged Hampshire ladies: rose catalogues; getting the Aga serviced; the latest Karl Lagerfeld collection and the growing nuisance of New Age travellers toting mongrel dogs on lengths of string. One of the dogs had jumped the privet at the vicarage and ravished the curate's poodle. All agreed that the potted shrimps were delicious.

As Gunter woke, propping himself up drunkenly on his elbows, the talk returned to punishments and pain. At his feet, the small trophy cup brimmed with his semen.

Babs sat on the chair Angela had used when breastfeeding the German coach. Signalling to Jane and Angela, she squatted her buttocks heavily on to the leather seat, her nylon tights crackling as their sheen grazed the hide. With the silent, stern brunette supervising, Jane and Angela dragged the still-bound Gunter to Babs and hauled him across her knee, leaving him bare-bottomed for her intimate perusal.

'You propose to merely spank him?' the brunette asked, failing to conceal a note of disappointment.

Babs nodded, pausing to suck at a piece of shrimp wedged in her tooth. 'An old-fashioned method of discipline, but one which I have every confidence in. Very

18

effective,' she murmured, dimpling Gunter's left buttock with firm fingertips, 'and so very pleasurable, I must confess. Actually owning a naked man's bottom. Having it completely in your control. And observing how it grows pink and then crimson under one's relentlessly spanking hand. Delicious.' She giggled.

Gunter groaned. He squeezed his thighs together.

'No, young man. We'll have none of that nonsense. Relax your cheeks. That's better. Legs a little wider apart. Now get your bottom up a fraction higher. More. Good. Now a fraction more.'

Gunter strained to obey these pre-punishment instructions, his toes whitening as they dug into the wooden floor. As he did so, Babs thumbed his cleft fleetingly and then, cupping her spanking hand into a slight curve, gently palmed the swell of his buttocks.

'Are you going to spank him until he comes?' Jane asked, tilting her strawberry-blonde head inquiringly.

'Not until *he* comes,' Babs replied, nodding as she emphasised the pronoun. She smoothed the crown of the buttocks she proposed to blister. 'Gunter is to be severely spanked until *I* come.'

And for the first time since they had intruded into his private work-out over three hours ago, Gunter knew the meaning of fear. He had known – and endured – pain, the dark pleasure of punishment, the bitter-sweetness of surrender and the anguish of humiliation since their visitation. But now it was the raw taste of fear that soured his mouth. Bare-bottomed, and with his hands in tight bondage, he was helpless across the ample lap of this large Englishwoman. This slightly tipsy Englishwoman who was probably just a little bit mad. She proposed to spank him soundly until her pleasure was achieved in orgasm. He shuddered. The others, he remembered painfully, had disciplined him with a ruthless economy. Justice had been dispensed swiftly. But this hugely breasted giantess the others called Babs was approaching his punishment differently. Her shrill giggling haunted Gunter – as did the cupping, squeezing hand at his bare bottom.

'Wicked, wicked Gunter,' she wheezed. 'And who is going to get a thoroughly smacked bottom, hmm?'

For the very first time since the eight white pumps had interrupted his press-ups earlier that fateful evening, Gunter heard himself begging aloud for mercy. As the sound of the severe spanking echoed around the gym after four sustained minutes of her harsh palm across his suffering buttocks, his cries became curses. Gunter, as the brunette had unerringly predicted, howled aloud, blaspheming as his cheeks reddened beneath her cruel spanking hand.

'Faster,' Angela urged, thumbing her pussy fiercely.

'Harder,' encouraged Jane, busy at her nipples.

'Excellent,' cried the brunette, rubbing the tennis ball trapped by her right hand against her clitoris.

Babs ignored her appreciative audience. Concentrating on the bottom before her, she continued to spank it harshly, raining down a storm of hot pain across the blazing cheeks. In a desperate bid to escape, Gunter lunged across her thighs – but merely succeeded in gouging his glans into the rasping sheen of her tights. Screaming as he came, he splashed and soaked her. Vaguely aware of his hot seed seeping into her nylon-sheathed thighs, Babs continued her furious onslaught upon his bare buttocks, noting with satisfaction that the spanked cheeks were now deeply crimsoned.

Suddenly, the crisp echoes of the spanking hand ceased. The three watching women blinked as if emerging from a trance, their wet fingertips fixed at their pouting labia as if frozen in the very act of masturbation. Gunter, sobbing gently, collapsed down across the semen-smeared thighs of his punisher.

Babs broke the spellbound silence, asking Jane to bring her a bottle of Pilsner from the little white fridge. Gunter yelled out in protest, bucking and jerking violently, as the chilled bottle was positioned along his cleft between his reddened cheeks.

'There,' the spanker whispered, her tone soothing and gentle as she knuckled the ice-cold bottle deep into his cleft.

Flattening her palm down, Babs began to roll the Pilsner bottle up across the outer buttock then back, across the red and ravished cheek just below her bosom. Gunter inched his cheeks up, eager for the cold glass upon his hot torment. Deftly grasping the bottle, Babs inverted it, probing his puckering anal crater with the top. Gunter came immediately, his audible squirt splashing her stockinged feet. Babs giggled as she scrunched her toes and paddled in his slippery puddle.

'Mad woman,' the German cursed harshly. 'Crazy Englander. Damn bitch.' Normally so exquisitely polite, his outburst – and subsequent stream of oaths – thrilled the naked women encircling him in his shame and pain.

Placing the bottle down once more along the length of his sticky cleft, Babs applied the cold surface across the contours of her chastised victim's blistering cheeks for several minutes – then, having tossed him unceremoniously down on to the wooden floor, used the green bottle at her slit. Trapping it between her heavy thighs, she pumped hard. The glass rasped her wet tights' mesh. Above her panting gasps, the crackle of her punished pubic fuzz was distinct. Rising in a sudden surge of frustration, Babs bestraddled the German who lay prostrate at her feet. Treading down triumphantly upon his reddened buttocks, she resumed pleasuring herself with the bottle, bruising her erect love-thorn with the glass. Gunter, pinioned beneath the semen-soaked stockinged foot, cringed in an anguish of shame as Babs finally exploded aloud in a shriek of orgasmic pleasure. Tossing the bottle aside – it splintered on the floor, the shaken lager seething curdled spume – she sank down upon the tennis coach. Capturing his red bottom between a pincer of powerful thighs, she rode him, jerking up her broad buttocks and raking her pantihosed pubis down across his punished rump: her final flourish of supreme dominance.

It was dusk. A light breeze shivered the leaves of the beeches outside. Inside, four electric light bulbs blazed. In their harsh glare, Jane and Angela were struggling to dress

Gunter in the soaking pair of tan tights Babs had discarded. As they snapped the darker-hued waistband around his hips, his trapped shaft strained against the wet sheen stretched across his groin. Naked still, apart from the grotesque tights, and still helplessly bound at the wrists, he knelt before his tormentors. They were dressed and ready to depart. The gym stank of spilled lager, sweat and semen.

The stern brunette assumed her role as leader of the perfumed, predatory pack. 'I am not completely unfamiliar with your tongue, Gunter.'

Angela, who had become intimate with the German's hot mouth, giggled as she stroked her pussy beneath the tiny, pleated white tennis skirt.

'I refer to the German language. More specifically, the writings of Grimm.'

Gunter, swaying slightly on his knees in a lust-exhausted stupor, blinked stupidly.

'Not Hans von Grimmelhausen, whose torrid work, "Simplicissimus", I find somewhat too picaresque,' the brunette continued suavely. 'I mean the brothers Grimm. You are no doubt hoping for a fairy-tale ending, Gunter. I am afraid you are to be disappointed.' She brandished his black diary and flipped through the pages. 'You are hoping that each mother will replace her daughter-in-law for your special coaching sessions.'

Gunter denied the charge – but the jerking cock probing the tan tights both betrayed and confirmed his secret desire. To silence his loud protestations, they gagged him once more, using a pair of cotton panties.

The stern brunette tore the diary into a thousand tiny pieces. 'No, Gunter. There is to be no fairy-tale ending. We are going now. In a little while, the Club Secretary will receive an anonymous phone call. Attracted by the lights here in the gym at a late hour, he will lead the investigation and they will find you. I am sure they will come to some satisfactory arrangement – but your expulsion from the club will be automatic. A grim ending, I am afraid, to your little fairy-tale, Gunter.'

Scooping up the brimming Challenge Cup, she trickled the silvery semen over the bound, kneeling German – taking care to soak the tights where they strained at his shaft. Dropping the golden cup to the floor, she stamped on it, crushing it completely beneath her dominant pump.

2

Sticky Fingers

The April sunshine blanked the screen of her monitor with a blaze of gold. Yvonne stretched her hand out and, fingers fumbling for the cord, found it and snapped down the blinds. London's West End traffic became a dull roar. Glancing back into her monitor, she smiled.

'Come and take a peek at Trap 2.'

Bostick, her partner on the afternoon security shift – so called because she stuck to suspects like glue – joined her at the screen. Their hands collided as they both made a grab for the joystick. Yvonne withdrew, allowing Bostick to take control.

'I'll zoom in,' she grunted urgently, teasing the stubby joystick.

The surveillance camera, cunningly mounted above the unsuspecting customers, angled and dipped in response to Bostick's command. Trap 2, a changing cubicle in the lingerie section, filled their screen in big close-up. In it, a Greek beauty in her late thirties was struggling into a black satin basque. As the nude battled with the basque, she tossed her long, black hair tempestuously. Her bouncing breasts seemed to fill the entire screen.

'A bit to the left. No, your left,' Yvonne whispered excitedly.

Bostick's thumbtip stroked the joystick. They watched in silence as the superbly buttocked Greek finally squeezed her heavy breasts into the underwired cups of the stretchy black satin.

'She needs a bigger size,' Yvonne remarked. 'Vain cow.'

Bostick nodded. 'Yep. Look. She's going to try that red one now.'

They continued to watch in silence as the voluptuous Greek unzipped and wriggled out of the black basque, her breasts bulging as she peeled away the tight cups. As she bent to scoop up the red basque, the Greek's naked buttocks pressed against the mirrored wall. All four walls of the changing cubicle were lined with glass, allowing the dry-mouthed voyeurs a deliciously frank appreciation of their unsuspecting prey. The Greek, her breasts and belly moulded within the second skin of the red basque's fierce embrace, examined herself critically. In the glass, her eyes spotted a stray wisp of pubic hair. Yvonne and her dominant partner craned eagerly as the Greek guided her fingertips down to her pussy to tidy away the wanton coils.

Bostick twiddled the joystick. She was rewarded with a captivating shot of the breasts, thrusting out proudly in the supporting cups. Bostick's grey eyes narrowed as she trained the prying lens down on the swollen bottom. Watching intently, the grey eyes feasted on the naked buttocks bulging against a glass panel, the dark cleft wide between the splayed cheeks.

'I'd love to cane that,' she grunted. 'Imagine having those cheeks to lash and stripe.'

Yvonne, her throat tightening, swallowed noisily.

'Still,' her partner whispered, patting Yvonne's bottom proprietorially, 'I've always got yours.'

'You've lost her,' Yvonne murmured, wriggling away from the dominant hand across her cheeks.

Bostick recaptured the Greek. In her red basque, tossing her dark hair back, she was admiring the cleavage the underwired cups had brought to her proud breasts. In another big close-up, the two watchers admired the cleavage as well. From its steep angle, the lens lingered over the swell of the shining breasts. The Greek used body lotion, giving her ripe flesh a satin sheen. Yvonne bent closer to the screen. Reaching out her straightened index finger, she traced the outline of the breasts nestling in their cupped bondage.

'Cut that out,' Bostick snapped, her jealous tone unmistakable – a sharp tone Yvonne thrilled to hear.

'Sorry,' she whispered penitently.

'You will be, when I get you home.'

'Please, I didn't mean –'

'Let's take a look in Trap 3,' Bostick said suavely, dismissing her partner's anxious whimper.

Two young blondes, stripped down to their white cotton panties, were helping each other into bras. This time – to Yvonne's silent resentment – it was Bostick who responded. Twiddling the joystick, she probed the mirrored cubicle, lingering over the thighs and pubic mounds of the pantied young lovelies below.

Yvonne grew jealous. 'Try Trap 1,' she suggested, attempting a casual voice.

'Be quiet,' Bostick hissed, 'I like what I'm seeing.'

'Yes, but –'

'Shut it.'

Yvonne lapsed into sullen silence.

'And don't sulk,' Bostick continued, savouring the peach-cheeks within their stretched white cotton panties, 'or I'll give you something to sulk about right here and now.'

Yvonne shivered with pleasure at the delicious threat. Bending so close to the screen that her breath misted the glass, Bostick ogled the nubile blondes. In the confines of Trap 3, they jostled for space. Colliding, thigh to thigh, pubis to rump, they finally managed to face a mirror and, between them, fit on a cotton sports bra. Bostick growled as the girl behind adjusted the cups for her partner in front. Pressing her face into the screen, she licked then kissed the big close up of the apple breasts being sheathed and squeezed in the crisp, virginal cups.

Sulking over by the wall, Yvonne stood with her arms folded, her face a mask of misery. Bostick's head of cropped hair spoiled her view of the screen, but she briefly glimpsed the playful, fluttering hands of one blonde nymph capturing and pleasuring the braless breasts of the other.

The phone buzzed. A long, continuous snarl.

'Internal. I'll get it,' Yvonne volunteered.

Engrossed at her screen – the blondes in Trap 3 were now cuddling and tongue-tip teasing each other – Bostick ignored both the phone and her partner.

Yvonne murmured into the phone, then hung up. 'Jewellery. They've just had a punter.'

Bostick swivelled round, her alert face raised. Over her shoulder, on the neglected screen, one young blonde was kneeling before the parting thighs of the other.

'Was there a lift?' Bostick demanded.

Yvonne nodded. 'It was a lift. Punter in a yellow Chanel suit. Black gloves. Asked to see eternity rings. Diamond solitaire's gone.'

'She's palmed it. Neat. How much?'

'Eleven thou.'

'Greedy. Has there been a door alert yet?'

Yvonne shook her head. 'She's still inside.'

'Cool,' Bostick purred. 'Better do a sweep.' Back at her screen, operating the joystick deftly, she soon spotted – and tracked – their target. They held her in a long shot as she dallied on the edge of the lingerie section toying with a leather bustier. Yvonne joined her dominant partner at the screen.

'She'll go into Trap 1 with that. That's where she'll do the business.'

They tracked the slender, elegantly dressed brunette's progress between the displays of bras and panties, switching to a big close-up as their quarry sidled into the seclusion of Trap 1. They watched as she tugged off her black gloves with her teeth, tossing them down on to the floor, then wriggled out of her chic Chanel jacket and skirt.

'Think I know her,' Bostick murmured. 'Sure of it.'

Yvonne turned, her eyebrows raised inquiringly. 'Have you pulled her before? Is she on file?'

'No, not that. But I'm sure I know her.'

In her cubicle, their target was palming down sheer, black tights. Braless, she stood before the mirror, a silk thong moulded her pubic mound. Her breasts bunched as she struggled with a ring, prising the stone from its setting.

'Cool little cat. Just look at her.' Bostick nodded. 'She'll plug the stone and waltz out of there bold as brass.'

They held their breath as they watched the brunette toss the gold band away, drag the thong from her deep cleft and finger the gleaming gem up inside her rectum. Bostick snarled softly as the thief's long, white finger slipped out from between her soft, swollen buttocks and probe the silk thong back into position.

'She's plugged it. Door alert.'

The exclusive emporium – favoured by European royalty and rock star babes – boasted not one but two impressively liveried doormen. Former Coldstream Guards RSMs, they now manned the smoked glass and onyx portals to the off-Bond Street boutique wearing orange toppers and black frock coats with grey frogging. Both wore discreet earphones.

They had been studying the beauty of a cream-and-azure Bentley when the alert came. As if stung by wasps, they both sprang up the marble steps and, in silent unison, sternly faced the smoked glass double doors.

The brunette emerged, fishing daintily for Raybans. The orange top hats converged, offering impeccably polite assistance. She smilingly declined their gallantry. Undaunted, they insisted. The doors whispered apart – Bostick emerged, blinking in the strong sunshine after the dark surveillance room. Adroitly gripping her target's elbow with fingers of steel, she propelled the brunette back inside the emporium. Adjusting their improbable top hats, the two doormen turned to resume their perusal of the sleek Bentley.

Keeping up a pleasant banter about a new range of fragrances, Bostick steered the yellow Chanel suit unswervingly across the ground floor then down a flight of uncarpeted steps to a basement room. Pushing through the bland, beige door, she shoved her captive inside and closed the door, locking it silently. Yvonne was busy loading a cassette into a VCR.

'What the hell do you think you are doing?' the target demanded icily.

'My colleague and I have reason to believe –' Yvonne began.

'Cut the crap. Name?' Bostick demanded.

The brunette tossed her head imperiously and remained silent.

Yvonne, setting the VCR on rewind, snatched away the black bag and pushed the thief down on to a hard, wooden chair.

'How dare you? I demand to see –'

'Shut it, sweetie,' Bostick snapped. 'Who is she?'

Fishing out a gold card, Yvonne read out the brunette's name – a name frequently gracing the gossip columns of the glossies.

'Cross-check. It could be hot.'

The brunette glared at Bostick as Yvonne exhumed more evidence of identity: a cheque book, driving licence and dildo with their captive's first name etched along its gleaming length.

'If it's on the chick-dick it must be true,' Bostick chuckled. Then she clapped her hands. 'Gotcha. I knew it. Never forget a face. You're his ex, aren't you?'

Yvonne framed a question with her eyebrows.

'Our MD, of course. Him upstairs, when he's ever there. This –' Bostick gestured '– is last year's hot tottie. Dump you, did he? Come back for a final instalment for services rendered?'

The brunette rose and snatched back her black purse. 'I popped in to buy a bustier. I didn't like what I saw –'

'Neither did we, sweetie,' Bostick broke in, patting the VCR.

The brunette paled, then flushed angrily. 'That's outrageous – I mean – I didn't – But you just can't do that –'

'If that's a confession, I'll buy it,' Bostick laughed.

The thief made a rush for the door. Neither of her captors moved. Scrabbling at the locked door, the thief thumped it impotently with her gloved fists.

'Get back over here and strip. Or do you want to do this the hard way?'

The brunette did it the hard way – squealing as Bostick and Yvonne handled her roughly – dragging her Chanel jacket and skirt off before snatching down her black tights. The shivering young thief, dressed in nothing but her slender thong, cupped her naked breasts protectively.

'Across the table. Face down and legs apart,' Bostick instructed.

The thief tightened her folded arms defensively, causing her squashed breasts to bulge. Her chin rose a fraction in defiance.

'I'm waiting, sweetie. In your own time,' Bostick continued laconically.

'N-no,' their captive stammered. 'You c-can't –'

'Across the table for a strip search, sweetie. Do it now.'

Exposing her bosom, the brunette dropped her hands down to her thighs. Surreptitiously inching her fingertips around to the swell of her buttocks, she furtively scrabbled at her cleft.

'Leave that alone,' Bostick snarled, taking two menacing paces towards the nude. 'I'll get the stone out. Pleasant little perk that goes with the job.'

Yvonne giggled; her dominant partner silenced her with a scowl. Suddenly grappling the cowering brunette, Bostick twisted the nude around towards the table, then forced her face down across it, ordering Yvonne to grab and secure the thief's wrists. Yvonne obeyed, pinioning the nude down in helpless surrender.

'Legs apart,' came the crisp command.

The splayed nude whimpered. *Crack*. Bostick spanked the upturned cheeks savagely, swiping her flattened palm dominantly down across their proffered swell.

The spank elicited a shrill squeal of outrage from the writhing nude across the table.

'I said get your legs apart, bitch,' the spanker warned the spanked.

Her reddening cheeks wobbled as the thief sullenly obeyed, inching her thighs apart. 'Please don't –'

Snapping on a pair of disposable plastic gloves, Bostick demanded silence. Submitting to the stern command, the nude slumped down across the table, rolling slightly to ease her crushed breasts.

'And stay absolutely still,' Bostick warned.

The nude shivered at the ominous command. Gazing down at the superbly rounded buttocks which she had just spanked, Bostick saw each cheek dimple with fearful expectation. She patted them, her plastic-sheathed finger-tips drumming the rubbery globes of naked flesh. Snarling softly, Bostick suddenly swept her thumbtip down between the buttocks, raking the warmth of the dark cleft. The nude moaned. Bostick withdrew her thumbtip and scrutinised the dulled plastic sheath.

'A bit sticky, aren't you?' she queried, wiping the thumbtip on the nude's left buttock. 'We know you've got sticky fingers.' Her plastic-gloved hand swept down – twice – to spank the naked buttocks harshly.

'No,' the nude shouted, then cursed her tormentress.

'Yes, you have, you little thief. Sticky fingers and a sticky bottom.' Demanding absolute silence, Bostick snap-ped her fingers at Yvonne for the box of tissues. Taking a tissue, Bostick wedged it roughly between the spanked cheeks, then dragged it up along the cleft in a single sweep. Face down into the hard wooden table, the pinioned nude hissed aloud.

'That's better,' Bostick murmured, tossing the soiled tissue aside after examining it briefly. 'Now I think it's time we took a little look inside Aladdin's cave for the jewel. Open sesame.' Bostick chuckled, kneeling down and press-ing her face into the softness of the right buttock.

An eerie silence filled the small room. For a full two minutes only the muted scratching of the pigeons jostling for space on the window ledge beyond the drawn blinds could be heard. Up in the bright sunshine, the orange-toppered doormen saluted the Bentley as it purred away from the pavement. Bond Street was busy and bustling: mobile phones chirruped, taxi brakes squealed and elec-tronic tills silently accepted whispering plastic cards. Down in the silent room, where two women held a nude in their thrall, only their heartbeats were audible.

Deftly probing the nude's rosebud sphincter with her straightened index finger, Bostick explored the tight warmth of the rectum. The nude contracted her inner muscles, denying the plastic-sheathed finger deeper access. Bostick pressed her lips into the naked buttock, then, peeling her lips apart, bit softly into the firm cheek. The nude screamed, collapsing her belly down into the table in abject surrender. The probing finger met no more resistance. Bostick twisted her wrist – the nude rose up on her scrabbling white toes – then raked the rectal warmth with her fingertip.

'Got it,' Bostick grunted softly as she located, and slowly retrieved, the secreted gem. 'That just about clinches it,' she whispered, depositing the recovered stone down on the table. It glittered under the harsh neon above, almost as brightly as the tears squeezed from the thief's tightly shut eyes.

'Police?' Yvonne murmured, relaxing her grip on the pinioned wrists slightly.

'Yep,' Bostick replied, her stern tone belied by the grin she flashed her colleague over the bending nude. 'Get on the phone.'

The brunette wriggled and broke free. Staggering back, her buttocks squashed up against the wall.

'Hope you brought your toothbrush, sweetie. No bail for a stunt like this,' Bostick said, palming the precious stone. 'Bed and several breakfasts in Holloway.'

The nude paled as she sank slowly down to her knees, dragging her buttocks against the wall. Bostick peeled off the plastic gloves, finger by stretchy finger. Yvonne picked up the phone and started to dial.

'Of course,' Bostick murmured softly, 'we could wrap this up here and now.'

Yvonne paused, her finger an inch above the button. The nude glanced up quickly.

Yvonne replaced the receiver. Reaching across to the VCR, she stroked it. 'Tapes can be wiped so easily.'

'And we've got the stone back,' Bostick rejoined, ignoring the anxious face of their captive.

'Save on all the paperwork –'

'Get away on time.' Yvonne nodded in agreement.

'So which is it to be, sweetie?' Bostick demanded, harshly interrogating the startled thief. 'Punishment – or the police?'

Their captive looked up, blinking in the glare of the neon uncomprehendingly.

'Choose.'

'Not the police.' The brunette shook her head. 'Not that.'

'Punishment it is, then.' Bostick nodded judiciously as she rubbed her hands together with brisk and evident relish. 'You first,' she gestured to Yvonne. 'She's your pull. You took the call.'

Yvonne grinned, basking in her stern partner's generosity. She crossed over to the slumped nude, then grasped her wrist and dragged her to her feet. Arranging a chair next to the table, Yvonne sat down, then forced the naked brunette across her lap.

'Pass me her tights.'

'No – please –' the thief squealed, wriggling frantically.

Bostick scooped up the shrivelled black tights and tossed them to her partner.

'Hands together,' Yvonne commanded, dragging the writhing girl's arms up behind her.

The brunette hesitated, protesting plaintively.

Yvonne took the tights and shook them out into a shining skein. She started to bind the captive wrists tightly. The nude made a lurching bid for freedom.

'You chose. I can make that phone call if you really want me to,' Yvonne whispered, pinning the thief down firmly by the nape of her neck.

Slowly, reluctantly, the nude drew her arms back together as instructed, submitting her wrists to the bondage of the tights.

'Sensible girl,' Yvonne purred, caressing the naked buttocks with the open palm of her spanking hand. 'Sensible girl.'

'I'm sorry – Please don't –' the thief whispered, squeezing her cheeks tightly together beneath the increasingly dominant caresses of Yvonne's firm palm.

The punisher ordered her victim to keep still – and silent – but the strict warning only succeeded in triggering the nude into a frenzy of wriggling and loud protest. Yvonne looked to Bostick for direction. Bostick tapped her left breast in silence, then turned her hand into a claw at her own bosom. Yvonne nodded, then reached down to cup and squeeze her captive's left breast. The solid sphere of satin warmth bulged as it filled her hand. Yvonne squeezed harder; the brunette squealed as the controlling talon bunched the naked bosom ruthlessly.

'She's going to yell the place down,' Bostick observed impatiently. 'Better use this.' Picking up the gleaming dildo from the table, she examined it closely – thumbing the cool length appreciatively – before approaching the bare-bottomed thief sprawled across her punisher's lap.

'Open wide,' Bostick commanded.

The thief, twisting her face around, glimpsed the dildo. She parted her thighs instantly, dipping her tummy and proffering herself up on whitened tiptoe for the shaft. Bostick snorted, suppressing a grim laugh, and briefly teased the outer lips of the wet pussy with the blunt snout.

'Not those lips, bitch.' Bending down, Bostick inserted the dildo into the thief's protesting mouth, silencing her squeals as the smooth ivory slid between the parted lips.

The first seven spanks – swift as they were savage – rang out crisply. Yvonne gripped the brunette dominantly by the nape of her neck and pinned her down as she administered the flurry of searing spanks with her flattened palm across the rounded buttocks. The dildo rendered the brunette's shrill squeals into barely audible whimpers. Yvonne paused, fingering the hot cheeks firmly, then knuckling them – and the cleft between – as she briefly released her grip on the nude's neck and used her free hand to toy with the dildo, driving it deeply into the thief's mouth.

Bostick barked her disapproval. 'This is work, not play. Get on with it.' Her eyes narrowed jealously.

Yvonne blushed under Bostick's anger, her cheeks reddening as warmly as those she had just spanked. Returning her left hand to the thief's neck, she spanked the girl again, very hard, with another stinging seven. The blistering cheeks blazed beneath the furious onslaught, their pinkness deepening into a plum's shade of pain with each cruel swipe. In their stockinged bondage, the bound hands writhed, the fingers of the spanked nude splaying out in mute protest. Bucking and writhing across her chastiser's knee, the brunette squirmed in her struggle to escape, her joggling buttocks enflaming Yvonne into a renewed onslaught. The small room echoed to the harsh cracks of the punishing palm across the burning buttocks as Yvonne scorched them into the stillness of submission.

Bostick, gazing down at the thief in abject surrender, nodded curtly. 'Much better.'

Yvonne glanced up, basking in the approval, then lowered her eyes to the hot bottom at her mercy. Her victim had slumped – utterly tamed and subdued – across her thighs. Yvonne sensed the naked bosom nestling into her stocking's sheen, felt the stubby nipples prinking with excitement. Placing her spanking hand down across the swollen contours of the spanked cheeks, she relaxed her grip on the thief's neck and tenderly stroked the bowed head. Bostick's soft growl brought Yvonne's hand back to the neck instantly. Yvonne looked up anxiously at her stern partner.

'Another dozen,' Bostick prescribed, swiftly dragging her straightened index finger down along the cleft between the crimson cheeks. 'The bitch needs to learn. Let the lesson be painful.'

Yvonne nodded eagerly, closing her eyes and opening her mouth obediently to receive Bostick's finger – fresh from the brunette's hot cleft. She shrank a fraction from the feral tang anointing the dominant finger, but Bostick drove it deeper, filling her submissive partner's mouth with the acrid taste of the suffering brunette.

Keeping the finger firmly in place, Bostick gazed down upon the hot buttocks below. 'You're doing a good job there. Excellent,' she whispered. 'Proceed.'

Yvonne sucked hard on the finger, relishing her stern partner's approval. Bostick made no attempt to remove her finger, remaining, feet planted apart, towering above both the punisher and the punished.

'I said, proceed.'

Guzzling on the finger filling her mouth, Yvonne spanked the bare-bottomed thief with a measured dozen, delivering each searing swipe slowly and deliberately. Dizzy with the delicious delight of dominance and discipline, she sank her breasts down into the scrabbling fingers of the suffering nude, allowing the frantic fingernails to ravish her nipples, then crushed her bosom down into the hot cheeks.

Bostick, withdrawing her finger from her partner's mouth, turned away, her fingers now busy at her slit. More cruel spanks rang out. The protracted punishment drove both chastiser and chastised towards orgasm.

Bostick, skirt riding her hips, was strumming her pantied pubic mound. 'Harder,' she hissed, 'and faster.'

Another flurry of spanks – harder and faster, as Bostick had decreed – echoed around the room. The brunette jerked, raking her exposed slit repeatedly against her punisher's nylon-stockinged thighs as she approached her climax. Yvonne, thrilled by the wetness of the spanked nude, drummed her feet in ecstasy as her own delicious spasms soaked her cotton panties. Suddenly, with their eyes closed and their heads tossed back, both punisher and punished came together in sweet unison.

'That's enough of that,' Bostick thundered, turning around swiftly in response to the silence of the stilled spanking hand. 'The bitch is here for pain, not pleasure.'

Yvonne opened her eyes, blinking guiltily. The jealous anger of her partner replaced the delight on her upturned face with fear. She clamped her thighs together in a futile attempt to deny the second climax threatening to explode within her. Above her reddened cheeks, the bound hands of the nude twisted in ecstasy as she succumbed to her renewed orgasm.

'I warned you,' Bostick snarled, advancing on Yvonne. 'Give her to me.'

The dildo fell out of the thief's mouth as Bostick grappled her up and across to the table. Red-bottomed and stumbling, she was helpless in her captor's fierce grip. Bostick forced the bound nude face down before spread-eagling and arranging her for more pain. Scooping up the dildo, she returned to the bending thief and drove it between her spanked cheeks. The brunette's left foot rose up, treading the empty air.

'Feet down and spread your legs,' Bostick commanded.

The brunette, crushing her breasts into the table, obeyed.

Bostick gave the ivory shaft a quarter-turn twist. 'Submit.'

The cheeks tightened, denying the dildo access. 'No –'

'Submit,' Bostick hissed, twisting the dildo cruelly.

Gasping, the brunette slumped in surrender, her breath clouding the table's polished surface.

'Eleven thousand buys you quite a lot of pain,' Bostick snarled, tightening her grip on the ivory shaft. 'A lot of pain.'

The dildo probed the dark anal whorl, inching into the muscled rectal warmth. Soon, the firm shaft filled the thief completely: she kissed the table in a frenzy of anguish then lapped eagerly, her swollen tongue flattened into the wood.

'I'll be back,' Bostick warned, pincering a finger and thumbful of the upturned bottom and twisting it savagely.

Yvonne, who had fingered herself into a third orgasm as she watched Bostick dominate the thief, dropped her hands down as her dominant partner turned.

'You,' Bostick snapped. 'Strip.'

Yvonne blinked. 'But –'

'You belong to me, girl. I own you, absolutely. And any pleasure is mine to give, mine. Not hers,' she hissed, jerking her thumb at the nude face down across the table.

'I didn't mean to –'

'I saw you,' Bostick snarled, almost choking on her words in her fury. 'Enjoying yourself during her punishment. Pain is pain and pleasure is pleasure. If you don't know the difference, I'm quite prepared to show you. Now get undressed and alongside her across that table.'

Pale and trembling under her partner's display of wrath, Yvonne rose up from her chair and pleaded with Bostick

– but the dominant remained unmoved, feigning indifference as she slowly unbuckled and removed the thin leather belt from her waist.

'I'm waiting,' was all she replied.

Yvonne, head bowed in defeat, kicked off her shoes and, unzipping her skirt, wriggled out of its tight embrace. She shuddered as, palming down each shear nylon stocking, she touched the wetness bequeathed by the spanked brunette's weeping pussy. Bostick, snapping her fingers, demanded the soiled stockings. Bringing them up to her nose – and tongue – she inspected the damning evidence intimately. Yvonne blushed, fumbling with the mother-of-pearl buttons which remained stubborn at the cuffs of her blouse.

'Just get your panties down and get across that table,' Bostick whispered, tossing the incriminating stockings aside.

Yvonne thumbed her cotton panties away from her cleft and pubis, gasping softly as the spindling thread of her sparkling arousal stretched, then snapped, splashing in against her naked thigh. Stepping out of her panties, she inched timorously past the belt dangling from her partner's clenched fist. Bostick retrieved the cotton panties, inverting and exposing them with the splayed fingers of her free hand. Glancing anxiously over her shoulder, Yvonne saw Bostick sniffing the wet patch.

'Face down across the table,' Bostick commanded, snapping her belt harshly.

Yvonne approached the edge of the table, her fingertips trembling as they caressed the shining wood. The belt snapped again. Down across the table, the naked thief shivered at the cruel sound of supple leather, tightening her cheeks in a reflex response of fearful expectation. Between her clenched buttocks, the shaft of the dildo suddenly straightened. Yvonne watched, enthralled, as the bending brunette relaxed imperceptibly and the rigid dildo drooped. The thief squealed as Bostick brusquely snatched the ivory shaft away, leaving the pouting anus pink and glistening.

'No, don't touch,' Bostick warned as Yvonne, bending obediently down alongside the thief, nestled into her, thigh kissing thigh. 'I can make this stretch far enough for two naughty bottoms,' Bostick whispered softly, fingering the leather belt affectionately then cracking it loudly; its blood-curdling bark filled the room with the ominous promise of pain.

When Yvonne's bare buttocks rose up for the lash, quivering two inches away from the proffered cheeks of the naked thief, Bostick positioned herself alongside her victims, her leather belt dangling down from her right hand.

'Sticky fingers,' she announced. 'I'm going to punish you both for your sticky-fingered sins. You –' she tapped the brunette's bottom with her furled belt '– used your fingers to take that which was not yours to take and you, –' she continued, teasing Yvonne's upturned cheeks with the tip of the belt '– abused yourself with your fingers, taking for yourself what is mine and mine alone to give you.'

She ordered them to roll over, breasts upwards. 'Now get your hands up. Palms up. Yes, that's right, bitch. Over your breasts.'

Bostick swiped the short length of leather down repeatedly, reddening their upturned palms and splayed fingers. Whimpering under the fierce rain of pain, both of her victims flinched and withdrew their hands – only to shriek aloud and reposition their hands instantly as the belt whistled down to lash their breasts savagely. Dreading the burn at their exposed nipples, both submitted to having their sticky fingers punished until Bostick, grunting her satisfaction, ordered them both face down across the table once more.

Standing alongside them, Bostick flexed the leather. The belt rose, hovering for a deliciously dreadful moment above both bare bottoms, then whistled down, biting into both double domes of defenceless flesh. The single swish-slice stroke elicited a double squeal. Again, the punisher's arm rose, pausing for a heart-stopping moment, then cracked the belt down viciously across the writhing cheeks.

Ignoring their piteous cries, Bostick shifted her weight on to her right foot and levelled the lash, whipping it suddenly inwards against the outer curves of the bare bottoms. Three times in rapid succession, she plied the belt at this angle, leaving reddening lines across the swell of the bunched cheeks where the fierce leather had planted its burning kisses.

'Sticky fingers,' Bostick grunted, drawing her thighs together and raising the belt aloft.

Snapping the lash down four more times, she relished the sight of the punished treading their pain into the carpet beneath their grinding toes, snarling with delight at their smothered moans of suffering and feasting over their tightly clenched whipped cheeks.

She administered two more searing strokes, then placed the curled length of leather down on the table before their tear-dimmed eyes. Picking up the dildo, Bostick squeezed it in her palm and knelt down alongside the thief's trembling thigh. Weighing the ivory in her open palm, Bostick kissed it fleetingly before nudging it in between the shining labial folds.

The brunette hissed out her willing acceptance this time; her bound hands splayed in ecstasy above her striped cheeks as the dildo inched up inside her wet warmth. Her reddened cheeks joggled as she squeezed them together, accepting the cool delight eagerly. Slowly, at first, then with increasing vigour, Bostick wielded the phallus, frequently twisting it to enhance and heighten the pleasure-pain. The brunette cried out aloud, then struggled to bring her thighs together to trap and contain the fierce delight: but Bostick remained in strict control. Kneeling down between the thief's legs, she positioned herself so that her powerful knees, splayed, kept the nude's ankles far apart. Leaning in against her victim, she buried her face into the brunette's punished buttocks, mouthing the striped cheeks and tonguing the belt-weals as she plunged the dildo deeper.

A piercing wail of anguish filled the room. It was not the pre-orgasm shriek of the writhing thief but Yvonne's shrill whine of resentment. Bostick chuckled, then returned to bite the buttocks before her as her submissive partner sobbed aloud.

'Me – Not her – Me – Please –' Yvonne begged, whimpering brokenly for the stern touch of loving dominance Bostick was deliberately denying her.

Bringing the thief to a loud, uninhibited climax, Bostick slowly withdrew the dildo and, shuffling around to kneel before Yvonne's bare bottom, tenderly nuzzled the glistening tip at the heat of the eagerly widened sphincter.

'Yes –' Yvonne hissed, jerking her hips in her frenzy for the shaft. 'Yes –'

Nuzzling the anal whorl gently, Bostick smiled as she saw the straining buttocks desperately attempting to capture and contain the elusive shaft. Tip-teasing the sticky rosebud crater for several agonising minutes, the dominant ravished her submissive into a paroxysm of frustrated yearning.

At the table, face down and sobbing, Yvonne begged. She hammered her fists furiously down on to the wood: but Bostick denied her, cruelly punishing her by slowly withdrawing the tantalising tip of the dildo, after a final, raking flourish down along the yawning length of the hot cleft.

'No,' Bostick pronounced solemnly, wiping the snout of the ivory dry on Yvonne's curved cheek. 'No pleasure for you, my girl. At least, not now. Later, perhaps,' she added, holding out the threat of a delicious promise. 'In bed, tonight.'

Yvonne moaned.

'Now kneel, both of you. Come on. Down on the floor.' She untied the nylon tights that bound the brunette's wrists.

They knelt obediently, gazing up at their tormentress. Bostick stood before them, her skirt once more riding her hips and her panties stretched down, with her dark pubic nest exposed. Both penitents eyed it hungrily.

'I think you've been punished enough,' Bostick murmured, fingering the thief's upturned face. 'In a moment, I will blindfold you, and you will pay full homage to me. Full homage, understand?'

Yvonne began to protest – and was silenced by her stern partner.

'Understand?' Bostick whispered, inching her pubic mound towards the brunette's lips.

'Yes,' the thief murmured, licking her lips.

Bostick used Yvonne's panties – bound tightly with a single nylon stocking – to blindfold the brunette. As Yvonne, kneeling alongside, sniffled miserably, Bostick drew the brunette's head towards her parted thighs. Seconds later, a soft, liquid lapping sound filled the room. The brunette sucked hard and tongued deeply. Soon, her unbound hands fluttered up to Bostick's plump hips, framing and steadying them; then the hands slipped around to cup the heavy buttocks, drawing Bostick firmly into her upturned face.

Bostick rose up on her toes, shivering with delight at the fierce hornet down at her oozing hive. Excluded from the tender violence, Yvonne wept bitterly, until Bostick's fingers reached down and tilted the sobbing girl's face upwards. Gazing down into the tear-filled eyes, Bostick smiled – signalling her forgiveness.

Yvonne ceased her weeping instantly and opened her mouth to receive and accept two fingers from her stern partner. In rhythm with the darting tongue at her slit, Bostick probed Yvonne's mouth. For six minutes the three were locked into their private world of pleasure: the thief served her captor devotedly; the captor rode the face of the thief – and forced her stiff fingers into her kneeling partner's sucking mouth.

Bostick came, wiping her slit repeatedly down across the brunette's blindfolded face. Yvonne, sensing her dominant partner's sudden spasms, collapsed down on to the carpet in a violent orgasm. Bostick trod the writhing nude down beneath her foot, increasing her squeals of raw pleasure to fever pitch. Turning her wet face blindly towards the sounds, the brunette struggled to understand.

'No,' Bostick gasped aloud, taloning the brunette's hair and bringing her shining face back between her hot thighs. 'I'm not finished; neither are you.'

'And you can use this,' she added, placing the dildo in Yvonne's hand. 'In the special place.'

Eager to outperform the brunette, Yvonne shuffled around, gripping the shaft between her teeth. Kneeling down behind Bostick, she guided the shaft between the heavy cheeks, which Bostick held impatiently apart. Lunging forward, Yvonne drove the dildo in deeply until her face was cushioned, then buried, in the softness of the buttocks.

'Harder,' Bostick grunted, dismissing Yvonne's efforts and praising the brunette busily lapping at her slit.

In a frantic fit of jealousy, Yvonne dropped her hand down, snaking it between Bostick's parted legs, and tugged at the kneeling thief's pubic fuzz. The brunette screamed into Bostick's slit.

The phone rang, breaking into the intimacy of the moment.

'Get that,' Bostick ordered, her voice seething with anger.

Yvonne smothered her disappointment, rising up on one knee reluctantly, her face still buried in the bottom before her.

'At once,' Bostick prompted curtly.

Easing back from the heavy buttocks, Yvonne stood up and scampered across to the phone. Picking it up, she listened attentively, acknowledged briefly and hung up.

'Dodgy gold card being used in perfumery,' she whispered, reluctant to break into Bostick's intense pleasure.

'Better get dressed and get down there.'

'But –' Yvonne hesitated.

'Just go and get it sorted,' Bostick hissed angrily, waving the submissive away and returning to concentrate on her pleasure.

'That's not fair. She –' Yvonne shouted, jabbing her finger down at the kneeling nude. 'That should be me.'

'Then watch and learn if you want to take her place,' came the cruelly whispered retort.

'But, Bostick –' Yvonne whined, tears sparkling in her eyes.

Bostick ignored her. Gazing down almost tenderly at the busy-tongued brunette, she gently stroked the nude's face in both acknowledgement and reward for the hungry lapping at her slit.

Weeping softly, Yvonne struggled bare-bottomed and stockingless into her tight skirt. Zipping it up, she flounced out, banging the door tempestuously behind her.

'Has she gone?'

Bostick ignored the question and stared at the big close-up on the VCR. Captured in a freeze-frame, the thief was plugging the stolen gemstone up between her plump cheeks. Yvonne watched jealously as her partner tapped the bulging cheeks with a dominant fingertip – and turned away in a pretence of unconcern as Bostick switched the VCR off and rose from her chair.

'Sort out the card?'

'Yep. Well over the limit and no repayments for at least six months. Kuwaiti. Stacks of dosh. Accounts extended their limit by a couple of thousand.' Yvonne paused. 'So she's gone, then?' She managed to keep her tone bright as she bent down to retrieve her stockings and panties.

'Don't bother with those,' Bostick murmured, approaching her partner and snatching them out of her hand. 'Just go and lock the door.'

'Going to watch the VCR again?'

'Just lock it.'

'But –'

'And then slip out of that skirt. I want you bare-bottomed for your punishment.'

'P-punishment?' Yvonne faltered.

'Naked and bending, if you please.'

'No – you can't –'

'Oh, but I can and I will,' Bostick purred softly, gathering up her leather belt once more and furling it twice around her right hand. 'Punishment. Double punishment, for you, my girl.'

'D-double?' echoed Yvonne's squeal of protest.

'You dared to turn her punishment into a cheap chance for your own pleasure. Punishment is a serious business, girl, as you are painfully about to discover. Skirt off and bend over.'

The zip slid down despite Yvonne's trembling fingertips. Seconds later, she was touching her toes like a naughty sixth-former before an angry Head Prefect.

'And then you dared,' Bostick continued curtly, skimming her fingers lightly over the buttocks she was about to beat, 'to show sullen, spiteful resentment when I was doing my duty. I saw your hand go between my legs. I saw you tormenting her –'

'She was –'

'Obeying me completely. I was establishing my supreme authority and your petty jealousy nearly ruined my domination and her proper punishment –'

'I'm sorry. I didn't think. I hated seeing her –'

'Silence. You know the rules of the game. Break them at your peril, girl.'

The belt cracked down four times in blistering succession, leaving crimson weals where the leather had lashed the naked buttocks. Bostick paused, took a step back, and flicked the belt up between Yvonne's parted thighs, whipping the leather up into the pussy above. Yvonne squealed.

'She was a common little thief. I was only teaching her a lesson. You must curb this possessive, jealous streak, my girl. I was only doing my duty. Like I am doing now.'

Swish-cracking the belt four more times, Bostick whipped the suffering cheeks mercilessly – again bringing the brutal hide up between Yvonne's thighs to scald the chastised girl's weeping slit.

'No – Please –' Yvonne wailed, stumbling forward in her delicious agony.

'Back in the punishment position, girl. Bottom up.'

Sobbing, Yvonne obeyed, straining her splayed fingers down to touch her white toes and offering her whipped cheeks up to the hovering belt. But the burning lash did not explode across her cheeks. Instead, Yvonne felt Bostick's lips at her stripes – and then mewed as Bostick's tongue lapped at the length of her cleft.

'So next time, when we have her in here again, naked and at our mercy,' Bostick murmured, mouthing the words into the punished cheeks, 'I will only be doing my stern duty.'

'Again?' Yvonne hissed, blinking away her tears and jerking her buttocks back into Bostick's face.

'She'll be back, like a cat to its cream. And,' Bostick whispered, 'we'll be ready for her.'

The two top-hatted doormen were furtively ogling a leggy model promenading across the street in the blazing sunshine. A taxi nosed up to the curb. One orange topper was doffed as the taxi door was opened; the other was smartly raised in salute as the brunette in the chic yellow Chanel suit skipped up the marble steps and disappeared through the smoked glass door opened for her.

Swishing her black gloves like an angry cat, the brunette stalked the perfumery. Out of the corner of her eye she saw the security camera up above stalking her progress. She slunk across to the jewellery display, closing on her prey: a large rope of lustrous pearls. Stretching out with feline grace, she snatched up the pearls, enclosing them in her gloved fist. The fist brought the pearls to her cleavage. She shivered slightly as they slithered down between the warmth of her bunched bosoms. Glancing up, she stared directly into the unblinking eye of the camera. The camera dipped and nodded, acknowledging her.

Trembling slightly, the brunette turned and headed – not too quickly – towards the exit. She trembled with fear, with delicious dread: not the fear of being apprehended and frog-marched down to the basement room with the bland, beige door, but with delicious dread of what awaited her once that beige door was firmly locked behind her.

3

Rough Shoot

Lady Alice strode purposefully down the draughty corridor along the east wing of Strachayle Castle. Approaching a large, mullioned window, she stopped abruptly, turning to instruct her maid scurrying in her wake.

'As for the Godolphin girls, Miss Edwina will have this bedroom and I shall place Miss Charlotte in there. During their visit, as their personal maid, you shall occupy the box room at the end of the landing, girl.'

'Yes, ma'am.' The maid nodded obediently.

'Strictly speaking,' Lady Alice continued as she fingered the window sill for traces of dust, 'the rough shoot is a gentleman's sporting weekend but I am obliged to Lady Godolphin and so have agreed to receive her daughters. It will complete their coming-out season.'

Heather, the maid, relieved to see that her mistress had failed to discover any dust, merely nodded. Lady Alice would have dispensed brisk discipline if her finger had detected any evidence of a lazy maid. But the moment of danger, and the threat of a sore bottom for Heather, had passed. She sighed.

'London debs frequently prove to be as spirited as they are inexperienced,' Lady Alice pronounced as she inspected the curtains closely. 'See to it that there are absolutely no nocturnal adventures. Understand me, girl? No midnight excursions.'

'Yes, ma'am.'

Lady Alice drew her lorgnette swiftly up to her piercing eyes. The lenses flashed as the mistress inspected her maid.

'Girl,' she barked, 'did not the housekeeper issue you with a clean, starched apron this morning?'

Heather blushed. Squirming under the glinting lorgnette, she nervously palmed the crisp apron at the curve of her thighs.

'You have managed, I see, to soil it already. I shall see to it that tuppence is deducted from your wage this sabbath to defray the extra laundering costs. I will not abide slovenliness in my maids. Go straight down to the housekeeper's office and ask her for a clean apron, girl.'

'Yes, ma'am.'

'And for two strokes of her tawse.'

Heather bowed her head, meekly accepting the prescribed punishment. Behind her back, her hands fluttered before instinctively cupping and shielding her buttocks.

'And, girl –'

'Yes, ma'am?'

'Come back upstairs to me directly you have been punished. I wish to see your stripes. I want you properly punished and so I will examine your bottom for my own satisfaction.'

'Yes, ma'am.'

Three hours out of London and four hours from Inverness, the powerful train thundered northwards, its thick ribbon of smoke curling away over the flat Fenlands.

Watching the gold and brown patchwork of autumnal fields flash by from the luxury of their first-class carriage, the Godolphin sisters lapsed into companionable silence. Since leaving London, their excited chatter had been of the Season so far. Dances, suppers and more formal dinner balls. Their presentation at Court – before a diminutive, plump little Queen dressed in funereal black. Goodwood. The opera. Encounters with virile men ruined by the oppressive vigilance of chaperones. Equally thrilling for the debutantes was their introduction to bustiers and corsetry that squeezed and to the cool kiss of silks and satins upon their trembling young flesh.

Now they were heading for Scotland and the weekend rough shoot. To Strachayle Castle, which would be bristling with desirable males. Their hearts hammered behind their heavy, swollen breasts. To be alone amongst men at last. Alone, unaccompanied and unchaperoned.

Edwina closed her eyes and recounted the intimate highlights of her coming out season so far. She shivered as she remembered the fierce mouth, and the warm, probing tongue, of a Hussar. He had twirled her away from the dancefloor during a waltz, kissed her savagely out on the balcony and then spun her back into the respectability of the ballroom that night in Cadogan Square. She had, later that night in bed, played with her pussy properly for the very first time, the memory of his hard lips and punishing tongue soaking her frantic fingertips.

Edwina flushed at the memory, then shivered with pleasure at the thought of other waltzes, other gallant officers. Dominant men who had gripped her fiercely, held her closely, their proudly erect manhoods urgent against her moistening maidenhead. And that evening in the opera. Yes. She shuddered and moaned at the delicious remembrance. A decorated Major in the Blues, his leathery face masterfully stern, bending down in the darkness to retrieve her gloves. She had held her breath and squirmed as his hands had caressed her upper thighs. She blushed and grew pleasantly hot at the thought of his sure and certain touch, at the bold impudence of his hand sliding beneath her buttocks to squeeze and fondle them throughout the entire second act of *Turandot*.

Edwina, a brown-eyed, softly lisping brunette, delighted in the easy arrogance and supreme confidence of older men. Experienced, mature men. Melting in their presence, she often felt the soak of her excitement at her silk cami-knickers. She yearned to know their power more intimately. But during the Season, the rules of engagement between the sexes were strict and the codes of propriety severe.

As the train thundered onwards, she lapsed into a waking dream. Behind coyly closed eyes whose lashes frequently flickered with excitement, she conjured up deliciously naughty dreams and desires for the weekend of

49

rough shooting. But Edwina scorned the dubious pleasures of roaring guns, barking dogs and chill mists on freezing grouse moors. For her, the game to be bagged was men. Preferably older men. Worldly men of experience. A Tory grandee, perhaps. Stern and accustomed to command. He would curtly insist upon a midnight assignation, instructing Edwina to attend him in his chamber. Risking the shame of scandal if discovered, she would rush on tiptoe to him. Behind his locked door, he would remain attired in his black velvet smoking jacket, sipping brandy as she shrugged her white lawn chemise off and stood in its puddle at her feet, naked and gleaming before him. He would approach, judging her as he would a horse or dog. Inspecting her intimately, he would run his firm finger from her chin down her throat to her bare bosoms. The fingertip would close into a cruel pincer with his thumbtip at her nipple. Gazing dominantly into her wide eyes, he would tease and tame the painfully peaked flesh-bud then bring his cruel lips down upon it to suck, then bite.

Moaning slightly, Edwina tossed and turned in her sumptuously upholstered leather seat. At the join of her thighs, a warm ooze signalled her delicious distress. Despite her tight clothing, the corset and crinolines, she managed to spread her buttocks wide, almost crying out softly as a dull ache burned deep in her cleft. Lulled by the rhythms of the wheels and seduced by her waiting fantasy, she drifted back into her dark reverie: her wicked desire for naked submission and meek surrender to the sharp appetite of a mature, dominant male.

Behind closed eyes, she imagined him once more, still attired in his velvet jacket, in stark contrast to her soft nakedness. The contrast rendered him more powerful, more masterful. Naked, she would be his plaything for an idle hour. She would uncover her body for his perusal and pleasure. Yes. But, withdrawing his brutal hand from her punished breast, he would ignore her and return to sip his brandy. In her daydream, Edwina whimpered her soft sigh of pleasure. To be naked and ashamed before this man, this silver-haired statesman who forsook her breast to bring his lips to his brandy. She thrilled to the imagined humiliation – and her pussy wept with joy.

'Put your hands up behind your head, my girl,' he would instruct her.

Burning with both pleasure and shame, Edwina saw herself obeying with reluctant eagerness. Her breasts would swell and burgeon as her arms rose up, elbows angled, in obedience to his command. At her coiled, dressed hair, her fingers would undo her careful locks, spilling them down in a wanton tumble. Utterly naked now, and lewdly exposed, she would inch her thighs apart. Like a harlot. A shameful harlot one furtively read about in the Bible or the lurid Sunday papers taken by the servants below stairs. Dizzy with the thrill of her sinful lust, and shyly eager to be deservedly punished for that sinful lust, she would name for him – touching them, as she did so – her maidenly parts.

'And what does my little whore call these?' he would demand, tapping her nipples with the tip of his crop.

Cupping her breasts and offering them to him submissively, she would whisper her shameful response.

The crop would rake down across her belly and drag intimately through the dark nest of her curled body hair below.

'And what name has my little wanton tart for this?' he would growl, probing the sticky fleshfolds of her private place.

Rising up on her tiny white toes, she would confess the name.

'Not fanny?' he would counter sharply. 'Or cunny?'

Then, at last, the hoped-for – dreaded – command.

'Kneel.'

Bowing her head down so that her lips kissed the carpet at his feet, she would crouch, quivering, awaiting his pleasure and her pain. Treading her down with his foot upon the nape of her neck, he would guide the tip of the crop down along her spine to the soft warmth between her raised buttocks. Soon, he would ply the crop less tenderly, more violently. With a vicious affection, to slice-swipe her naked cheeks and kiss them with crimson that would burn to a deeper red. But before the sweet strokes across her helpless buttocks, she would have to endure the bitter-bliss of abject humiliation as she knelt, naked, in his thrall.

The mournful screech of the train's whistle opened her large brown eyes instantly. Blinking away her fantasy, Edwina gazed out through the carriage window. In the far distance, just visible against the purple smudge of the horizon, she saw that a hunt was up and in full cry. Red-jacketed riders on tiny horses were following a speckled pack of miniature hounds. The master of the hunt saluted the train, acknowledging its whistled greeting with two muted notes on his horn. Thundering on, the train gave a farewell blast. The hunt vanished from sight. Edwina closed her eyes, her mind dwelling on a set of sepia prints she had glimpsed when staying with a great-aunt who rode with the Quorn. Sepia prints of huntsmen erect in the saddle, their crops alert and aquiver. Conscious of the wet seethe between her thighs, a moist warmth that rendered her fluffy little pubic fringe soaking, she seized upon the conjured image of her nocturnal visit to the lair of the silver-haired politician, her Tory squire, in Strachayle Castle. She wanted him still fully dressed, to sharpen her sense of his mastery over her trembling nakedness. A nakedness he would straddle as he flexed his cruel crop. Soon, the pleasurable pain would commence.

Down on the carpet beneath him, she would clench her small fists and willingly inch her bare bottom up. *Crack*. The first swipe of leathered cane across her waiting cheeks. Taloning the carpet, she would jerk in anguish at the bite across her rounded buttocks. Then, almost immediately, another short thrumming hiss as the crop lashed down. *Crack*. Another searing swipe – one of many, many more to blaze down and bite-slice her flesh. She would grunt her response into the carpet, the shrill yelp softened by a sweeter note of dark joy. Between the strokes, she would squeeze her cheeks together as if to extinguish the tiny tongue of fire licking the length of her cleft. But nothing, she feared, would damp down the blaze deep in her tiny anal whorl.

* * *

Sitting opposite her sleeping sister, Charlotte Godolphin remained wide awake. Her summer months had been long and lonely ones and her Season had not been a success. With short, bobbed blonde hair the shade of pale champagne and glittering green eyes, Charlotte was almost exactly the opposite of her younger sister in every respect. Where Edwina was shy and timid, Charlotte was bold and strong-willed. Where Edwina sought maturity to take her firmly in hand, Charlotte desired to dominate youth.

Early nursery experiences with a tough nanny had allowed Charlotte frequent glimpses of naked male buttocks being firmly chastised. With two brothers and Thomas, a cousin, in the nursery and later at their small desks in the school room, Charlotte enjoyed the spectacle of nanny being fierce with the unruly boys. She had frequent cause to relish the ritual of their bottoms being bared to receive the flurry of stinging spanks.

The intervening years had afforded few crumbs of comfort to feed her growing appetite for the punishment and strict discipline of males. Three summers ago, she had contrived to get her cousin Thomas whipped when he was down for Michaelmas from Eton. She had lied, telling her mother that it had been Thomas who had introduced the grass snake to cook's bed. Lady Godolphin had plied the dog whip across the howling boy's bare bottom behind closed doors – but Charlotte had listened at the door, her pulses racing and her breasts feeling inordinately heavy in their sweet ache.

There were rumours, of course. Whispered asides between visiting dowagers. Whispered accounts of the caning of pantrymen suspected of stealing claret – and kisses from squealing maids. Charlotte had also overheard mention of a salon in Ebury Street where young bucks were tied up and flogged with bundles of birch twigs. Charlotte would bring these scraps and morsels to bed with her at night to feed her hot imaginings as her fingers flayed her pussy.

Charlotte was sure that there existed a private world within London society, a secret world where young men sought pleasure in being punished by ladies who found pleasure in dispensing discipline. But the doors to that world remained closed. Not so the doors to the library. She had passed many instructive hours among forbidden books, poring over Sadean texts and alighting, by chance, upon the poet Swinburne. She became acquainted with his professed penchant for pain, for strict punishment. In his confessions, the florid rhymster freely owned his need for cruel stripes to inspire sweet strokes from his pen.

Now, at last, she was heading for Strachayle Castle and the possibility of adventure. Such weekend gatherings always included poets and painters. Yes. There would be several young men, foppish in their long hair and peacock attire. Pale young men who would be eager for her strict attentions. She pictured herself in a drawing room, alone, perusing a small book of French verse. She would be smoking a small, slender cheroot and sipping a pink gin. One such young man, timorous, with delicate hands and shyly averted eyes, would enter. Avoiding her gaze, he would approach the pianoforte, seat himself before it and commence playing. It would be Mozart. She would join him, allowing the ash from her cheroot to spill down upon the white keys. Her presence would make him increasingly nervous. His fingering would become less sure. At his third blunder at the keys, she would sharply rap her folded fan down across his knuckles. With a soft moan of delight, he would bury his fist between his thighs. The bond would be forged between them. Later, in the moonlight of her bedroom, he would be naked and kneeling – hers entirely to do with as she pleased.

Charlotte concentrated hard, just as she did when reading German novels. Concentrated hard, anxious not to miss the slightest nuance. She imagined her bedroom after midnight. They would both be naked, young debutante and kneeling youth. He would be begging to kiss her breasts, belly and below. She, like La Belle Dame Sans Merci in the book in her father's library, would only deign to allow him to lick and lap at her feet. Whimpering softly, he would obey, his hot, wet tongue busy at her toes. After a strict spell of this delicious homage, she would turn languidly and offer her bare buttocks to his eager, up-turned face. Further homage would then be paid, his flushed face buried between her soft, rippling cheeks.

Her sovereignty established, they would enter into the night of discipline and domination. She would select a silken stocking to bind her kneeling slave, bind his ankles together into burning helplessness. Another silken stocking would visit his wrists and render them useless and immobile above his naked buttocks. Whimpering with fearful anticipation, he would writhe. Stern and silent, she would motion to him to be still, and out of pity allow him to peep as she donned a crisp white basque. His eyes would widen in wonder as she drew the laces tightly, squeezing her breasts until they bulged. Smoothing her belly and thighs, she would gaze down, smiling contemptuously at his thickening manhood raised in a smart salute. Capturing it between her knees, she would squeeze it as tightly as the satin at her bosom squeezed her ripe flesh. She would feel the warmth throbbing between her controlling flesh.

The train clattered over a set of points, jolting Charlotte out of her vivid reverie. Opposite her, her gloved right hand scrabbling fitfully at the silk dress stretched across her lap, Edwina dozed. Charlotte watched the gloved fingers suddenly splay out like a starfish as Edwina, in her turbulent dreams, palmed her inner thighs.

Charlotte studied her younger sister's face. The mouth was slightly open, the lips moist, the pink tongue-tip protruding as it would to lick at the ripeness of an oozing plum. Edwina was clearly enjoying a very wicked dream. Charlotte closed her glittering green eyes and returned to hers.

She revisited her boudoir in Strachayle Castle, where her naked slave-lover would beg for his pain. As he became both loud and impatient, she would have to kneel down before him and silence his pleading whine. Charlotte clenched her small paw-fists twice and purred as she anticipated finger-forcing her slightly soiled cami-knickers into his mouth. Further dark joy would flow from the binding of his imploring eyes with calico. Silenced, and denied sight, he would be all hers – the green-eyed cat had

55

captured her quivering little mouse. Let the tantalising teasing and exquisite torments commence.

With a gloved hand, of black velvet and stretching tightly up to her elbow, she would finger her captive intimately: rubbing, stroking and then probing as she explored all the secrets of the naked male so far denied to a well-bred debutante. Fear and excitement would bead the temples of her willing victim. The only sounds audible would be her panting breath and the soft creaking of her crisp basque. Utter wickedness. She would then experience the forbidden delight of his hot erection nestling against the soft curves of her bosoms and then, guided by her gloved fist, his twitching length between her satin buttocks. Would she dare to press the glistening tip of his captive shaft into that hot little hole buried deep between her cheeks? Squirming in her carriage seat as the train sped on, Charlotte grunted thickly. In her imagination, her night of perverse pleasures in Strachayle Castle was yet young.

Pain. That was what she desired to delight in – punishment and pain. The punishment and pain of a submissive male. She anticipated every single moment of her impending dominance. After undoing his blindfold to gaze down into his fear-clouded eyes, she would show him the instrument of chastisement. With neither crop or cane to hand, it would have to be her silver-backed hairbrush, stiffly bristled and glinting with the promise of pain. Then she would slowly bind a pink ribbon around the knout of his erection to stem and stay his spurt of vital juices elicited by the severe strokes of brush on bottom.

Forcing his head down into a cushion, and pinning him firmly as his gagged mouth mutely kissed the velvet, she would palm his upturned buttocks with her gloved hand. The sweep of the controlling hand would grow firmer. She would pause, briefly, to finger-stroke his cleft. As his sac swung gently between his splayed thighs, the time would come for the gloved fingers to close around the handle of the silver-backed hairbrush, grip it tightly and raise it aloft. The chastisement would commence: again, and again, the polished surface would crack down mercilessly across his punished buttocks. Her bound slave would writhe before buckling under the savage onslaught but, helpless in her thrall, he would not be able to escape her vicious tenderness.

After nine strokes, she would quickly invert the bristled face of the brush to tap the ribboned knout of his pulsing cock. The dancing pink ribbon would signal his desperate need for release but, cruel mistress that she was, Charlotte would deny him his desire and revisit his suffering cheeks to blister them harshly with the spanking brush. As his bottom reddened to an almost unbearable shade of pain, she would thrill to the knowledge that her own cami-knickers were silencing his howls of anguish.

And when the prinked fingers of her velvet-gloved hand released the ribbon? What then? Charlotte had as yet no direct knowledge of the erect male organ exploding and ejaculating. Forbidden texts in her father's library had prepared her but she enjoyed only a vague notion of how her punished slave would respond. The pink ribbon, dancing excitedly at the end of the twitching erection. With her dominant gaze quelling his submissive eyes, she would talon his hair and force him to worship her as her gloved hand slowly teased the ribbon loose.

Candle wax. Hot, sticky and quicksilverish. That was what it would be like. A squirt-splash of his seed up on to the swell of her bosom. Perhaps a pitter-pat upon her face. Would she dare to tongue-tip catch a pearl of his liquid devotion? It would be warm and creamy and waxy to the touch. The forbidden books had prepared Charlotte for the wet excitement of a whipped man. But no book yet printed, she acknowledged, could ever prepare her for the muffled scream of agony torn from her punished worshipper's gagged lips.

With a long, unbroken screech of its whistle, the shuddering train plunged into a long, dark tunnel. Charlotte gasped and sat bolt upright, blinked then twisted her face towards the black carriage window. Her green eyes glimpsed their own cruel reflection in the darkened glass. The eyes of a cat, hungry for her mouse.

* * *

The pony-cart trundled up along the mud track slowly. Shivering in the back, exposed to the chill mist, the Godolphin girls suffered the delights of a rough shoot. Heavy tartan rugs around their knees failed to keep them warm. Soon the moorland rose up too steeply for the labouring pony. Dismounting – cursing softly as they slipped and shivered – the sisters trudged the final mile to where the guns had assembled. Higher up, where the mist was thicker and more penetrating, the men stood in a ragged line, muffled in tweeds and frequently sipping from hip flasks.

On the crest of the rolling moor, beaters appeared, advancing slowly down towards the guns. They were shouting and waving sacking and thrashing the heather with long sticks. Rabbits bolted down into the bark and blaze of the guns. The beaters advanced, fanning out to cover the hillside. Small, fat grouse whirred up from the wet cover. Another salvo reverberated across the moor, bringing the dead birds down into the heather.

It was a dreary, dull sport for the girls. They shrank back from the noise of the guns and the reek of acrid cordite. They soon grew numb from both the boredom and the cold. They recoiled delicately from the sight of blood-spattered grouse being bundled and trussed as the game was bagged – and shuddered as rabbits were held aloft to have their necks stretched and their full bladders squeezed dry. The interminable Saturday shoot had not been a sparkling success. The Godolphin sisters bumped back in the cart to Strachayle Castle in the chill of an autumn dusk.

'Shall I run a bath, ma'am?' Heather inquired, helping Edwina out of her mud-spattered attire. 'Or would you prefer to wash and dress your hair before dinner?'

'I think I had better bathe, please.'

Please. Heather's eyes widened a fraction at the word. It told her that the young lady she was briskly disrobing was not the customary assured daughter of the aristocracy. Haughty young debs never used 'please' or 'thank you' to their maid. This girl, Heather mused, unlacing the strings of the corset and allowing the trapped breasts within its strict confines their freedom, was a shy little thing. The maid smiled as she stripped her mistress bare. Her shy, somewhat submissive mistress.

Edwina, her soft buttocks joggling as she trod the carpet, murmured a shy question to the maid.

'Oh, no, ma'am,' Heather replied emphatically. 'You'll not be seeing any of the gentlemen this weekend. Most strict about that, Lady Alice is, ma'am. Gentlemen dine separately, then retire to their port and cigars. It's billiards for them, ma'am. The ladies read religious texts or sew their pretty samplers.'

'Oh.' Edwina's sigh could not conceal the deep note of disappointment.

'Any particular gentleman was there, ma'am?' Heather prompted.

Edwina replied guardedly that she had hoped for some instruction from Sir Julian Fox, one of the weekend guests.

'Instruction, ma'am?' Heather echoed, retreating to the bathroom. She shivered as she remembered the old roué's consummate skill with the cane during a brief visit earlier in the year.

'Yes,' Edwina replied, hurriedly explaining, 'I need to be schooled. I remain such a novice and he is surely a man of rich experience.'

'Bath's ready, ma'am. Look sharp. Mustn't be late to table.'

The maid assisted her mistress into the bath tub and, unrequested but not refused, used the soap flannel vigorously. Edwina surrendered to the deft, capable hands of the busy maid, submitting her soft, pink nakedness to the soaped yellow sponge. Heather exchanged the sponge for a loofah. Edwina gasped aloud as it raked her shoulders and spine. Heather grew bolder with the loofah, using it at first in the cleavage between the wet, shining breasts and then angling it down to nuzzle the dark patch of pubic hair beneath the curdling soap suds. Edwina, grinding her buttocks into the dimpled rubber bath mat, shyly opened her thighs to receive the rasping length.

59

The snout of the loofah teased her labial fleshfolds as the eyes of the naked mistress met those of her attendant maid. Heather saw in Edwina the disappointment and the yearning. Reaching down, she caressed the bather's naked thigh as she insinuated her hand to wrench up the plug.

'Up,' she ordered, her tone crisply polite.

Edwina rose up as instructed, the creamy suds annointing her breasts and belly.

'I'll rinse you then dry you.'

The 'ma'am' had been dropped. The maid was now in control of her mistress.

'Turn around.' The curt command brought a slight flush to Edwina's cheeks. Her shining buttocks wobbled as she obeyed.

'Close your eyes.' Heather mounted a small foot stool and emptied the ewer of ice-cold water in a sluicing cascade over the nude.

Edwina gasped and squealed, hugging and squeezing her breasts protectively. The cold water raised her thick nipples up instantly.

'Stop that silly noise.' *Spank*. Heather slapped the wet bottom sharply. 'Hurry up and get out.'

Edwina half turned towards the maid, her lips parted in wonder. Her left hand was at her spanked buttock, soothing the reddening cheek.

'Leave that alone or there'll be another,' Heather snapped.

Edwina dropped her hands, exposing her bare bottom to the whim of the maid's spanking hand – the maid who was now utterly in command of her mistress shivering before her.

Roughly towelled dry, during which operation her breasts suffered cruelly, Edwina trembled eagerly as she waited for the fine sprinkle of dusting powder to be applied. Heather guided the nude to the bed in the adjoining chamber and arranged her captive face-down upon the bedspread. Cupping her right hand, she sprinkled the rose-scented powder until her palm was pale. Applying the dusting powder gently at first, Heather's touch became increasingly dominant as it swept down the dimpled spine and firmly caressed the proffered buttocks. Moaning into the pillow, Edwina inched her hips and thighs up so that her bare bottom could enjoy the delicious sensation of the sleek palm at her swollen curves. *Spank*. The sudden blow caused her heavy cheeks to wobble. Edwina hissed her pleasure – the necessary signal for the punishment to begin in earnest.

Heather mounted the bed, dimpling the bedspread as she knelt, using her left hand to pin her naked mistress down by the nape of the neck while her right hand cupped and squeezed the buttocks beneath its controlling touch. Edwina wriggled and squirmed in a token show of resistance, rubbing her nipples and pussy-lips into the rasp of the bedspread. Four harsh spanks rang out, the small, firm hand cracking down across the helpless cheeks. Edwina writhed in delicious pain, her sinuous jerking and sensuous wriggling immediately inflaming the hand into a furious, blistering staccato. The quickened hand caused the pink cheeks to redden as the crimson flush of pain spread across their delicious curves. Tiny red blotches betrayed the harsh imprint of the spanking hand's fingertips along the outer buttock's swell.

Squealing loudly, Edwina tried in vain to twist out of the maid's pinioning grip.

'Be still,' Heather commanded. 'I know when.'

Slumping down in submission, the mistress moaned as the maid ravished the bare buttocks with her spanking hand. Curving her hot palm, Heather shuffled her knees a fraction and stretched across to reach the outer cheek. Edwina writhed as the unblemished flesh burned pink then as uniformly crimson as its already punished twin. Satisfied, the maid addressed the soft sweep of the lower buttocks at the point where they melted into the swell of the upper thighs. Her angled hand swept up into the helpless flesh, causing her victim to scream.

'Silence.'

Obediently, Edwina bit the pillow to muffle her moans. In a swift test of her sovereignty, Heather relaxed her grip, releasing the spanked nude from her thrall. Edwina remained prone and still, squeezing her reddened cheeks spasmodically. Whimpering softly, she gestured for the return of her punisher's controlling hands. Smiling, the maid cupped and sharply squeezed both of the crimson buttocks then, lowering her face down into their inviting swell, licked and softly bit the chastised bottom.

Edwina's fists pummelled the bedspread. She jerked her nakedness against its rough weave, rasping her pussy so that the juicy outer lips splayed wide and her tingling inner fleshfolds raked the fabric deliciously.

'No. Stop that,' Heather warned, tapping the naked bottom with an admonishing forefinger. 'Not now. You must not be late for dinner. Tonight,' she murmured, fingering Edwina's sticky cleft lightly before scratching at the hot sphincter within, 'I will come to you. And I will bring something special. Something special for your naughty, bare bottom.'

Dinner was dispiriting. Lady Alice's fare was in itself quite acceptable – oyster soup, turbot, a baron of beef, a baked, spiced ham, Orkney cheese and fruits from the hothouse – but the company was dull and the conversation duller. The men dined separately. From time to time, gusts of coarse laughter bellowed from their secluded lair. Later, they would withdraw for cigars, brandy and ribaldry behind firmly closed doors. Lady Alice conducted her table with crisp propriety. Tomorrow, she informed her female guests, there would be a bracing walk to the kirk with religious texts and samplers to sew after lunch.

Edwina, her bottom still stinging after the severe spanking, squirmed and squashed her hot cheeks into the hard seat of her wooden chair. To her delight and shame, her belly tightened and her juices flowed freely as the baked, spiced ham was brought to the table. Its pinkness was just like that of a freshly chastised bottom; as the succulent meat surrendered to the carving knife, she felt her inner muscles spasm and implode.

Between the removal of the Orkney cheese and the arrival of the fruit, Lady Alice saw fit to complete her young guests' social education, launching into an interminable disquisition on the etiquette of rough shooting. Edwina fiddled with her ivory-handled fruit fork. Would midnight never come?

'It's a tawse. For your backside. Like I promised.'

Edwina shrank a little from the brutal length of leather. Her sudden movement caused the candle flame to flicker.

'Touch it,' Heather urged, offering the supple tawse to the young lady in the bed.

Edwina stretched out a curious finger and traced it along the shining hide. Emboldened, she accepted it across the palm of her upturned hand. Feeling its weight, she shivered.

'Smell it.' The maid's tone was curt. Only her eyes betrayed her fierce excitement.

Edwina obediently sniffed.

'Taste.'

Her flickering tongue-tip darted forth, retreating instantly from the haunting tang.

'Face down. I'll take the pillows,' Heather grunted softly as she gathered them up, 'and put them here.'

Edwina, turning over in the bed, felt the pillows between her naked hips and the cool linen sheet beneath. She nestled her pussy into their softness.

'Makes your bum nice and big and round,' the maid remarked, dragging the top sheet and blanket down to the end of the narrow bed. 'Hands up to the bedstead.'

Edwina's fingers blindly sought and found the brass-work at once. She gripped the dull metal tightly.

Crack. The broad belt whistled down, searing the proffered cheeks viciously. The punished nude squealed and clenched her whipped cheeks in a reflex of sudden agony. A second, then a third sharp crack followed, the swift strokes lashing down harshly across the naked bottom. At the brasswork, the gripping fingers splayed in an ecstasy of anguish. The punisher's grunts of exertion were drowned by the punished nude's choking sobs of joy.

'Silence,' Heather warned, raising the tawse once more above the quivering buttocks. 'Especially when you reach your satisfaction.'

Whimpering softly, Edwina tightened her grip on the brass bedstead and buried her face in the mattress.

The maid teased the hot buttocks of her mistress with the tip of the dangling tawse. Edwina jerked her whipped cheeks up and tried to capture it in her cleft. Heather grinned, snapped the leather aloft then swiftly cracked it down. The broad belt lashed the buttock's rounded swell, briefly flattening the double crimson domes. Edwina shuddered in response.

She'll be loud, this one, when she boils over. She's simmering nicely now, Heather thought as she fingered the tawse. Simmering nicely. Another three'll bring her to the seethe.

Crack. The leather barked. The nude jerked and squealed, her reddening cheeks wobbling deliciously.

Two more, Heather mused, and this little rabbit will be done to a turn. Flayed, skinned and all in a bubbling stew. Better let her bite the leather to silence her shrieking.

Eyes closed, her sphincter opening into a puckering crater, Edwina crushed her wet pussy into the pillows. The maid delayed the strokes. The mistress began to beg.

Strachayle Castle woke to a sharp frost. Lady Alice chivvied her guests to the kirk and back along the glittering lanes. After lunch in the draughty dining room, the women heard the men departing for more rough shooting. The Godolphin girls declined the invitation to sew samplers and retired to their respective rooms.

Edwina, claiming a headache, locked her door. She assured Lady Alice that all she required was a little rest. Listening to the retreating footsteps of her hostess, she started to loosen her bustle. Before the full-length looking glass, she raised her crinoline and petticoat and tucked them up at her waist. Slowly peeling down her cami-knickers, she thrust her bottom pertly towards the glass. Over her shoulder, she glimpsed the angry weals. The red stripes where the tawse had kissed her so savagely were still vividly imprinted across her rounded cheeks. Staggering across to the bed – hampered by her partial state of undress – she buried her face into the pillow which had captured the soak of her wet heat the night before. Moaning softly as her fingers scrabbled at her pussy, she sniffed the white pillow case, then kissed it devotedly.

Fuelled by the delicious memory of the tawse across her upturned cheeks, Edwina arrowed her arms down to the base of her belly. Just as Heather the maid had shown her, she nipped her little pink love-thorn between her thumb-tips. Moments later, Edwina bit the pillow, tearing it open with her clenched white teeth.

'Lady Alice wondered if there was anything you required, ma'am.'

Charlotte, bored and discontented, did not even bother to turn her gaze away from the window. Ignoring the maid, she shook her head.

'Sure, ma'am?'

'Nothing,' Charlotte snapped.

Heather hesitated, reluctant to depart.

'One moment, girl.'

'Ma'am?'

'Have all the men gone to the shoot?'

'Yes, ma'am. Lady Alice insists that all the guns go out.'

'Even young Hugh Lambton?'

'The poet, ma'am? Most reluctant, he was, but Lady Alice was firm.'

Charlotte received and accepted the disappointment in silence, but the maid, perceptive and shrewd, suddenly understood. What else would a stern young beauty like Miss Charlotte want with a poor stick like that long-haired poet Hugh Lambton if not for an afternoon of games – games in which the rules were strict and the penalties severe?

Heather was anxious that Lady Alice did not discover this green-eyed young vixen entertaining her young poet after dark. Somehow, she would have to amuse the cruel blonde here and now.

'Nothing I can do, ma'am? I'm here to serve.'

To serve. Charlotte whispered the words softly. 'Tidy up my dressing table,' she commanded.

Heather busied herself at the task, her mind less than half on her duties. Her knuckles swept a glass bottle on to its side. The room was instantly heavy with spilled perfume.

'Be careful,' Charlotte rasped, springing up and rushing to the dressing table. 'Just look what you've done. I've a good mind –'

'To punish me, ma'am?'

Silence, as suffocating as the sudden scent, filled the air. Heather bowed her head down and drew her hands together at her apron like a penitent schoolgirl before an angry Dame. Charlotte drew her left hands up to the pearl choker at her throat. Impossible possibilities flashed behind her green eyes. Could she punish this pert little minx? Bare her bottom and spank her hard? The desire to do so fluttered in her tightened throat.

'Just be careful,' she snapped, turning on her heel. 'Get my green gown out for dinner this evening. You can help me dress.'

In the silence of the late afternoon, with two lamps lit against the gathering gloom, the obedient maid knelt and slowly removed the last vestiges of silk and satin. Charlotte, her fluffy blonde bush sparkling in the lamplight, stood naked above her kneeling maid, naked and imperious, with her head tossed back and her hands planted firmly upon her hips.

Heather gazed up, seeking permission from the hard, green eyes. The nude inclined her head and stared dominantly down at the servant shivering at her feet.

'The perfume you spilt –'

'I'm sorry, ma'am, please –'

'Be quiet. I am thinking of a fitting punishment.'

Heather closed her eyes and bowed her head. It was brought up instantly by Charlotte's taloning hand. Heather's face was drawn closer to the gleaming pubic mound.

'Kiss me,' Charlotte murmured. 'Kiss me for not whipping you as I should.'

The maid's eager little tongue licked at the curved inner thighs, rapidly working its way towards the golden pubic

66

fern. With a soft crackle and a wet rustle, the tongue lapped the length of the pouting labial fleshfolds, then probed their salty interior. Charlotte snarled her pleasure and, gripping the maid's hair with both fists, forced the upturned face into her aching heat. Heather whimpered, her protest smothered by the hot pussy filling her mouth, but submitted to the desires of her mistress.

'Kiss,' Charlotte commanded. 'Do not lick or suck.'

Cradling the maid's head against her flesh, Charlotte spread her legs wide, ready to accept the sweet kisses. Heather defied the stern instructions, and sucked and bit the slippery fleshfolds with savage tenderness. Moments later, Charlotte buckled and collapsed, screaming softly as she rode the upturned face between her quivering thighs.

As she staggered forwards and stumbled, Charlotte forced Heather down on to the carpet beneath her. Her hips jerking now in the sweet frenzy of her gathering climax, the naked mistress straddled then squatted on the maid's face. Wriggling and burning her bottom on the carpet, Heather twisted her face to avoid the hot juices. The movement ravished the nude above. In her ecstasy, Charlotte squeezed her thighs, punishing the face below. In a spirited rebellion, Heather poked her short, thick tongue up in defiance, piercing the bitter sphincter. Choking on her lust, Charlotte savoured the ultimate submission and rose like a rocketing game bird into an explosion of delight.

'Impudence. Such wicked impudence. How dare you use me so? I'll show you who is the mistress –'

'Oh, no, ma'am, please don't –'

So far, both had played their parts to perfection: the outraged young aristocrat and the snivelling maid. But there was a touch of raw severity in Charlotte's tone, and a trace of real fear in Heather's pleading.

'How dare you put your tongue there?'

'I'm sorry, ma'am, please don't –'

'Silence. You must be taught a lesson, girl. A very painful lesson.'

67

Across the bed, her bottom bared – it had been soundly spanked – and her hands tied tightly together, the maid shivered beneath the menace of her mistress above.

'Keep absolutely still or I'll use the slipper on you.'

Heather whimpered. The wooden finger, smooth, straight and polished, approached her bottom an inch at a time. It grazed the curve of her left buttock. Heather spasmed, flinching as the finger briefly dimpled the soft swell.

'Be still.' Charlotte steadied the pearwood glove-stretcher then guided it directly into the shadowed cleft. Heather swayed her hips and, moaning softly, wriggled evasively.

'If you struggle you will suffer.'

'No, ma'am, don't. I didn't mean to –'

'I told you to kiss me, not feed upon my flesh as if it were a breast of boiled fowl.'

'But I thought –'

'Thought?' Charlotte echoed sardonically. 'Don't trouble your pretty little head with thoughts, girl. Just listen and obey.'

Heather squealed as the smooth finger nuzzled her wet anus. Her bound hands writhed helplessly as the glove-stretcher slid in between the soft mounds of her spanked cheeks.

Relishing her absolute dominance, Charlotte pinched her nipples and let her fingertips fall down to her prickling pussy. Stepping back from the bed, she grasped Heather's small, naked foot and brought the soft instep up against the wet flesh between her thighs. The maid cried out in shame and outrage at this usage, sensing where her tiny foot had been placed and hating the notion. Staring down at the tightened cheeks clenching the wooden finger between them, Charlotte ground the soft instep into her pussy, and came loudly. On the bed, helpless and humiliated, Heather sobbed.

Thrilling to the maid's sorrow-sobs – and the writhing bare bottom – Charlotte picked up the second glove-stretcher. Leaving the ivory kid leather glove impaled on the wooden finger, she knelt once more upon the bed and rested the tip in the hollow of the maid's knee.

'No –' begged the sobbing maid. 'Please. Not there –'

'The greatest impudence of all,' Charlotte purred, her green eyes dilated then sharply narrowed with lust, 'was your attempt to humour me. Don't deny it, girl. You dared to come to me and indulge my little whims.'

'I only meant –'

'You know what happens to a clever little maid who gets too big for her boots? Hm?'

On her bed, Heather sobbed brokenly.

'She's brought to heel, girl. Brought to heel.'

The little wet foot, sticky with Charlotte's wet heat, curled up in a reflex of fear.

Charlotte stroked the stretched finger of the glove down along the naked leg. At the wet ankle, she tapped the straightened finger upon the shining flesh. 'Brought to heel.'

'Please, ma'am, I've learned my lesson –'

'Not quite, girl,' Charlotte whispered, inching the tip of the erect finger up the leg towards the maid's wet pussy.

A week after the guests had departed from the rough shoot, Lady Alice sat at her desk in the estate office. The accounts books and green ledgers lay closed and set aside. She had more pressing business to attend to. Her right hand fiddled with a length of bamboo cane. It rattled on the polished surface of the desk.

'A very gushing letter from Lady Edwina, with no less than five pounds sterling enclosed. A similar note from her sister, with a curious gift. A tiny pair of gloves fashioned in beaten gold. Explain this largesse to me girl, if you will.'

Standing before the desk, Heather blushed but sought refuge in silence.

'Speak up, girl, or my cane will soon quicken your tongue.'

'I can't say, ma'am, I'm sure.'

'Cannot, or dare not? Don't be pert with me, girl.'

Heather remained silent.

'I can only conclude that you conspired with the wretched girls and procured for them forbidden assignations. What Lady Godolphin will say upon the matter of her daughters' violation, I shudder to think. I'll need the names of the men, of course.'

'But it isn't so, ma'am.'

'These letters and generous gifts tell me otherwise. Across that chair. Bare-bottomed.'

'But ma'am –'

'This instant.' Lady Alice rose from behind her desk, cane in hand. Striding across to the chair, she tap-tapped the seat impatiently with the tip of her quivering bamboo. 'I am going to whip you until you confess all.'

Across the chair, her bare buttocks trembling beneath the hovering cane, the maid softly cursed her own willingness to serve.

4

Stocking Filler

'Come.'

The door to his office opened timidly. Mr Faulkner drummed his fingers impatiently. 'Close the door, girl.'

Helen, a single parent with an eleven-year-old girl of her own, scuttled in, shutting the door behind her with a jerk of her buttocks. Stepping up to the desk, she hovered at the empty chair. Mr Faulkner did not invite her to sit.

'Just had region on the phone. Disappointing figures, I'm afraid. Very disappointing.'

He was lying. Returns at the call centre were soaring. Region had promised him a fat bonus. With Christmas coming, everyone was up for phone-a-loan easy credit.

'But the section is working flat out –'

'A section is only as good as its leader. Your section is well below performance targets, girl.'

'But I can't –'

He raised his hand to silence her protest, then eased himself back in his chair, staring directly at her breasts.

'There must be some mistake. Couldn't you recheck these figures?' Helen pleaded, squirming under his penetrating gaze.

'Only one figure I need to check. And –' he chuckled, '– you know which one that is, don't you, girl?'

Helen, a slender brunette with superb breasts, hung her head down. She blushed. Her fingers twiddled nervously. The spreadsheet she was clutching fluttered to her feet. She stooped to retrieve it, her bosom bulging at the stretch of her silk blouse.

'Leave it,' he barked. His tone softened. 'Half cups?'

Flushing deeply, Helen nodded.

'Underwired? Like I told you?'

'Underwired, like you told me,' she whispered.

'Show.' He snapped his fingers.

Mr Faulkner employed thirty-three females at the instant loan call centre. Ten to each section. Each section had a leader. All the girls busy at their terminals, sticking carefully to their scripts, had no problems with their manager. Mr Faulkner was very careful. But they hated their section leaders who drove them so hard. This isolated the section leaders. Outside the group safety of the flock, they were easy meat for the hungry office wolf.

'Show,' he snarled.

Helen, unable to share her dark secret with her colleagues, and struggling to bring up her daughter, was vulnerable. When the boss said strip, she stripped.

'Hurry up.'

Helen's fingers fumbled with the pearl button at her throat. She closed her eyes. She was already well overdrawn; Christmas without a wage would be grim. Her fingers quickened at the buttons of her blouse, leaving the flapping silk open to reveal her brassiered bosom exposed to his hungry gaze.

'Good girl,' he grunted, his greedy eyes blinking. He edged his chair back to the desk. His clenched right hand, knuckles whitening, slowly fisted his thickening erection, nursing it up into a fierce shaft.

'Shall I take my blouse off now?' Helen murmured, her voice husky with shame.

'Not yet. You know the routine.'

She did. Mr Faulkner liked her to finger each thin, white bra-strap, plucking them in turn from her warm flesh and snapping them, making the soft fleshmounds captured in their cups wobble deliciously. Helen gave him what he wanted, wincing slightly as the straps bit into her shoulders and her breasts bounced in their brassiered bondage.

'Stop teasing,' he growled impatiently.

Closing her eyes, she performed the weekly routine with sullen reluctance. Slowly wriggling out of her silk blouse, she peeled the straps down over her shoulders and bunched her breasts together. Thumbing the half cups down, she exposed each swollen breast for his perusal and pleasure.

He knuckled himself for a full two minutes. 'Now,' he barked.

She shrugged off the scanty confection of white lace, instantly palming up her gently bobbing breasts and offering them to him in utter submission. His fist worked furiously at the bulge in his straining trousers.

'Nipples,' he choked, his voice curdling with arousal.

Her thumbtips dragged down across each dark nipple, crushing the tiny flesh peaks, then flicked upwards immediately to coax them into erect little stubs.

'Faster.'

Her thumbtips became a blur at her painful, darkening nipples.

'Down,' he hissed, slapping the leather desk top with his left palm.

Massaging her breasts fiercely, her face contorted by both disgust and delight, Helen lowered herself down, half kneeling, and settled her naked, swollen breasts upon the leather. They shivered as they nestled into their own reflections. The cleavage between the trembling satin orbs was deep and inviting. The pert nipples strained in their painful arousal.

'Beautiful,' he whispered thickly.

Helen gasped aloud, jerking her head back sharply, her shoulders suddenly hunched, as he stretched his left hand out to tweak then pinch each dark nipple in turn. Blinking through her tear-filled eyes, she glimpsed his right fist knuckling the bulge in his trousers. She squeezed out her tears and closed her eyes, shutting out the sight of her total humiliation.

His excited, sweating left hand pawed her curves, squashing them, then – tightly fisted – kneading her warm flesh intimately. His knuckles dimpled her exposed curves, dominating their helplessness. Four and a half minutes later, he grunted and spasmed, eyes screwed up, face perspiring. His right knee shot up and cracked the desk above. Squirming in his chair, he cursed aloud, then moaned as he sagged in orgasm. Opening her eyes fearfully, Helen shuddered as her boss came, knuckling her nipples and his wet trousers in unison.

Tossing her head to one side, Helen gulped and blinked fresh salt tears from her eyes. Braless, she snatched up her abandoned blouse and struggled into it. Her breasts bounced as her arms filled the silk sleeves. Seconds later, her trembling fingers buttoned down and trapped the rebellious bosom, leaving the nipples prinking the tight stretch of concealing silk. She scooped up the white bra and scrunched it up in her right hand. She would take it home and wash it before wearing it again.

'Good girl,' Mr Faulkner grunted softly. 'Good girl. I'm sure those figures will be OK. No need for you to worry your pretty little head. Your job's not on the line. This month.'

'Thank you, Mr Faulkner.'

Susie, a lithe and leggy blonde, unzipped her black pencil skirt. It slithered from her hips, down her thighs to her feet. Arching each foot in turn, the blonde stepped out of its puddle daintily.

'Tights?' Mr Faulkner snapped. 'I said stockings.'

'But it's freezing at the bus stop, so I wore –'

'Tights,' he repeated angrily. 'Make you look like a bloody maths teacher. Here, get these on.' He pulled open a desk drawer, snatched out a packet of nylons and tossed them down at her feet.

Susie, with two of her section's ten terminals down, was eager to please. With no qualifications other than her leggy looks and no hope of a reference, her job as section leader was a priority. Her impatient landlord pressing her for rent arrears made her job at the call centre a priority over her principles. She picked up the packet of nylons and slit the cellophane open with her silvered thumbnail. The wrapping crackled loudly in the heavy silence.

74

'Self support, 15 denier and fully seamed. Autumn beige,' Mr Faulkner intoned like a priest at prayer. 'Autumn beige.' The office wolf licked his dry lips. Between his legs, his tail flickered with interest.

Keeping her chunky red sweater on, Susie dragged the vacant chair before the desk towards her. Planting her raised left foot upon the leather seat, she plucked at the dark blue above her swollen buttocks and yanked the waistband down over her bunched cheeks. As her silvered thumbnail grazed the shadow of her deep cleft, the office wolf growled his approval. Susie palmed the dark tights down over her thighs then, sweeping her foot down from the chair and positioning it alongside her other, wriggled and squatted slightly as she thumbed the tights down to her ankles in one swift movement.

Mr Faulkner, scrutinising every gesture, nodded appreciatively. As she struggled to remove the tights, he dragged his moistening palms across his leather desk top.

'Slowly. You're two terminals down, girl. No need to hurry.'

Susie crimsoned. Two terminals down gave him even more power over her. Tossing her blonde mane, she twisted around and guided her bare bottom down on to the leather seat. Her buttocks dimpled the polished hide, the heat of her cleft clouding its sheen. Jerking her knees up, she snapped the tights from her toes.

'When will I ever know?' the watcher purred, peering between her parted thighs at her shaven pubic mound.

It was a ritual. Susie dreaded the question – but with two terminals down she was ready to play the game.

'Know, sir?' she replied, licking her lips before answering.

Mr Faulkner's cock rose up and raked his Y-fronts in an instant salute to the authority conferred upon him. He thrilled to her 'sir'. The wolf insisted upon total respect from the sheep he preyed on.

'If you shave your pussy, girl, how do I know you're a natural blonde?'

Free from her tights, Susie, naked from the waist down, buried her silvered fingernails into a small side pocket of

her red sweater. Extracting a golden pubic coil, she
stretched across to the desk. Her thighs parted, revealing
the yawn of her darker flesh-lips at the base of her belly.
She placed the sleek wisp down upon the glinting leather.
'I saved one for you, sir.'

He craned forward and, licking his thumbtip, jabbed it
down. Bringing the golden coil of pubic hair up before his
narrowed eyes, he smiled. Trapping the fragile hair between a cruel finger and thumbtip pincer, he rubbed it. It
rustled faintly as he held it to his left ear, judging it as he
would a delicate cigar. 'Put the stockings on, girl.'

Susie bowed her head, instantly curtaining her blushes
behind a cascade of tumbling blonde hair. Elbows angled,
she drew the rolled-up stockings one by one over her feet
up to her ankles. Squashing her soft buttocks firmly into
the leather chair, she raised each knee in turn as she slowly,
seductively palmed the nylons up towards the supple sheen
of her thighs. The hem of her red sweater hung an inch and
a half above the golden tan of the stocking-tops, affording
a provocatively tantalising glimpse of her milk-white naked
flesh. Faulkner choked slightly as his tongue thickened and
his throat tightened with mounting excitement.

'Do they please you, sir?' Susie murmured, splaying out
her silvered nails along the dark bands of the taut nylons.

'Stand.'

She obeyed, her bare buttocks joggling enticingly beneath the loose cloth of her red sweater. She twisted away
from him, submitting her new nylons for his inspection.
She drew her legs smartly together. Again, her naked
cheeks wobbled above the shining nylon-sheathed thighs
just below. A faint crackle of whispering static broke the
loud silence as her stockinged thighs briefly kissed.

His fingertips drummed the leather desk top. 'The left
seam,' he barked. 'Not straight. Not perfectly straight.'

Lips parted a fraction, Susie twisted her face around to
peer at the swell of her left calf. She rose up on tiptoe, then
balanced on one foot as she flexed her knee. Her left heel
rose up, deeply dimpling the hollow behind her left knee,
as she strained to inspect the offending seam.

'Leave it, girl. I'll fix it.'

This was the moment Susie hated. Actual physical contact. Being touched. She hated the sound of his chair being pushed back away from his desk. She tensed and stiffened at the soft menace of his approaching footsteps. She shuddered at his heavy gasp as he sank down on to his knees immediately behind her.

'Absolutely still, girl, while I straighten your seam.'

'Yes, sir.'

She sensed the heat of his excited breath through the fabric of her red sweater stretched across her bottom. Then, the dominance of his controlling fingertips busy at her left seam.

After pinching the seam straight, he palmed the entire length of her nyloned leg with brutal tenderness, muttering softly to himself. He wiped his sweating forehead against the hem of her sweater, butting her cheek gently, then eased back to examine the ribbed seam.

'Must be perfect,' she heard him murmur.

His thumbs returned to her sheathed flesh, centering the seam to his satisfaction. Susie, despite her shame and humiliation, felt her wet heat juicing her labial folds. Soon she would be perfuming the office with her reluctant arousal.

His hands fell away from her captive flesh. 'Lovely,' he whispered excitedly. 'Lovely.'

Susie gasped and clenched her hands as his wet tongue rasped at her nyloned flesh, tracing with its quivering tip the entire length of the thick seam. As he strained to lap at the darker bands of each stocking-top, once more his forehead butted her rounded buttocks. Soon, the stocking-tops were soaking. He kissed them feverishly and started to suck. Susie felt his fierce erection, pulsing through his trousers, rake her flesh as he twisted on his knees behind her. Her belly tightened as his nose penetrated her clamped thighs. She heard him sniffing deeply.

'Fishnets next time.' His lips mumbled the words into the shrine of her trembling legs. 'With a black suspender. Understand?'

'Mm.'

'Say it, girl.'

Susie repeated the instruction, deliberately prolonging the vowels. She dropped her voice to a husky whisper when announcing the words black suspender belt. His erection jerked against her. He groaned, burying his face into her thighs.

'Still behind with your rent, girl?'

'Yes, sir.'

'You need not worry. As long as you make sure the fishnets are tarty. Tarty and cheap. OK?'

'Tarty and cheap fishnets, sir, with a black suspender belt.'

His grunt became a prolonged moan. Susie flinched as the spurt of his orgasm soaked through his trousers on to her shining legs.

The calendar on the wall showed a cute little brunette squashing snowballs into her bare breasts. Above the cupping hands, her red lips formed a perfect circle of coquettish surprise. Below, fine powdered snow dusted the nude's dark bush between her splayed thighs. Debbie Does December. Mr Faulkner's office was one of the remaining few where such a calendar could be openly displayed.

Christmas was almost about to break out. Outside, the pavements were congealing with shoppers and ungritted slush. He liked Christmas. It was, Mr Faulkner thought happily, a time for giving. He liked presents. What would he be getting from his three section leaders? he wondered. Obedience. It did not matter how they wrapped, then unwrapped it – as long as they offered him their obedience and submission. In satin basques, in half-cupped lace bras, in satin panties or in glossy nylon stockings. No, it didn't matter how they gift-wrapped their surrender to him. Half-dressed, then naked before him, subject to his slightest whim, it was his thoughts that counted. His fantasies made flesh.

Annette closed the door gently. He glanced up, his eyes raking her wolfishly. He grinned, revealing his white teeth.

The office wolf's tail thickened and grew erect as the lamb approached his desk.

Annette worked hard to pay for her singing lessons. With good looks and a great figure, all she needed was another six months' voice tuition. Then she would be ready, her agent promised, for her career launch. But not for another six months.

Mr Faulkner liked having Annette in his thrall. A cool, upper-crust brunette with a private education, she had at first been both a threat and a challenge. Her clipped vowels and perfectly modulated tone had made him acutely aware of his estuary vowels and coarse glottal stops. He had at first never risked anything tricky – like naming a French cheese or wine – in front of her, dreading her contemptuous disdain for his clumsy pretensions. Then he had found out her weak spot and pounced. She needed her job desperately for the tuition fees. In his thrall, she became tender meat for the hungry wolf.

'What are you going to sing for me, eh?'

Annette fingered the edge of the dark leather desk top, avoiding his direct gaze.

'What are you studying these days?'

'French chansons,' she whispered, jabbing her straightened index finger into the leather sulkily.

'Chansons,' he echoed, mangling the pronunciation.

Annette winced, but masked her contempt carefully.

'Offenbach. I'm studying his Tombal-Cazar –'

'Sounds like a Kraut name to me. Sing some.'

Her hands drew together at her belly. Moistening her lips with a darting tongue tip, she raised her head a fraction up from its dejection and started to sing. Her tone was sweet, each cadence perfectly captured.

Mr Faulkner raised up his hands and executed a crude attempt at conducting her. A gathering tear sparkled in her eye.

'Aren't you forgetting something?' he interrupted bluntly.

Annette blushed, turned slowly and, without missing a single note, presented her bottom to his greedy gaze. An inch at a time, she raised the hem of her skirt up until her pantied buttocks were fully exposed.

'Keep singing, girl. Nice little tune.'

Annette obeyed, but the shame of her humiliation brought a tremble to her voice.

He gripped the edge of his desk. 'Now bend over.'

The song became more ragged, more discordant, as Annette bowed to his wishes. Her brunette curls tumbled to curtain her tear-stained cheeks as her hands, fingers splayed, touched the shining black toes of her kitten-heeled court shoes. Facing the desk, and the man sitting behind it, her rounded buttocks burgeoned within the stretch of their taut white cotton panties.

'Good,' he murmured, rising up from his chair. Striding around the desk, he approached the exposed, pantied bottom of the bending girl. 'Nice white panties. Posh. Clean, white cotton. I like that. I like that very much. Upper-drawer drawers.' He chuckled at his own cruel humour, his quivering forefinger tracing the outer curves of each swollen cheek with increasing dominance.

'Tell me again about the uniform they made you wear at that snooty boarding school.'

She told him. He thumbed the engorged head of his erection through his trousers as Annette detailed the vests, navy knickers, ankle socks, pleated skirts, crisp shirt-blouses and striped blue-and-silver ties of her uniformed boarding school days.

'No bras?'

Annette told him that, when they entered the Lower Sixth, Matron would measure the pubescent bosoms and send away for cotton bras which the girls could wear instead of the tight vests. Knuckling himself frantically, he ordered Annette to repeat it all over again.

'Now continue singing,' he grunted.

Squeezing the tears from her eyes as she squeezed her thighs tightly together, she resumed her piece from Tombal-Cazar.

'Now I want to see it.'

Annette sobbed slightly but kept her thighs pressed together.

'Open up, girl, or you'll have to sing somewhere else for your supper.'

Her cleft became a thin crease as she clenched her cheeks protectively.

'Now,' he hissed savagely, seething with impatient lust.

The thighs, sleek and soft, parted, revealing the soft shadow of her cleft deep between the pantied cheeks.

'Wider,' he thundered, choking on his arousal. 'I want to see it.'

She sobbed. Obedient to his whim, she continued singing as she positioned her bulging buttocks for his intimate inspection and prolonged perusal.

'Excellent.' She heard him giggle as he inched his face down against her swollen curves. His parted lips fleetingly brushed against the white cotton sheathing her buttocks. Her belly churned and she missed her note. Faltering, she struggled to resume the chanson.

Mr Faulkner started to come. His bulging Y-fronts caught most of his warm seed, soaking them and his trousers. The dark stain spread as he whispered sweet obscenities into the tight panties. He glanced down. His eyes widened as they saw the tiny stray wisp of dark pubic hair trapped by the white cotton trim. His shaft pulsed, the wet glans raked upwards and dribbled more glutinous semen. His eyes darted to the contoured swell of her pubic plum undulating beneath the stretch of soft fabric.

'Hands,' he ordered in a voice neither of them recognised.

Slowly, reluctantly, her clear-varnished fingernails appeared across the swell of each cheek, almost but not quite touching at the dip of her cleft. Slowly, reluctantly, she started to drag her cheeks apart. She sensed him bending closer, felt his hot breath. Already, her nostrils flared in repugnance at the sharp tang of his orgasm.

'Perfect,' he pronounced, peering at the small dark circle of her shrivelled sphincter. 'Perfect,' he repeated, probing its soft warmth with his index finger pressing through the white cotton panties.

As his fingertip grazed her sensitive anal whorl, Annette gasped – and hit a shrill A sharp Offenbach never scored.

Annette toyed with her pudding, prodding the apple crumble and cream listlessly with a sulky spoon.

'Not struggling with another diet?' her lover, Jane, asked with ironic concern.

Annette placed her spoon down and, forcing a smile, shook her head.

'Come to bed,' Jane decided firmly. 'You need cheering up.'

Naked, bosom to bosom, belly to belly, they cuddled and embraced beneath the duvet. Jane, maturer and gently dominant, rode the nude below, sweeping her hips from side to side to rasp her pubis across Annette's fluffy nest. But tonight, there were no sharp little squeaks of response. Soon, speech was impossible as their mouths met and pressed fiercely together. Jane, as usual, took the upper hand, probing Annette's mouth with her thickening tongue. Again, the nude in her embrace remained mutely passive. Driven by both panic and impatience, Jane slid her left hand down to cup and squeeze Annette's buttocks. Bridling at the continuing lack of response, she taloned the left cheek savagely then slipped her finger deep into Annette's rectum. The cheeks tightened, signalling resistance and resentment. Jane sensed no welcome in their warmth.

Dragging her prinked nipples across those of the submissive nude beneath her controlling body, Jane eased herself up on her elbows, sighed and rolled over on to her back. They lay, thighs just touching, in the silence of the darkened room.

'Is there someone else?' Jane whispered softly. 'I think you should –'

Her anxious voice was drowned by a loud sob. Jane scrambled to snap on the bedside light and returned to her naked lover, cradling the weeping girl.

Annette refused to explain at first, but Jane coaxed her gently. Soon the shame and humiliation experienced under the predatory boss was laid bare.

* * *

Later. 'Drink this,' Jane murmured.

They sipped brandy alternatively from the same glass, each girl carefully placing her lips where the other's had been.

'I'm sorry –' Annette sniffled.

'You're sorry?' Jane gasped, her face pale with fury.

'I just couldn't say no –'

'Leave it all with me, darling,' Jane soothed. Her grey eyes were as cold and as hard as pressed steel. 'Just leave your Mr Faulkner to me.'

Three days before Christmas Eve. Party time. For all the girls busy at their terminals, this meant two mince pies on a paper plate and a free can of fizzy drink each. Some had softened the harsh neon-lit sterility of their work place with festive decorations. For most, it was just another busy shift.

Inside his office, Mr Faulkner almost trembled with excitement. Soon he would be receiving his presents from the three section leaders.

Helen brought her gift in to him just after eleven-thirty. Eyes lowered, her hands fluttering nervously, she approached his desk. Faltering slightly, she steadied herself, both palms spread down upon the leather. Her bending posture offered him a generous glimpse of her bulging breasts and the deep cleavage between. His eyes accepted, feasting greedily.

'What little Christmas treat am I in for?' he chuckled, stretching up his curled finger and hooking it into her blouse just beneath her bosom's swell.

Helen squirmed free and stood up, blushing furiously before the desk. Shame fuelled her reddening cheeks, as did the double vodka she had tossed back neat moments before plucking up the courage to enter the wolf's lair.

'Come here and give it to me,' she heard him bark. He sounded like some monstrous little spoiled brat.

She skirted his desk and approached his chair, kneeling down on the carpet submissively before him. Her hands unbuttoned her blouse slowly, her fingers clumsy with both vodka and shame. They plucked at the buttons, working upwards from her lower belly to her throat.

'Faster,' he half shouted, half whimpered.

Shrugging her pale green blouse free, she revealed the scarlet bustier within which her swollen breasts bulged in strict bondage. In one fluid motion, as graceful as it was sensuous, her fingers found his zip and, seconds later, fished out his lengthening shaft. It pulsed expectantly within her curved, cradling grasp then seemed to fill her fist of fingers with its urgent heat. Shuffling closer, her knees now positioned between his feet, she drew his hot cock to the cool curves of her proffered bosom.

'Yes,' he moaned, grasping the sides of his chair. He inched his buttocks up from the leather seat so that his glistening snout could kiss her soft flesh. It left a thin snail slick of pre-come across the bunched breasts' outer curves.

Helen, head bowed, teased his foreskin back with a trembling thumbtip. The gesture rocketed him into a juddering ecstasy. Behind her back, just below her shoulders, her fingers worked blindly to release the bustier's clasp. It gave. She sensed the weight of her loosening breasts burgeon. Peeling away the cups from her heavy flesh mounds, she let the scarlet bustier slither down to her thighs. In their freedom, her rounded breasts, nipples thickening, bobbed gently. She heard him curse as she raked his gleaming glans across each stubby nipple.

'Kiss it,' he choked.

Bowing down in utter submission, her dark hair spilling over her eyes, Helen tongue-tipped the hot snout of his shaft then pressed her lips upon it.

Witch, he screamed softly. Or was it bitch?

'Suck.' She heard that clearly enough.

He jerked his hips, thrusting two and a half inches of his shaft into her mouth, spearing the flesh of her throat. Inching back a little to accommodate it, she closed her lips around the cock and sucked hard.

'Santa's coming,' he warned, twisting in ecstasy.

Helen quickly drew her head away and guided the engorged cock swiftly down into the warmth of her cleavage between her breasts. The jerking action milked him into a searing release. As he splattered her, she cupped her breasts, trapping the spurting shaft, and squeezed hard. He groaned sweetly in response as she rocked back and forth, her buttocks bouncing on her heels. The groan deepened into a prolonged howl of delight as the office wolf emptied himself over her, the thick gobbets splashing her chin, neck and left shoulder.

'Happy Christmas,' Helen whispered, shuffling away from the chair. As she did so, her wet breasts bounced. Droplets of semen gathered at her stiff nipples splashed down to scald her thighs with shame. Behind her dark tumble of hair, her eyes sparkled with unshed tears.

Mr Faulkner, his erection still exposed, sank back into his chair. Twisting around, he lowered his sweating face down on to the leather of his desk top.

'I'll leave this for you,' Helen murmured, gathering up the scarlet bustier and cramming it into his bottom drawer. 'For your private pleasure, later,' she added. 'You can pretend to whip my naughty bottom with it and then come into the silk cups, mm?'

At the leather, his fingers splayed out like a speared starfish as the whispered words exploded softly in his swirling brain.

Out in the Christmas rush, Mr Faulkner was a nobody. In the bustling deli, where even the salami sausages were threaded with silvery tinsel, he waited in a long line before reaching the glass counter to ask for a chicken and salad roll. No mayo. The acne-troubled youth wearing a pair of glittering antlers and, given his skin condition, an unfortunate red Rudolph nose-cap, wasn't listening. Outside of his realm, the king of the office often found it difficult to make his presence felt.

He got a turkey bap. With mayo. Out in the slush, he bit into the festive fare. He swore, knowing that the rich stuffing would trigger off his bloody heartburn. A sudden surge of shoppers edged him off the slippery pavement. A taxi horn exploded behind him. The cabbie cursed him roundly. Shaken, he dropped his turkey bap into the gutter and loped back to his lair.

Back in his office, he was king once more. Perched upon his leather throne, he rubbed his hands. Three-fifteen. His subject was due any moment. Soon the leggy blonde would be seeking an audience to pay full homage.

Susie was bare-legged when she entered. Mr Faulkner's eyebrows rose. Anger and disappointment flickered across his eyes beneath. Susie held up a single black Fogal stocking in her clenched right hand. The eyebrows dropped. Below, the wolf licked its lips.

Mr Faulkner rose, paced around the desk and sat on it, his hands unbuckling his trousers and dragging them down to his knees. Susie, her blonde mane shining as it veiled her bowed head, sat beside him, her soft buttocks squashed into the leather. Her naked thigh nestled intimately against his.

'I like Christmas stockings,' he grunted, rubbing the black nylon between a pinched finger and thumbtip.

'Good things come in stockings,' she countered playfully, swallowing her resentful rage.

'Stocking filler,' he whispered as she stroked his cock slowly but firmly until it rose up, nodded and acknowledged her.

'Will you fill my stocking, sir?' Susie asked demurely, teasing his glans with a gentle brush of the wispy sheen.

Sir. It erased the ignomy of his turkey bap. Mr Faulkner eased himself up a fraction, peeling his heavy buttocks from the leather. Susie's fingers played with his shaft, stroking it deftly as she whispered her pretended admiration for his potency. Capturing the throbbing erection carefully, she threaded the black nylon stocking over it until its bulging flesh filled the shiny mesh.

'Will you fill my stocking, sir?' Susie whispered, masturbating him slowly, skilfully, taking pains to rasp the glans.

He shuddered in his delicious anguish, pounding the leather with his naked buttocks. His hands gripped the edge of the desk as he thrust his hips forward. Pumping him with vicious assurance, Susie braced herself for his orgasm.

'Talk to me,' he ordered, his eyes screwed up tight. 'Say those things you know I like to hear.'

Like a perverted nun at her dark catechism, Susie whispered the words he burned to hear, her shining red lips a warm breath away from his ear. Glossy. Fifteen denier. Self-support. Sheer. Ribbed seams.

'Yes,' he choked. 'More.'

'Cool nylons on warm thighs. Stretching up to the tight suspender above. The suspender's bite into the dark stocking-top. Stockings,' she tantalised, 'tightly stretched and shining.'

Each phrase was expertly accompanied by a subtle double-jerk of her controlling circled fingers. The controlling fingers within which the sooty black nylon rasped his quivering shaft.

He came like a bull, snorting and pawing the carpet as he squirted his hot release. Susie did not hurry, letting him slump down on to the desk. She slowly unwound and then peeled off the sticky black nylon. Holding it aloft before his bleary eyes, she allowed him to watch the slow drip-drip of his seed silvering the dark sheen.

'Where is the other one?' he grunted, after recovering from his intense climax.

'The other one, sir?' Susie replied in a coy pretence of unknowing.

'They come in pairs –'

'What are you suggesting, sir?' she bantered.

He loved it. He was almost dizzy with delight.

'The other black stocking. Show me.'

'Why, here it is, sir. I was keeping it warm for you,' Susie whispered, plucking the second black Fogal from her cleavage with a teasing display of shy reluctance. 'I thought you would like to see me use it on my wet pussy, sir.'

She was giving it all she'd got. The voice. The teasing words. The tongue-tip wetted lips. Driven by her desperation, Susie knew she had to make this Christmas present secure her uncertain future.

His sweating face distorted in a twisted grin of eager lust. He half choked, spluttering. Good, she thought. His response was all that she had calculated for.

'Pussy,' he grunted. 'Do it,' he almost shouted. 'Put it on your pussy now.'

'Sh,' she cautioned, nodding briefly to the closed office door – and the busy girls beyond it. 'Our little secret.'

Her last three words raked through his body. He crumpled at the knees, about to come violently. Susie dropped down to her knees instantly, her skirt riding her white hips, her panties stretched at her knees. Nimble fingers threaded the second black stocking up between her splayed thighs. The twisted skein of shiny nylon bit softly into the labia at her shaven pussy. Taut between her two clenched fists – one above her buttocks, the other level with her heaving breasts – the sliding stocking rasped her wet flesh.

His cock quivered and jerked. 'Faster.'

Raking her sensitive flesh as she plied the Fogal expertly, Susie squeezed her cheeks together in response to the scald deep in her cleft. Faster. The command echoed in her brain. Her fists became a white blur. Her belly tightened. Slumped back against the desk, hips pumping the air frantically, he shot his load with a sweet curse, leaving her upturned face sticky and shining.

Suddenly, the door burst open. Blinking through the semen silvering her eyes, Susie twisted around in alarm to glimpse a red mini-skirted, black thigh-booted female Santa entering the office. Susie screamed softly, clenching her buttocks in a reflex of surprise, trapping the stocking in her hot cleft. Faulkner cried out angrily. Santa kicked the door closed with her jabbing black boot. Unshouldering her white sack and trailing it along behind her, she approached the boss and the kneeling blonde.

From behind her red domino eye mask, Jane took in the scene before her. It was just as her lover Annette had described it. Worse. Brutal lust and dominance. Female humiliation and abject submission. Jane's grey eyes flashed dangerously as they drank in every detail. The kneeling blonde, her black stocking biting into her pussy and buried up between her swollen buttocks. The semen-splashed face. Submission and humiliation. Submission and humiliation which others – including Annette – had suffered repeatedly at the eyes and hands of Mr Faulkner.

'Happy Christmas,' she burbled, managing a light note. 'I'm your Santa Stripper.'

Extracting a small sound system from the sack, she planted it on the carpet and clicked it on. The office was instantly flooded with the insistent boom of a turbo-charged Jingle Bells.

Susie, wiping the semen from her face, scrambled to her feet and arranged her clothes.

'Leave us,' Santa commanded, jerking her thumb over her scarlet shoulder at the door. 'And see that we are not disturbed.'

Susie scuttled out, ignored by her boss who ogled the nubile Santa, thrilling to her white fur-trimmed mini-skirt, black fishnets, sleek dark thigh-boots and pert little bobbled hat.

'Who –?' he started.

'Special little treat for Christmas,' Jane whispered.

A raunchy strip ensued, leaving Santa bare-breasted. Little red silk tassels quivered at her nipples as she dragged her palms slowly up the shining length of her black boots then rasped her fishnets with splayed fingernails. Slumped in his chair behind the desk, Faulkner sat transfixed. He grunted as Santa mounted his desk, swinging her sack down on to the leather. Kneeling, her thighs deliberately parted, she allowed him a peep of her white-pantied pubis.

Jingle Bells thumped out its relentless beat. Faulkner reached up with greedy fingers to play with the tassle dangling down over the curve of Santa's left breast.

'Not yet,' Jane teased, flinching from the cruel thumb at her exposed nipple. 'I've got some presents for you. Special toys,' she whispered, 'for a very special little boy.' Her grey eyes shone behind the red domino mask.

'Show me,' he demanded.

She opened the white sack and spilled its contents down on to the leather surface of the desk. He picked each item up and nodded excitedly, jingling the handcuffs, swishing the supple sprig of mistletoe and rustling the packs of coloured condoms.

'Party time,' Jane whispered, peeling away the fur-trimmed mini-skirt from her thighs. She shook out a two-foot artificial silvered Christmas tree from the sack. Burying her hand in the farthest corner of the limp material, she extracted a fat, juicy orange.

Faulkner rattled the handcuffs impatiently but Santa merely drew them up to her glistening red lips, kissed the cold steel playfully, then placed them down on the leather. 'Later,' she whispered. 'All in good time.'

As he writhed in his frustrated torment before her, Santa weighed the orange in her outstretched palm. Bringing the swollen fruit fleetingly up to his nostrils, she ordered him to sniff. Faulkner's eyes widened in wonder then closed tightly. He dug his nose down into the gleaming rind.

'Sniff,' Santa commanded.

He obeyed, head bowed and nostrils flaring.

'You like to sniff, don't you?'

He nodded, digging his nose into the fruit. He parted his dry lips and attempted to lick. Santa glimpsed the white teeth of the office wolf.

'Bite,' she whispered, forcing the orange into his mouth.

As he sank his teeth in response to her command, she rammed the orange into his mouth. Faulkner opened his eyes in surprise. He tried to speak. Imprisoned by his deep bite, the orange filled his mouth, gagging and silencing him completely.

'Good boy,' Santa murmured. Skidding off the desk, her thigh-boots squeaking as they scuffed the leather, she was behind his chair in seconds, snapping the handcuffs into place.

Beyond the office door, all was quiet and in darkness. The abandoned phones remained silent. The late shift had gone. The call centre was now on a 48-hour Christmas shut-down.

In his office, Mr Faulkner knelt on the carpet, naked, gagged and handcuffed. A tight blindfold rendered his helplessness complete. Santa was erecting the small artificial Christmas tree on the leather desk top. Helen, Susie and Annette sipped red wine from the white plastic cups.

'Merry Christmas,' Helen mimed, raising her cup.

Susie and Annette raised their cups in response. Annette approached the desk and embraced Jane, crushing the tasselled breasts of Santa to her own. They kissed.

'What are you going to do with him, Jane?' Annette whispered, giggling as their tongues licked and probed slowly.

'I'm here to make sure he gets his presents. Gets what's coming to him. Santa has emptied her sack,' she continued softly, 'so that he can empty his.'

In his naked subjugation – Susie had him pinned down beneath the firm tread of her stockinged foot – Faulkner moaned through his gag. Behind his back, above his buttocks, his handcuffed wrists twisted in a frenzy of dread. Susie trod him down dominantly, then scrunched her stockinged toes up into the sac swinging between his thighs.

'Security comes on site in four hours,' she warned, gazing down at him pitilessly as she grazed his balls with her rasping nylon.

'We'll have to work faster than that,' Santa replied, grinning mischievously. 'I phoned the managing director earlier. Told him it would be worth his while coming in. Pay a little surprise visit.'

Faulkner twisted, straining to rise. Susie trod him down firmly.

'Even on Christmas Eve?' Helen asked in disbelief.

'Even on Christmas Eve,' Santa purred. 'He'll be here in time to find you three out there loyally processing applications and credit ratings while Faulkner entertains Santa.'

The three section leaders squealed their delight.

Santa became serious. 'Helen,' she said sternly. 'It's time you gave him his present.'

Helen, dressed from the waist down in a tight skirt, nylon stockings, panties and blue court shoes, wore only a cotton sports bra above. It fitted her breasts perfectly, cupping and controlling the warmth of their weight. Bending down and taloning his hair, she dragged him across the carpet towards a chair. His pinioned hands bounced helplessly above his naked buttocks as he shuffled behind her in painful obedience.

'Get him across the chair for punishment,' Santa advised. 'Unless you want the naughty boy across your knee for a spanking.'

'No spanking for him,' Helen announced savagely, hauling him belly down across the seat of the chair. 'He likes the feel of a bra,' she continued, drawing her hands together behind her back to unclasp the sports bra. 'Let's see how he likes the feel of this.'

Her breasts bounced as the crisp cotton cups fell away. Helen wound the white stretchy strap twice around her right knuckled fist and dangled the bra down, deliberately skim-teasing the clenched buttocks below. With a soft snarl – remembering all the humiliation she had endured – she flicked her wrist and angled her elbow, whipping back the bra's length over her right shoulder. Planting her feet slightly apart, she ground her blue court shoes firmly into the carpet and bent over her naked, quivering boss.

A soft whistle and sharp crack announced the first slicing stroke. The thin white band left a thinner scarlet line across the whipped cheeks. Faulkner grunted and spasmed in pain, sinking his teeth deeper into the orange that smothered his screams.

'A dozen strokes,' Santa said softly, fingering the feathery branches of the silver Christmas tree. 'To begin with.'

The bare-breasted whipper traced the tip of the spindling bra across the naked buttocks of the whipped man helpless beneath her. 'A dozen strokes –' she nodded, bending to pin him down at the nape of his neck '– to begin with.' She plied the lash with vicious willingness, a keen venom behind the administration of each and every searing stroke. Again and again, she lashed the twisted cotton bra down across his ravished flesh.

'Wait,' Santa hissed. 'Christmas comes but once a year. Let's make this one memorable.' She positioned herself at the chair, parting her black shiny thigh-boots. Shuffling forward, she trapped his face between the polished hide, drawing her thighs tightly together. 'Another dozen,' she commanded, squeezing her boots into his sweating face.

The strokes blistered down, snapping across his redden-ing buttocks. Choking into the oozing orange, the whipped man writhed, grazing his face against the polished boots that gripped him fiercely.

Dropping down before him, brushing Santa aside, Helen smothered his spluttering face with her heavy breasts. Taloning his hair dominantly, she forced his face merciless-ly, contemptuously into her swollen warmth. Santa skip-ped around and knelt at his whipped cheeks. Splaying her fingers wide, she dragged the scarlet nails slowly down across his burning cheeks.

'Santa Claws,' she whispered, raking his upturned but-tocks viciously.

Helen dressed, tidied her hair and slipped out to the outer office, leaving Susie to the pleasure of administering revengeful pain.

'Stockings?' Santa murmured. 'Nyloned torments for his Christmas box?'

'Stockings.' Susie nodded, dragging Faulkner down from the chair and roughly forcing him on to his knees.

The naked man struggled but Susie was firm, tightly binding his veined shaft with one black stocking and fastening it with a butterfly bow before threading the second black stocking up between his whipped cheeks.

'A perfect humiliation,' Santa approved, stepping back a fraction to admire the kneeling wretch submitting to nyloned dominance.

Susie squatted down beside her boss. Grasping the two ends of the black stocking, she jerked its skein deep up into his soft cleft. Faulkner bit deeply into the orange. Susie dragged the nylon back and forth, burning and scalding the sensitive flesh of her captive. After six minutes, Faulkner, quivering in exquisite agony, buckled into complete surrender, his chin shining with dribble from the savaged orange between his teeth. The skimming nylon continued to punish his cleft with deep, probing tongues of flame but the orange wedged between his teeth quenched his screams. The black butterfly knot at the base of his belly fluttered as his bound shaft pulsed and twitched in its torment.

Forcing the black stocking up his anus with one, and then two fingers, until only a ribbon peeped from his burning sphincter, Susie stretched her hand out to his shaft. Playfully, she dabbled her fingertips on his glistening glans. Faulkner almost bit the orange in half as his erection strained for release. With a flourish, one hand at his stocking-bound erection and the other plucking at the stocking crammed up between his whipped cheeks, Susie pulled at both nylons. He came with an audible groan, shooting out his pent-up stream, pumping his hips helplessly as he emptied his agony into the air. As the nylon was ripped out of his anus, a second orgasm exploded almost immediately, churning his sac as he shuddered and jerked. Biting savagely into the orange, he soaked his chest, leaving it yellow and shining. On the carpet, unseen by his blindfolded eyes, the stains of his squirting seed slowly darkened.

With both Helen and Susie pretending to be busy outside, Jane and Annette shared the final humiliation and punishment of the office wolf. Slicing open the first of three packs of coloured condoms, Santa applied a red one to Faulkner. 'Rudolph the red-cocked reindeer,' she hummed tunelessly, applying the sheath roughly. 'That tree needs decorating,' she observed. 'You use the mistletoe on him. Whip him long and hard.'

Annette swished the supple sprig down across Faulkner's already punished buttocks. Tiny white berries danced in the air, landing on the carpet. One waxy bead settled in the crease between his clenched cheeks. Annette paused, lowering her lash, and fingered the berry out of his cleft and flicked it away. By the time Faulkner had filled his third condom – which Jane hung daintily from the silver branches of the artificial tree – there were no berries left on the cruel sprig.

'Leave him to me, now, darling,' Jane whispered. 'The manager will be looking for a replacement in the New Year. Go out and pretend to be busy. When he comes through here, he'll find Santa taking this lucky little chap for a ride.'

Dressed and composed, Annette turned, one hand on the office door. On the floor, still handcuffed but with his gag and blindfold removed, Faulkner scrambled on all fours as a naked Santa, her slit nuzzling his creased neck, urged him on. Black shiny boots dug into his pale thighs and a whip of berryless mistletoe reddened his already thrashed buttocks.

5

The Mousetrap

The sleepy village of Steeple Creighton stirred as it woke to the sound of the 6.40 milk train from distant Lessingham. Dark smoke rose into the pale dawn sky from the engine huffing through the cutting behind the apple orchards. The train whistled its approach to the village station, scattering the chickens in the garden of Bramble Cottage.

Upstairs, in the low-ceilinged bedroom of Bramble Cottage, Miss Allensby, the young village librarian, rolled over in her crisply laundered sheets and tried to resume her delicious dream. In that dream, the County Librarian had just pressed an ink date stamp into the nape of Miss Allensby's neck. Naked and trembling as she bent over her issuing desk, her breasts squashed into the narrow tray of small, yellow tickets, Miss Allensby held her breath. The cold kiss of the date stamp, fleetingly pressed between her shoulder blades, caused her to cry out softly.

'Silence,' the County Librarian hissed sternly, briskly spanking Miss Allensby's bare bottom.

In her dream, the naked librarian clenched her spanked buttocks and shivered as she waited for the ink date stamp to imprint itself down her dimpled spine. Soon, it would be pressed firmly against her left buttock.

In her dream, the village librarian parted her lips to squeal. A train whistle shrieked. Chickens clucked noisily.

'No chickens in the library,' the County Librarian said crossly, raising a spanking hand up above the quivering buttocks below.

Miss Allensby woke and rubbed her eyes – and then her warm, moist pussy. Rising reluctantly from her bed, she stood naked before her full-length mirror. Her fingers strummed at the dark patch of coiled hair at her pubis, then dipped in between the wet velvet of her sticky labia. Her nipples, dark and stubby against the smooth cream of her generous breasts, thickened and peaked as she remembered the date. Today, the County Librarian was visiting the village to inspect the tiny library in Back Church Lane.

Miss Allensby cupped her breasts and squeezed them. The thought of the County Librarian, an austere brunette in her early forties, always made Miss Allensby's pussy grow moist as it softened. Squeezing her captive breasts more urgently, and pretending to herself that it was the controlling hands of the dominant County Librarian that brought such pleasurable pain to her bosom, Miss Allensby considered what she should wear. A crisp white blouse with a black velvet choker at her throat. No. The broader band of blue velvet with the exquisite white cameo, she decided. A sensible skirt, belted. Nothing pleated or frilly. Seamed stockings, of course. A light tan, and her black lace-up brogues. Girdle or bra with suspender belt? Miss Allensby hesitated. Twisting slightly at her hips, then turning fully, she glimpsed over her shoulder at her bare bottom. In the mirror, it loomed large. Large and inviting, with a temptingly dark cleft between the heavily fleshed cheeks. Inching her bare bottom into the cold glass briefly, she hugged her breasts fiercely and shuddered with pleasure. Girdle, she decided, recovering from the frisson of the mirror's stern kiss. A girdle – hoping that the strictures of the stiff white foundation garment would accentuate her waist and hips and tame and mould her swollen cheeks. Tame and mould them, presenting her bottom in the most flattering, the most seductive way to her important visitor.

Taking down her skirt and blouse and fishing out her stockings and panties from her lingerie drawer, Miss Allensby suddenly remembered that her best white girdle was still hanging out on the clothes line in her back garden.

* * *

The sharp whistle of the 6.40 froze the crouching figure in his tracks. Seconds later, he rose from the protective screen of blackcurrant bushes and, avoiding the betraying crunch of the cinder path, tiptoed over the soft loam towards the two pear trees flanking a decent-sized but uncut patch of lawn. Strung between the two pear trees, a line of washing fluttered gently in the warm air of a late summer dawn. Crouching down once more, the man glanced up at the bedroom window. The curtains remained drawn. Rising, he loped forwards, stumbling once as he slipped on the dew-silvered turf. At the clothes line, he ignored the two hand towels and the stark white pillow cases, reaching up with a trembling hand to delicately finger the stiff contours of a white girdle. Closing his eyes and swallowing hard, he squeezed the empty cup that had held the warmth of the wearer's right breast. Grunting softly, he pinched the fabric of the cup where the berry-hard nipple would peak proudly.

A crow fluttered in a nearby elm, cawing noisily. The man opened his eyes and wiped the sweat from his brow. Snatching the girdle down from the line, he buried his face into the garment. He breathed in deeply, fleetingly intoxicated by the haunting perfume of washing soap and female fragrance. He kissed the stretchy, starched fabric and licked at the gusset flap which had strained at the pungent pussy of the girdle's owner.

Up above in the tall elm, the crow flapped its ragged wings, fluttering restlessly. In the distance, the faint whistle of the milk train leaving the station brought the man clutching the stolen girdle to his senses. Turning, he scuttled across the lawn, the white garment gripped in his tightened fist. As he scuttled through the blackcurrant bushes, the hens scattered, clucking their annoyance.

Drawn to her bedroom window by the noise of her distressed poultry, Miss Allensby twitched her net curtain. Down in the garden of Bramble Cottage, all seemed peaceful and undisturbed. Pressing her naked breasts against the window pane, and causing her already erect nipples to peak in sharp pleasure, Miss Allensby frowned.

Stepping back into her bedroom, she fingered her nipples, her thoughts on the white girdle she had pegged out on the clothes line in yesterday's sunset. Back at the window, her net curtains parted, she peered down and gasped. Between the pillow cases and the hand towel there was a gap. A gap that should not have been there. Miss Allensby's frown deepened into an angry grimace.

Set back from the village green, in the shadow of the squat-steepled Norman church, the vicarage of Steeple Creighton was already astir. Bacon, fried bread and mushrooms sizzled on the Aga, filling the airy kitchen with their delicious aroma. From the polished beechwood Cossor radio, the Third Network filled the air with gentle music.

'Vaughan Williams. So very English. And quite right for a warm September, don't you think?' Harriet Bentley pronounced as she gently placed an opaque majolica vase down into a deep white sink.

'Delius for me,' her inseparable companion, 'Fierce' Bierce, replied, busy bullying the bacon.

Harriet Bentley nodded. Taking up a pair of scissors, she snipped the purple Michaelmas daisies into suitable lengths and crammed them into the majolica.

'Better take George his through to the study on a tray,' Fierce Bierce declared aloud. 'No, not like that, dear. Honestly, you're quite hopeless with flowers.'

'Would you?' Harriet sighed, abandoning the daisies. 'He's got the Somersby funeral today and is worried about the eulogy.'

'Colonel Somersby had a decent war. We need men of his kidney now, with Suez brewing up. Tell your brother to say that.'

'No, darling,' Harriet murmured. 'Best keep politics out of the pulpit.'

With her brother brooding over his funeral in the study, Harriet enjoyed her breakfast with Miss Bierce. They had hardly slept a wink last night, their lovemaking had been so ferocious. Harriet's breasts and thighs ached sweetly. Dark purple bruises mottled her upper arms and buttocks where Fierce Bierce had bitten and sucked. That was why she had plucked the purple Michaelmas daisies and not the bronze-gold chrysanthemums.

Biting into a sweet mushroom, Harriet gazed across the spotless table cloth at her lover. They had breakfasted together, without exception, since the age of sixteen when they had boarded together. Their schoolgirl passion had proved long-lasting, and when the Reverend Bentley had assumed the living at Steeple Creighton, extending an open invitation to his sister to join him and run the vicarage, it was inevitable that her chum would be joining her. Nicknamed 'Fierce' because of her strict administration of the slipper to naughty bare bottoms in the dorm, Miss Bierce had been given a room at the end of the draughty landing. Every night, when the Reverend Bentley dozed over next Sunday's sermon, or nodded over his translation of Horace, Fierce would steal out of her bedroom and join Harriet in her large, warm bed. Just as they had breakfasted together for over fourteen years, so they had shared the same bed.

The telephone rang.

'Now, who on earth could that possibly be?'

Village etiquette was quite strict on the use of the telephone.

'I'll go. Finish your bacon,' Fierce said, wiping her lips with her napkin.

She returned, minutes later, and gently closed the dining room door.

'Well?' Harriet's eyebrows rose inquiringly as she sipped her tea.

'Bit more of that funny business going on,' Fierce said softly. 'You know, our washing line thief.'

Harriet placed her cup down in its saucer. 'Who –?'

'Bramble Cottage. Miss Allensby. Didn't see anything. Lost a girdle. Pretty cut up about it, our librarian is. Damn furious, in fact.'

Harriet closed her eyes, imagining the village librarian in her white girdle, her breasts and heavy buttocks squeezed within the figure-hugging stretchy fabric. With the poppers on the gusset pressed into place, how those splendidly ripe cheeks would bulge –

'Harriet,' Fierce warned.

The vicar's sister flushed and opened her eyes to meekly meet her lover's stern gaze. 'Sorry, I was just –'

'I know very well what you were just –'

'I wondered,' Harriet continued quickly, 'when the telephone rang. People simply don't ring quite so early. It had to be some sort of emergency.' She paused. 'Fierce,' she murmured, 'why do they always ring us?'

'You mean?'

'The school mistress, when her nylon stockings were taken, and only last week, young Susan at the Fox and Goose –'

'Young Susan won't see twenty-nine again,' Fierce snorted, 'and barmaid or not, she should be ashamed to even admit to owning fancy black lace panties, let alone having them pinched. These unfortunate women telephone us, my dear,' she continued imperiously, 'because no woman wants to discuss her lingerie with that oaf Perkins.'

Harriet nodded. That oaf Perkins, the village bobby, must – like her brother the vicar – be kept in ignorance of the recent outbreak of intimate thefts plaguing the village of Steeple Creighton.

'No,' Fierce observed, fiddling with the Michaelmas daisies until she had them all standing to attention, 'it is better that we girls stick together. And we don't want *The Gazette* to get wind of any of it. Just imagine having those Sunday dreadfuls down from Fleet Street if they got hold of the story.'

'No,' Harriet agreed, secretly envying her lover's way with flowers. 'But something must be done, Fierce, don't you think?'

As her brother gazed upon the respectful lowering of the late Colonel Somersby's yew coffin into his freshly dug earthen grave, Harriet, squatting naked on a cork-topped stool, watched the heavy buttocks and smooth thighs of Fierce Bierce being lowered into the steaming bath.

Approaching, then kneeling down at the edge of the bath tub, she gathered up the loofah and plied it with wicked innocence. Fierce writhed and gripped the sides of the steaming tub as the loofah nuzzled impudently between her splayed thighs.

'Little devil,' she chuckled, her knuckles whitening.

'It can't be the fish. That's every Tuesday and Friday,' Harriet murmured, absently twisting her wrist and driving the loofah home.

Grunting her pleasure, Fierce managed to nod. It couldn't be the fish. The village received its supply of skate, herrings and cod on those two mornings – usually after ten o'clock – from Lupins of Lessingham. True, young Lupin had been observed coming out of Old Forge cottage adjusting his blue-and-white striped apron after giving the widowed Mrs Cakebread her weekly turbot – but the timing – and the days, too – were all wrong. No, it wasn't the fish.

'And the coke and coal is fortnightly,' Harriet mused, jabbing the snout of the loofah now with vicious tenderness.

'No, not the coke and coal,' Fierce screamed softly, grinding her soft buttocks into the rubber mat in a paroxysm of ecstasy.

'So we're looking for somebody –'

'Some man,' Fierce managed waspishly.

'Some man,' Harriet conceded, 'who is out and about very early almost every morning. Fierce,' she squealed excitedly, ramming the loofah savagely.

Fierce moaned and sank beneath the bubbles.

'It's the post. It's got to be. Early morning run. Daily deliveries. And nobody really notices –'

'The postman,' Fierce announced, surfacing with a splutter. 'Well done, my dear.'

The glistening nude eased herself back so that her bobbing breasts shone as they rose up. Splaying her thighs wide, she gestured impatiently for the return of the loofah to her smiling labia.

'But how are we going to catch him?' Harriet murmured, kneeling down to dry her lover's legs and thighs with a large white towel.

'Don't worry,' Fierce smiled, gasping slightly as the towel raked her deep cleft firmly. 'No dawn patrols in Wellington boots or skulking in dripping laurel bushes with field-glasses.'

'Then how?' the kneeling woman repeated, dabbing at the pubic plum with a fistful of towelling.

'Brains,' Fierce pronounced decisively. 'First, we'll get some sort of proof. If not proof positive, something highly suggestive. Some evidence.'

'Like an actual pair of panties?'

'Like an actual pair of panties. Then, when we're sure of our little mouse, we'll set a trap.'

'Rat, dear, surely?'

'Mouse. We're looking for a shy, timid man, I think. One who cannot get close to women in the flesh but who likes to finger and possess their scanties.'

'Mouse it is,' Harriet agreed, thumbing away a stray pubic coil from the outer labial fleshfold.

Fierce spasmed slightly in response to the thumbtip, her heavy buttocks joggling. 'We know,' she continued, sighing contentedly as Harriet kissed and sucked at her hot pussy, 'the sort of cheese our little mouse prefers. So we'll bait the trap and snap –'

'And snap?' Harriet mumbled, slurping at the juicy fragrance at her lips.

'Snap, my dear, denotes the leather strap whistling down across our naughty postman's backside.'

'Oh,' Harriet grunted, biting softly now. 'That sort of snap. As in snap, crack.'

'As in snap, crack,' Fierce gasped, battling helplessly against the surge of her imminent climax.

Harriet's swollen tongue was now buried too deeply to reply. She merely nodded enthusiastically, rasping her nose down against the erect little clitoris. Fierce buckled at the knees, her loud cry of sweet agony echoing loudly against the white tiled bathroom. So loudly, that their spinster neighbour, Miss Violet Pye, dead-heading late tea roses in nearby Little Paddocks, shuddered – and nipped a prize specimen off with her glinting secateurs.

'I was thinking of taking Boris out for a little spin. A pre-season trial run. Best not leave it until some winter morning when we'll really need him to perform.'

The Reverend Bentley looked up from his well-thumbed Horace and vaguely murmured his assent.

'Jolly good,' Harriet nodded. 'So glad you agree.'

The long habit of coupons and then post-war rationing still held the village in its austere grip. The vicarage only used Boris, a venerable Humber, in the months of winter. Springtime, the long summer days and autumn frosty mornings saw the vicar, his sister and her companion bicycling around the parish.

Boris needed a little nursing in the garage. Harriet teased out his choke. Boris responded with a deep growl.

'So we break down close to the postman's cottage?'

'We pretend to break down, my dear,' Fierce corrected, stretching the fingers of her splayed hand into the tight warmth of a leather glove. 'We'll get the bonnet up, whip out the fan belt and then knock on his door.'

'Damsels in distress routine, eh?' countered Harriet, treading her brogue down firmly on to the clutch.

'Damsels, as you say, in distress,' Fierce echoed, steadying herself against the walnut dash as Boris lurched violently.

They bowled down the leafy lanes, putting the sedate Humber through its gentle paces. Just as the church bell tolled two, the Humber whispered to a halt in front of a white-painted thatched cottage at the lower end of Station Road. After an elaborate pantomime featuring the raised car bonnet, a struggle with the fan belt and some rueful scratching of perplexed heads, Fierce and her companion approached the front door. Late sweet peas perfumed the air as they spilled over from their hanging basket. The knocker echoed loudly. The door was opened at once.

'Boris has let us down, I'm afraid,' Fierce said, mustering her pretty-please voice. 'Could you help, do you think?'

Douglas, the young village postman, squinted shyly into the afternoon sunshine. He dragged his fingers through his dark, wiry hair and shrugged. 'I'll take a look, ma'am.'

'So kind.'

'Fan belt, ma'am,' he pronounced, seconds after ducking down beneath the raised bonnet.

Harriet shrugged in a pretence of helplessness, mentally brushing aside the image of her own hand cutting the fan belt with a bread knife not half an hour since.

'Can anything be done, just to get us back?' Fierce asked anxiously.

'Don't rightly know, ma'am.' He was ill at ease, clearly uncomfortable in their company.

'Of course,' Harriet prattled naively, 'if we were wearing stockings I suppose we could have used one, couldn't we? But we aren't,' she sighed, raising her hem three inches, revealing her shapely leg above her knee to the lower thigh.

Douglas blushed and averted his gaze.

'Or couldn't we?' Harriet continued, dropping the hem of her tweed skirt. 'Fellows do it in books.'

'They do say that a stocking does the trick, ma'am. Temporary, like.'

Fierce and Harriet remained silent.

'I might be able to –' Douglas muttered, anxious to rid himself of the unwanted visitors. He withdrew into the shadows of the cottage, emerging several minutes later with a shrivelled nylon stocking in his hand. 'Found an odd one, ma'am.'

'Pull over here,' Fierce nodded.

The Humber brushed back the nodding cow parsley as Harriet nosed it gently to a halt in the secluded lane. It was the work of a moment to replace the nylon stocking with a spare fan belt.

'Hold it up,' Fierce commanded. 'Let's see.'

Harriet obliged, allowing the nylon stocking to dangle down from her fingertips. 'And what was our girl-shy young postman doing with a nylon stocking, do you suppose?' she whispered. 'Never seen walking out with any of the belles of this parish.'

'Or any other. Hold that stocking up higher, my dear,' Fierce ordered. Taking a pace forwards, she snatched at the seamed stocking and inspected it closely. Drawing it up to her nostrils, she sniffed. 'Stale semen. You can see the stain.'

Harriet squealed and let go of the stocking. Fierce snatched at it deftly and gathered it tightly around her gloved fist.

'I don't think my brother would –'

'It'll all be over before he surfaces from his morning prayers,' Fierce snapped impatiently. 'Now come along, do. Check through with me. Letters addressed to selves at vicarage posted yesterday?'

'Pretend post stamped and sent.'

'Wet paint – please use rear door – sign on front gate?'

'Yes,' Harriet nodded, rubbing dried flakes of green paint from her fingers. 'He'll have to come round.'

'Trap suitably baited with cheese?'

'Red satin basque dangling temptingly from clothes line.' Harriet giggled.

They crouched in the cool shadows of the pantry. Harriet twiddled with the waxed paper cover on a lid of a jar of honey. Fierce spanked her sharply, motioning for silence. Harriet squeaked and, reaching back to rub her sore bottom, dropped the honey. The glass splintered and the dark honey oozed.

'Leave it,' Fierce warned as Harriet dithered. 'Listen.'

The familiar clicking of the postman's pedals filled the silence of the vicarage, followed by the rattle of the front gate. They strained to hear Douglas following the garden path around by the greenhouse – and the clothes line. Soon his footsteps crunched on the gravel at the back door. They heard him forcing the post under it, heard him cursing softly as he grazed his knuckles on the boot scraper.

'Shall I go and see if –'

'Wait,' Fierce whispered.

'But we'll miss him. He'll get away,' her companion protested anxiously.

'That was the front gate,' Fierce announced. 'There's his bike.'

They strained, breath bated, to catch the retreating click-clicking of the departing postman's bicycle.

'He's gone,' Harriet whispered excitedly, scampering to the kitchen window. 'And so has the red basque. He's actually pinched it.'

'Knew he would. Excellent,' Fierce exclaimed, rubbing her hands briskly. 'Kippers for breakfast? Need to build your strength up for the task ahead, my dear.'

'But you let him get away,' Harriet pouted.

'Not entirely. Absolutely no need for any unseemliness here, at the vicarage. No, we know where to find him, after our kippers,' she continued, vigorously buttering the bottom of a shallow frying pan.

'Ever punished a chap, my dear?'

'N-no,' Harriet murmured.

They had waited until the heavy shower of rain had finished before setting off to walk through the village towards the cottage in lower Station Road. Along the wet lanes, blackberries and bright hips glinted in the drenched brambles. The musk of wet earth hung heavily in the air. Up in the clearing sky, fluffy nimbus clouds scudded away to the east.

'Of course you haven't whipped a man. Silly of me,' Fierce confessed. 'If you had, I would have known about it.'

'Have you?' Harriet whispered.

'Certainly have.'

'No. Who? When?' the vicar's sister cried.

'Two, no, three years ago. St Swithin's Day.'

'And where was I?' Harriet demanded.

'Parish bun-fight. W.I. show. Helping your good and godly brother.'

'I remember. You were late. And you were all flushed when you eventually came to help judge the jams and pickles.'

'Caught a young chap skulking in the vicarage garden. Down from Oxford to visit an aunt. Reading Modern History, I believe. Why do they insist on calling it Modern History when it ends long before Cromwell was born?' Fierce wondered aloud.

'Go on, Fierce,' Harriet urged. 'You found him skulking.'

'Had the nerve to claim to be a budding lepidopterist. Munching our gooseberries, cool as you like. Pockets crammed full of them. Made him spell it.'

'Gooseberry?' Harriet blinked, losing the thread somewhat.

'Lepidopterist. Couldn't, of course, and didn't. Wouldn't know a cabbage white from a red admiral. Lugged him down to the potting shed –'

'Fierce, really.'

'Bundled him inside, hauled him over my knee – gooseberries everywhere – and pulled his pants down –'

'You didn't!'

'Spanked him hard.'

'Spanked? But aren't there usually some canes in the potting shed?' Harriet asked eagerly.

'Capital canes of the most supple, whippy bamboo. As your bottom jolly well knows.'

Harriet shivered deliciously.

'Capital canes in the potting shed but no room to swish 'em. No, didn't bother with any of your Mistress Stern fancy Mayfair prominent Member-in-brothel nonsense, my dear, just gave it to him hot and hard.'

'Oooh,' Harriet sighed.

'Little beggar howled. Spanked him until my hand was too hot to go on. Spoiled my skirt.'

'Spoiled? You mean –'

'Spoiled as in soiled. Jerked like a gaffed salmon then wriggled like a weasel. Emptied himself all over my blue serge. Nasty, sticky stain. Had to go in and change before I went to judge the jams. Greengage, wasn't it?'

108

'Wasn't what?'

'Greengage. From Halls Farm. The winning jam.'

They were approaching Back Church Lane, avoiding the large brown puddles after the heavy shower. A jay flashed in front of them.

'Ever seen him again? I suppose not.'

'He writes, still. Christmas cards. I had a word with his teacher,' Fierce continued. 'Miss Robinson. Retired now.'

'Who?'

'Our postman. Young Master Douglas. She remembered him. Quiet boy. Kept to himself. Awkward and shy. Especially shy with the girls, even then. Only had to deal with him once.'

'What did he do?'

'Found him in the girls' changing rooms while they were having their gym class. Pair of navy knickers in his hands. Caned him. Six strokes for being out of bounds, another six for the knickers. So it would seem,' Fierce concluded, lengthening her urgent stride, 'that our young postman has form.'

'Well,' Harriet said breathlessly, trying to keep pace, 'isn't that interesting? But the basque, Fierce. What if he has hidden it? What if he denies it?'

'He won't.'

The sweet peas had suffered in the sudden shower. The doorstep to the postman's cottage was peppered with their pale petals. Fierce trod her brogues into them as she hammered the wrought-iron knocker.

Douglas appeared at the door. They shouldered past him without a word, leaving him stammering nervously in the doorway. Beneath their sensible brogues, sweet pea petals littered the carpet.

Fierce came directly to the point. 'Douglas, show me your hands.'

'Ma'am?'

'Hands, Douglas. Show.'

Douglas, blushing furiously, presented his hands for her perusal, knuckles upturned.

'Palms, please.'

He hesitated and scowled.

'I'm waiting.'

On examination, his palms were red.

'Caught you red-handed,' Fierce declared. 'That red satin basque you stole this morning –'

'Didn't,' he blurted.

'Dyed. Deliberately dyed with red stain. Upstairs with you, my lad.'

'No – please – you can't –'

'At once.'

Upstairs, the accused buckled under the stern questioning of Fierce Bierce. Brokenly, and tearfully, he confessed fully to all his crimes. The stockings, the black panties, the girdle. His red hands were proof positive of his guilt in stealing the basque.

'Naughty boy,' Fierce murmured, strumming her pubic mound beneath her tweed skirt. 'Such wickedness.'

The accused stood by the end of his bed, head bowed, his face burning with shame.

'What – what are you going to do?' he muttered. 'Who you going to tell?'

Fierce sat down on his bed, smoothing the skirt at her thighs. Her broad bottom sank into the mattress beneath her. She plucked off her leather gloves very slowly. Harriet, fidgeting nervously by the window, looked at her companion expectantly.

'No need to tell anyone, I think. You will go round to each of your victims. You will apologise and return each stolen item. They may punish you as they please. Miss Allensby has a super little riding crop. Her aunt rode out with the hounds,' Fierce added conversationally to Harriet. 'Nice little treat for both of you, I'm sure.' Her voice was bright but brittle. 'And there's certainly no need for anyone to mention this to that oaf Perkins. He drinks, I gather. Don't want him blabbing it all out in the Fox and Goose. Mustn't get into *The Gazette* or go before the bench at Lessingham magistrates. No, no,' Fierce continued briskly, 'I won't have that. No fuss. We settle this quietly. Just like Suez.'

'Ma'am?' Douglas blinked.

'Suez?' Harriet echoed faintly.

'Least said, soonest mended,' Fierce explained. 'No need to drag in the UN. All we have to do there is teach Mr Nasser a painful lesson. One he'll never forget. That's what we'll do, won't we, Douglas? Trousers down, please, young man.'

'No, ma'am, please, ma'am,' he whimpered, gripping the bedpost.

'Perhaps not.' Fierce seemed to reconsider. 'Did I say trousers? I'm so sorry. What can I have been thinking of, hm?'

Douglas looked up, the possibility of a reprieve giving him some slender hope of evading his impending punishment and pain.

'No, not trousers. Everything. I want you naked, young man. Naked for your punishment.'

The faint gleam of fragile hope died in his sorrowful eyes. He stammered his protest, whining and bargaining as he promised solemnly never to offend again. His voice trembled and rose to a shrill pleading – but Fierce was firm.

'At once,' she barked.

Harriet's mouth opened as he stripped, reluctantly and resentfully, under the cruel gaze of his tormentors. He twisted away as he dragged down his underpants, presenting his bared buttocks as he hopped on one foot and kicked them free. Harriet squeaked her disappointment at missing a glimpse of his cock.

'We don't want to see your bottom, Douglas, you rude little boy. Not just now, at least. Plenty of time for that. We have all afternoon for your naughty bottom. Turn around,' Fierce barked.

Harriet clapped her hands in delight as their naked captive shuffled round bashfully to face them, his hands cupped over his groin.

'Hands up on your head, young man,' Fierce instructed.

He blushed and whimpered, hesitating to obey.

'Douglas. It would be better for you to obey me instantly. Don't forget, in a little while you will be bare-bottomed across my knee. Completely at my mercy. Silly of you to vex me, don't you think?'

The threat was as powerful as it was polite. He obeyed.

'Your first cock, isn't it, my dear?' Fierce murmured as Harriet rose from the bed and approached the naked man.

'Mm,' her companion replied, bending down to examine him more intimately.

'Apart from those engravings of ancient Greeks and rude Romans who really should have known better.' Fierce chuckled, alluding to illustrated volumes which the Reverend Bentley consulted from time to time – blissfully unaware that his sister knew of their existence.

Fierce snatched up a small looking-glass, gripping the long handle firmly. Approaching the naked postman, she wedged the oval mirrow between his thighs. He rose up on his toes and grunted, his fingers digging into his wiry, dark hair. Adjusting the levelled mirror, Fierce skilfully captured his cock and balls, cradling them on the surface of the cold glass. He squirmed and closed his eyes tightly, flinching as his sac bounced gently on its own reflection.

'How very curious,' Harriet murmured, shyly stretching out a bold finger and caressing the flaccid member.

'Careful.' Fierce laughed. 'Those things can be quite beastly. Unpredictable, and liable to go off, you know.'

The postman shuddered in exquisite torment – but his cock unfurled on the cold surface of the mirror and slowly thickened, lengthening under Harriet's stroking fingertip. She gasped as his foreskin peeled back, and gasped again as the purple glans was revealed.

'Ooh, look, Fierce, it's changing.'

'Never mind that now, you can play with it later. Our purpose here is punishment, my dear. His pain, not our pleasure – although,' Fierce conceded, glancing down at where the veined cock's heat had clouded the silver glass, 'the two are not mutually exclusive.'

'You're a rotter,' Harriet pronounced with sudden venom, kneeling back and sinking her buttocks on to the heels of her brogues. 'Sneaking around and stealing things, private things, from those poor women. Don't you know how upset they were, how ashamed they felt?'

'That's it, my girl, you tell him.'

'How would you like it if your private things were fingered and pawed by some stranger, eh?'

'Let's see, shall we?' Fierce nodded judiciously, angling the mirror's flat surface in against his balls, trapping them so that only his erection showed. 'Finger his privates. See how he burns with shame.'

Harriet knelt up and enclosed a gripping fist of curled fingers around the postman's shaft. She squeezed. He whimpered, gasping aloud. Placing her thumbtip at his glans, she rubbed it gently. His left thigh tensed rigidly before he staggered back a pace.

'Keep perfectly still, young man,' Fierce whispered ominously, pressing the cold glass firmly into his scrotum. 'Perfectly still.'

Harriet amused herself for several minutes, intimately inspecting and fingering the captive cock. Then, gently brushing the mirror aside, she palmed his dangling balls then cupped them – and squeezed.

Tears sparkled in the postman's eyes. Hot tears of shame. Arms aching as he obediently kept them aloft, he moaned softly and begged for mercy.

'Nonsense,' Fierce laughed. 'We haven't even begun, young man.' She tapped the glistening snout of his cock with the mirror, then wiped the smeared glass against her thigh. 'Before I bend you over and beat your bare bottom, I want to see your collection.'

His eyes darted evasively. 'Ma'am?'

'Now don't be silly, Douglas. You know perfectly well what I mean. Let's see everything. Your pictures, cuttings from newspapers and magazines. And all the stolen garments. The lot. Wardrobe, chest of drawers, under your bed. Wherever you keep them, get them out at once.'

Harriet and Fierce sat, hand in hand, on his bed as the naked man scurried around his bedroom. Just as Fierce had predicted, a collection was quickly assembled and arrayed on the bed before them. Neatly folded and heavily creased advertisements cut from periodicals were exhumed, displaying a range of bras, girdles, bustiers and waspie suspender-belts. Coloured pictures of mature matrons bound and constrained by the strict bondage of their corsetry followed – as did voluptuously photographed models in nightwear and daringly styled swim suits.

'Look,' Harriet whispered, stretching her hand down to touch a cover torn from Vogue.

It was the infamous Lepape photomontage from July 1934, showing a bronzed model spread out on a beach towel, sporting a flimsy pair of oyster silk panties tied tightly at her waist with a drawstring.

'Daring for its day,' Fierce assented, scratching the dried semen splashed over the model's nipples and belly. 'French, of course. Dear Hardy Amies has us buttoned up to the chin.'

'He's got masses. Simply masses,' Harriet whispered as the display threatened to engulf them.

'Quite the little connoisseur, eh, Douglas? What else have you got for your private entertainment? Show.'

Sepia-tinted snapshots, modern but with a curiously Edwardian feel, were produced. Lithe legs, nyloned or bewitchingly sheathed in the sheen of seamless silk stockings. At the bands of darker material hugging the shapely upper thighs, suspenders bit deeply, drawing the stocking-tops up severely towards the swollen buttocks above.

From a shoe box tucked away at the back of his wardrobe, Douglas produced the pride of his collection – a catalogue featuring tightly pantied bottoms of plump, full-buttocked women. Permed and unsmiling, the arms folded across their bare bosoms, the gallery of mature beauties gazed up from the shining pages. Douglas knelt down on one knee as he surrendered his most prized possession.

'Follows the fuller figure most faithfully,' Fierce remarked, placing the open catalogue down on the bed. 'Most faithfully. Now, my boy. Fetch me all the stolen garments. Get them at once and no shilly-shallying.'

'Look at his thing. It's –' Harriet pointed a quivering finger down at the postman's straining erection.

'He's saluting these.' Fierce nodded, tapping the pantied bottoms in the catalogue, her fingertip brushing the bulging cheeks. 'See how his balls swing,' she continued, her tone crisply clinical.

Douglas, aroused and fully engorged by the images he had been forced to unearth and confront, stumbled awkwardly as he tried in vain to conceal his excitement. His proud shaft nodded, arching up stiffly to tap at his pale belly. He brought his hands together, desperate to cup and cover his hot shame.

'No, Douglas. Hands down, if you please. I wish to see the items of lingerie you have pinched. Stolen,' Fierce added, her voice sharpening with anger, 'at cock crow. We'll soon see if we can make your cock crow under the lash of my leather belt presently, shan't we?'

Harriet giggled and drew her knees up to her chin. She hugged herself excitedly, crushing her breasts. 'May I have a go, please? Oh, Fierce, please say I can punish his bare bottom, please.'

'I'm not quite sure that you are sufficiently –'

'Please, Fierce,' Harriet gushed, 'I want to whip his bottom with a belt and hear him howl –'

'Steady on, girl. You most certainly shall have his bottom all to yourself. All in good time. You may punish him as you please.'

They watched as Douglas stretched up on tiptoe against his wardrobe, raking the snout of his straining shaft into the door as he pawed blindly to retrieve his stolen trophies from the upper recess. He staggered, yelped and collapsed into the wardrobe, pressing his sweating face into the dull wood and squashing his fat cock painfully. They saw his cleft tighten into a severe crease as he clenched his buttocks in anguish, his left knee twisting inwards to nuzzle his right leg in an arabesque of agony.

'Stop horsing around, young man,' Fierce snapped waspishly. 'Just get those garments down at once.'

Turning away from the wardrobe, trembling with fear and shame, he presented the stolen underwear to Fierce, surrendering each item up to her outstretched hand.

'Kneel,' she thundered.

He obeyed, head bowed, his knees dimpling the carpet in fearful genuflection.

'Head up, my lad. Look at me.'

Douglas gazed up sorrowfully to the stern woman on the bed.

'I want you to show Harriet here what you steal these garments for, Douglas. Show her how you use them for your private, wicked pleasure.'

'No, ma'am, please, ma'am – not that –'

'We're waiting,' Fierce murmured, tossing him a pair of light tan nylon stockings. 'Commence.'

Closing his eyes, Douglas held both stockings aloft, dangling them down from his fingertips so that they teasingly brushed his face, belly and the tip of his twitching cock. With his right hand, he slowly wound one of the stockings around his thick shaft. With his left hand, he drew the matching stocking to smother his upturned face. Drowning slowly in the shining material, he sniffed deeply and sucked hard. The skein of glossy nylon stretched at his nostrils and lips. His wet tongue probed the taut sheen, darkening the tan as he lapped furiously. Down below his belly, his gripping fist pumped the nyloned cock, slowly but firmly.

'Open your eyes, Douglas. Look at me.'

He blinked, gazed up at her drunkenly and squeezed his eyes shut tightly once more.

'No, Douglas. Open your eyes and look at me.'

Through the veil of the flimsy stocking's tan gauze, his frightened eyes met her stern gaze.

'And you're not doing this properly, are you?' Fierce demanded accusingly. 'You usually say things, don't you, Douglas, when you are at your beastliness? Come along, boy; we want to hear you.'

Broken under her dominant spell, the naked, kneeling postman could not but obey.

116

'Her name? What is her name?' Fierce prompted.

'Angela,' he whispered hoarsely.

'And where is Angela? What is she doing, Douglas?'

He answered in a thrilling whisper, spellbinding his listeners as he took them – with his fevered imagination – into the bedroom of Angela. He described her as being naked and glowing after a bath. Softly towelled dry and gently dusted with talc, she stood before her mirror preparing to dress.

First, he whispered, her bra. He described her soft breasts bulging as they filled the snow-white cups. Panties next. Panties stretched tightly across her bottom and biting up into her deep cleft. The waspie suspender-belt being wound around her slender waist.

Angela, he muttered, Angela. Now she was searching for her nylons. Her pair of light tan, sheer, seamless stockings. Angela's nylons.

'We've pretty much got the picture. That's enough of that.'

The kneeling postman came out of his trance, slumped forwards and moaned. The nylon in his curled fist darkened suddenly with the wet stain of his spurting seed.

After forcing him to dry himself with the pair of stolen black lace panties, Fierce arranged herself on the bed and, splaying her thighs, dragged her protesting victim down across her lap. Pinning him firmly at the nape of his neck with her controlling left hand, she smoothed his upturned buttocks with her dominant right palm.

'I propose to spank you, Douglas. Spank your bare bottom until it is hot – and sore. Hot, sore and very, very painful. I'm afraid you've been very wicked, haven't you?' she continued, dimpling her fingertips into the curves of his helpless cheeks, 'and you must be severely punished, mustn't you?' She swept her thumbtip down between his buttocks, raking his cleft. He jerked in response, squeezing his cheeks and trapping her thumb in his warmth.

'No,' she murmured, extracting her thumb. She drew her hand away abruptly, then let it hover above the anxiously clenched cheeks below.

'Go on,' Harriet urged excitedly. 'Spank his bottom.'

Fierce shook her head. 'No need to hurry. No need for unseemly haste, my dear,' she murmured, lowering her palm down until it fleetingly skimmed the upturned cheeks. 'Like good wine, or a haunting piece of Mozart, punishment must be a pleasure slowly savoured.'

Douglas squirmed across her knee, drawing his thighs tightly together.

'See?' Fierce whispered, gazing down. 'He shivers with dread, knowing that soon the hot pain begins.' She finger-stroked his cleft. He bucked and moaned. 'Making him wait adds to his anguish, my dear.'

'Oh, please, Fierce, I can't bear it. Spank him.'

'Be patient, my dear. My,' she remarked, tracing her finger up his quivering thighs and drumming his left buttock dominantly, 'all that cycling has certainly left our young postman very fit and trim. Capital muscle tone, don't you think? That leather saddle has worked wonders for his bottom.'

For several more spellbinding minutes, the punisher continued to inspect and intimately examine the bare buttocks she was about to chastise.

'Wicked boy,' she snarled softly, suddenly sweeping her broad palm down harshly.

Douglas jerked across her lap, gasping aloud as his punished cheeks flattened then wobbled under the impact of the spanking hand. They reddened immediately the moment Fierce dropped her palm down against the tops of his thighs to steady his wriggling.

Harriet squealed her delight, drawing her hands to her breasts to squeeze their soft warmth as she stared intently at the pink cheeks.

A second – and then a third – harsh spank exploded across the postman's naked buttocks. Fierce grunted her satisfaction and quickened the tempo of her searing onslaught.

Harriet, almost swooning with delight, squeezed her breasts each time the spanking hand ravished the buttocks below. 'Harder,' she urged, 'faster.'

The spanking was a blistering instance of flesh punishing flesh. For a full seventeen minutes, Fierce brought her merciless hand down, eliciting howls from the writhing postman. His ravished cheeks blazed from pink-blotched crimson to a painful shade of scarlet. When her hand had grown numb from her efforts, Fierce planted it down across his burning cheeks.

Douglas blubbered noisily, choking on his deep sobs.

'Stop that silly nonsense at once, young man, or I'll really give you something to cry about.'

He sniffled and writhed across her lap, anxious to rid his hot bottom from the controlling presence of her dominant hand. Despite her aching arms, Fierce pinned him down ruthlessly, quelling his rebellion.

Harriet's hands fell away from her bosom. 'I'm wet. You know, down there,' she confessed in a tone of amazement and alarm. 'Soaking wet.'

'So am I,' Fierce grunted. 'Look.'

She pushed the naked postman down on to the carpet, then planted a well-aimed brogue down, trapping his spanked buttocks. Treading him firmly into submission beneath her pinioning foot, she indicated the glistening smear where the punished man had orgasmed into her tweed skirt. 'I'd best take it off. It'll sponge out later.'

'I'll join you,' Harriet's indistinct voice replied through the jumper being dragged over her head.

They stood over him, Fierce actually astride his naked body.

'You may have him for a spell,' Fierce declared, taloning the postman's wiry hair so that his sweating face was forced up into her pubis. 'First taste of dispensing discipline to a naked man, eh?'

Virginally, Harriet accepted the hairbrush, thumbing its stiff bristles. 'Those horrid pictures he keeps, Fierce. Oughtn't I punish him for that?'

'Most certainly. Get him bending across the bed.'

Fierce withdrew, watching Harriet – almost clumsy in her excitement – order and arrange the postman to bend over the bed.

'No, not like that,' Harriet rasped impatiently, swiping her victim's bottom savagely with the hairbrush. 'Up on your arms.'

Douglas, red-bottomed and eager to please, planted his hands down into the eiderdown. Bending, he gazed down at the array of pictures and cuttings spread out before him.

Crack. The hairbrush swept down. The postman smothered a soft scream. He sagged at the knees, burying his face in the lingerie illustrations scattered on the eiderdown.

Harriet inverted the hairbrush, bristled face upwards, and tapped his balls. 'Up,' she ordered, 'and keep still.'

Douglas shuffled painfully back into the prescribed punishment position.

'Take a long, last look at your collection, Douglas,' Harriet warned, raising the hairbrush up above his bottom. 'A long, last look.'

Twenty-three measured, deliberate strokes later, his knees betrayed him once more. Steadying himself on veined arms, the postman battled to remain upright. He sobbed brokenly.

'No, you don't,' Harriet hissed, glimpsing the pulsing erection. 'None of that beastliness.' Innocently unaware of the outcome of her action, she swept the bristled surface of the hairbrush along his shaft, burying the shining glans under the dark stubble.

'Don't do that –' Fierce shouted.

Douglas screamed softly as his hips pumped violently. He squirted his jet of liquid release noisily, splashing the cuttings and pictures of brassiered and pantied women below.

'Wicked, wicked man,' Harriet snarled, lashing his buttocks viciously as he orgasmed.

The remaining thick gobbets dripped down, splattering the semen-stained collection.

'Panties,' Harriet said primly, holding a pair aloft.

'Panties,' Douglas whispered thickly.

He was kneeling, head erect, his legs sheathed in the semen-drenched tan stockings in which he had worshipped

120

the image of Angela, two hours ago. Above the darker bands stretched at his thighs, his twice-punished bottom tensed.

Fierce, aiming the lash of her leather belt low, drew a thin bluish line of fresh torment across the punished cheeks.

'Basque,' Harriet announced, dangling the delicious confection before his eyes.

'Basque,' he echoed, gazing up in both desire and dread.

The leather belt whistled and snapped, biting into the swell of his proffered buttocks.

'Suspender belt,' Harriet teased, skimming his lips with the wisp of stretchy fabric.

'Suspender belt,' he groaned.

Once more, Fierce Bierce plied her length of cruel leather down across her helpless victim's striped buttocks.

'Careful, old girl.' Harriet giggled, plucking up a pair of black lace panties. 'Postman's about to make another delivery.'

6

Sachertorte

Otto Kitzler was proudly showing off his cellars to a circle of envious friends. The celebrated patissier paused before addressing them solemnly.

'It is all in the timing, the art of creating a magnificent success. A recipe must include a schedule,' he emphasised, betraying his Teutonic obsession with order and discipline. 'One must bring the necessary ingredients together with planning, method and perfect timing,' he concluded sententiously.

He waved his fat hands, gesturing to the lantern-lit, brick-walled cellarage crowded with boxes, jars, sacks and barrels. 'The finest flour from the Tsar's wheat fields in the Crimea,' he boasted. 'Choice cherries from Italy, butter from the flowered meadows on the lower slopes of the Swiss Alps, the smoothest chocolate from – ah, but that must remain one of my little secrets.' He clapped his hands and grinned. 'Bring these things together in the right order, at the right time, and the result is –'

'Another prize-winning *sachertorte*, *mein Herr*?' fawned one of his admiring circle.

'Exactly so. But if the timing is wrong – What do you want, girl?' Otto snapped, angry that his small moment of glory had been interrupted.

Gretchen paused at the bottom of the stone steps, her dark eyes shining in the lamp light. Within the tight stretch of her white blouse, her breasts rose and fell as she panted, blinking in the light. She smoothed her skirts at her hips and, drawing a deep breath after running down the stone steps, licked her dry lips. 'Mistress sent me down, sir. Ingredients for the special cake.'

'Special cake?' the medal-winning patissier echoed. 'Frau Kitzler told me nothing of this.'

'The footman came, master. From the Belvedere Palace. The princess herself has ordered a *sachertorte* for tonight. There is to be a party given in honour of the Crown Prince of Sweden.'

A murmur of delight rippled through the cellar from the suitably impressed visitors. When the Belvedere Palace set the pace, they consented, all of Vienna kept pace. Basking in his celebrity, Herr Kitzler beckoned Gretchen to approach. The girl obeyed, taking shy, uncertain steps across the stone flags. He grabbed her roughly, snatching at the long white tapes of her apron and plucking them loose. Gretchen squealed and wriggled but his fat hands held her fast.

'For the Crown Prince of Sweden, we will need flour as white and smooth as these thighs,' he laughed, dragging her skirts up to her buttocks.

His guests, brimming with schnapps and boorish bonhomie, clapped their loud applause.

'And butter as soft as these,' Otto grinned, his greasy lips splitting wide apart to reveal stained, yellow teeth, as his fingers cupped and squeezed Gretchen's exposed buttocks fiercely.

'And cream. As white as her breasts,' a cruel voice taunted. 'Eh, Otto? Cream as white as her breasts?'

Herr Kitzler's large hands snatched at the crisp lace sheathing Gretchen's taut bosom. A searing rip tore the blouse from her breasts, exposing their ripe swell to the greedy gaze of her tormentors.

'No, master, please don't –'

'And cherries, as red and ripe as –' another voice cried excitedly. 'Show us her cherries, Otto.'

The others brayed loudly. Gretchen squirmed in her shame but the master patissier's grip was tight and his fingers were nimble, despite his fat hands. Scooping out the soft warmth of her left breast, he palmed it, offering it up for their perusal. Pincering his finger and thumbtips, he teased up and pinched the dark, berry-bright nipple.

'And the exotic spice from Zanzibar,' they yelled, pointing down with quivering fingers at the girl's gently swelling pubic mound.

'Gretchen,' a harsh voice rang out from the shadows of the stone steps. 'Where is that wretched girl?'

Scuttling footsteps sounded the approach of Frau Kitzler. Her husband released his captive instantly as the yellow light of a bobbing lantern announced her arrival.

'Gretchen,' she snapped, holding her lantern aloft and playing its glare on the dishevelled girl. 'Wretched little slut. Get back up to the kitchens at once.'

Sobbing loudly, the girl scampered up the stone steps, scrabbling to hurriedly cover her naked bosom.

Up in the noise and heat of the kitchens, Gretchen dried her eyes and dutifully started to toast the shelled almonds in preparation for the delicious apricot paste that would coat the moist chocolate *sachertorte*. Herr Kitzler kept the recipe a closely guarded secret, allowing his workers to prepare only a small part of each cake – so that none knew the full secret. Gretchen, tossing the aromatic almonds, shivered as she heard the stern voice of Frau Kitzler ring out harshly above the clatter and the din.

'Where is that slut? Come here, girl.'

The master patissier's wife, her blonde hair gleaming in severely curled braids, her black bombazine skirts swishing the stone flags of the kitchen floor, grabbed the protesting girl from her place near the fiery oven into the white-tiled pantry where all was cool, calm and ominously silent.

The mistress shook the miserable girl violently. 'Flaunting yourself like a common street girl in front of Herr Kitzler and his important guests. I've warned you girl what would happen if I caught you –'

'But, Frau Kitzler, I didn't –'

'Silence, you little Hungarian slut. I saw you. I saw everything,' the mistress thundered, unbuckling a dark leather belt from her trim waist. She dragged a stool from beneath a table and positioned it with her foot in the centre of the red-tiled floor. It squeaked, grating harshly. 'Get across that stool, girl,' she commanded. 'I'm going to teach you once and for all. Across the stool, girl, at once. No, leave your skirts alone. I will arrange you and bare your bottom for the lash.'

'Please don't beat me –'

'Silence. Across the stool.'

Gretchen's dark eyes widened in fear. She begged aloud for mercy. 'Please, mistress, do not lash me. I truly didn't –'

'Obey my instructions, did you?' Frau Kitzler snarled. 'I warned you not to disport yourself before your master.' She jabbed her finger down dominantly to the awaiting stool and snapped the leather belt harshly.

Tearfully, the trembling girl lowered herself face down over the seat, settling her belly into the hard, polished wood. She whimpered softly as she felt the capable hands of her angry mistress dragging her skirts up over her thighs to her hips, fully exposing the swollen curves of her calico-sheathed buttocks. Grunting softly with exertion, one hand pinning the wriggling girl across the stool, the other hand gripping the belt, Frau Kitzler used her teeth to tug at the cami-knickers' laces, pulling them open with a savage toss of her head. Again using her teeth, she peeled the calico down across the plump cheeks. Gretchen moaned as the hot breath of her mistress kissed her bare buttocks. For a brief moment, Frau Kitzler sank her face into the bottom she proposed to beat, eliciting a shrill squeal from her victim squirming across the stool.

'Little Magyar witch,' the cruel Frau hissed, her words muffled by the soft flesh crushed up into her lips. 'I'll make you suffer for your wanton wickedness.'

'No –' the bare bottomed girl squealed her final protest, instantly squealing her torment as the leather belt whistled down to snap-crack across her rounded cheeks.

As the belt rose and lashed down repeatedly across her helpless buttocks, pinkish red weals deepened to a purpling shade of pain across their creamy flesh. Gretchen struggled to escape but Frau Kitzler's pinioning hand was steady – as steady as her unerring aim with the dark hide was sure. Plying the belt viciously in a mounting frenzy of jealous rage, the master patissier's wife lashed the jerking buttocks relentlessly. As the searing scald of her punishing stripes blazed, Gretchen clenched her fists tightly. Her sobs echoed around the white-tiled walls of the pantry. It was so unjust. So unfair.

Frau Kitzler paused, doubling the supple length of leather up in her hand. Bending back down, bringing her face to the whipped cheeks, she carefully examined the red stripes bequeathed by the belt across the upturned buttocks. First she fingered, then she licked, each savage weal, dimpling the ravished cheeks with her dominant tongue. Gretchen sobbed aloud, drumming her feet into the red-tiled floor as she jerked her buttocks up into the face of her punisher.

'Keep still, slut,' the stern Frau whispered.

Gretchen did not obey the strict command. The mouth at her hot cheeks opened. Seconds later, Gretchen screamed as the teeth of her tormentress bit deeply into the punished flesh.

Frau Kitzler stood up, rebuttoning the cuff of her right sleeve. She flicked the belt down once more across Gretchen's bottom, then coiled the suppled hide up into a tight curl. 'I've no time to whip you thoroughly now. There's work to be done. A special cake to be made. That was just a taste of what you'll get if I ever catch you at your lewd wickedness again, my girl. Understand? A taste,' she repeated, bringing the coiled belt to Gretchen's lips. 'Taste and remember,' the cruel Frau whispered.

Gretchen obeyed, flinching from the harsh tang as she reluctantly kissed and tongued the dark hide.

When not drudging in the heat and noise of the kitchens, Gretchen was forced to work as a waitress upstairs in the busy coffee house. There were over sixty white-linened tables beneath the carved oak ceiling from which hung huge bronze chandeliers. The walls of crimson velvet were hung with patriotic prints. Frequented by the cream of Vienna, Otto Kitzler's emporium was always bustling. Halfway along the teeming Hildburghausenplatz, it was the favourite haunt of musicians, spies, poets, anarchists, clerics, businessmen and the more raffish element of Viennese nobility. Mahler came for his mocha every morning, while Gustav Klimt argued art with von Zemkinsky every night.

When not eluding the lustful embraces of the greasy patissier, Gretchen was evading the jealous vengeance of his cruel wife. Quick and nimble as she was, the dark-eyed girl was frequently caught by both her tormentors.

Gretchen despised her Austrian masters. A Magyar from a remote village in distant Bohemia, she had made the difficult journey to Vienna to be apprenticed to the famous Otto Kitzler – whose delicious cakes and confections had reputedly held up the departure of the royal train to Trieste until they had cooled from his ovens and had been sugared by his hand. With Bohemia under the iron heel of the occupying Austrian army, Gretchen had come to Vienna, bringing with her all her impoverished family's hopes – only to find herself in servitude beneath the Kitzler yoke. They taught her nothing and used her as a mere slave. Denied access to the secret arts and mysteries of cake-making, Gretchen soon realised that her apprenticeship would be a long, miserable trial before she could return to her village to restore her family's fortunes.

At nine each night, Gretchen folded away her long white apron and slipped away out into the crisp snow-covered streets. Tonight, it was bitterly cold, with the silver stars glittering up in the black sky above Vienna.

She trudged along the Hildburghausenplatz, slipping frequently. Glimpsing into the blaze of the brightly lit windows of the shops, she saw the fine silks and satins of her Austrian oppressors, saw the virile lobsters they dined on and the carp-crammed barrels of brine. Cold and hungry, she longed for a slice of the pungent hams and fragrant cheeses displayed on the shelves, averting her shy gaze from the lewd wurst sausages at which black-stockinged schoolgirls giggled.

To reach her shabby attic at the top of her ramshackle lodgings in Kapellstrasse, Gretchen had to walk through the vast Prater, Vienna's notorious open-air amusement park. The Prater, as usual, was thronged with people wrapped in furs enjoying the music, lights and fairground rides. By the large wrought-iron bandstand, Gretchen saw the young prostitutes, masked and cloaked, tempting the soldiery and citizens, shopkeepers and noisy young students with their voluptuous charms. Naked beneath their dark velvet cloaks, they would fleetingly display themselves, shivering and smiling, their pale bosoms bouncing invitingly.

Gretchen scuttled past the gates of the Wahring Cemetery, making the sign of the cross hurriedly, and turned into the meaner quarters of the imperial city. Soon she was in Kapellstrasse. Up in her bleak, unheated attic, she boiled up some cabbage soup before carefully undressing. Naked, she draped the single blanket around her shoulders and drank her meagre bowl of soup, eked out with a slice of sour rye bread.

In bed, she fingered the weals on her bottom, shivering as she remembered the heat of the leather belt across her naked flesh. A peal of laughter rose up through the carpetless floorboards from the room below. Gretchen curled up in her narrow bed and tried to sleep. Laughter, a shout and the sound of breaking glass from below woke her from the very edge of sleep.

Sitting up in bed, she sighed. How much had she managed to save? she wondered. Taking her small leather purse from beneath her hard pillow, she emptied the coins on to her bed. Look after the groschen, her parents had warned, and the schillings will take care of themselves. The small heap of coins added up to very little – not even her fare back to her family. A silver schilling spilled down on to the floor, rolling across the uncarpeted floorboards to a shadowed corner of her spartan attic room. A whole schilling. Lost. Scrambling anxiously down from her bed on to her knees, Gretchen peered into the gloom. There, a soft gleam brought a cry of joy to her lips. She stretched out a trembling fingertip to touch the small coin – but found only a small hole through which the light from the room below glinted. Her left knee found the missing coin. Gretchen winced as she made the painful discovery, sitting back on her heels and clutching the schilling in triumph.

The hole in the floorboard fascinated her. Kneeling, she brought her dark eye down to its light. Through it, she saw the room below. Unlike the darkness of her own, it was warmly illuminated by five oil lamps. Brooding purple silk coverings dressed the walls, from which four huge sumptuously gilded mirrors hung, their large ovals of silver glass reflecting two naked figures on a single bed.

Gretchen gasped – with surprise at the unexpected splendour of the exotically furnished room in the Kapellstrasse slum, and with shocked delight at the kneeling woman, her wrists bound by black velvet ribbons, being mounted and savagely pleasured from behind by the naked man. Gretchen glimpsed the mask and dark cloak abandoned on a zebra skin rug and suddenly understood. Beneath her, a prostitute from the Prater was busily entertaining a client.

As Gretchen watched, the naked man, hips pumping and neck arching, groaned as he emptied himself into the kneeling prostitute's buttocks. The watching girl's breasts grew heavy, her nipples thickening pleasurably and peaking in a plucking pain. At the juncture of her tightly clamped thighs, a warm ooze moistened her labial folds.

Blushing with shame, Gretchen silently rose up from the hard floorboards and tiptoed back to her cold bed. Under her blanket, she shivered – not from the cold of her lonely attic but from the dark delights haunting her imagination. Her fingers strayed down from her hardened nipples across her belly to play at her wet pubic fringe. Closing her eyes, she conjured up the scene glimpsed through her spy hole – images of the bound, kneeling prostitute, writhing as she was ridden by the naked man at her buttocks.

Gretchen peeled her outer fleshfolds apart and furtively sought out her wet heat. Inexperienced, her thumbtip blindly probed to strum and stroke her clitoris. Frustrated and unskilled in the business of self-pleasuring, the village girl from distant Bohemia merely succeeded in tormenting and igniting her slippery slit. An impatient plunge of two straightened fingers into her pulsing heat caused her buttocks to clench and spasm. A low moan broke from her parted lips as her belly fluttered and then tensed. Driving her fingers deeper into her wetness as she squirmed her bottom into the mattress, she pumped frantically – just as she had witnessed the naked man spearing the proffered buttocks of the bound prostitute on the bed in the ornate room below.

But her joy eluded her. However hard she tried, the girl beneath the blanket in her narrow bed could not achieve the carnal ecstasy she desired. Even though the cleft between her swollen cheeks had become hot and sticky, and her brutally fingered pussy a tingling seethe, something in her subconscious mind forbade the ultimate delight.

Suddenly, in her simple, unlettered and unschooled way, Gretchen knew why. The naked, kneeling prostitute whose tightly bound hands symbolised her utter submission and surrender was like Bohemia, Gretchen's beloved home-land. Occupied by the brutal Austrians, Bohemia lay helpless like the girl below, while a stranger took pleasure in her prostration.

Gretchen snarled with both anger and frustration. Resting her sticky fingers up by her face on the pillow, she twisted and turned over in her bed, collapsing at length into a dream-troubled sleep.

Gretchen woke. It was bitterly cold. The nearby clock tower struck one. Gretchen had only slept for a few hours. She sat up in her bed, straining to listen. Soft noises rose up from the room below. Voices. The movement of furniture. Curious, Gretchen tiptoed across her uncarpeted floor back to the spy hole in the darkest corner of her bedroom. Kneeling, she peered down at the prostitute's gilded lair below.

There was a new client. An Austrian army captain, resplendent in his silver and blue uniform, was undressing with methodical care. His black polished boots and golden sabre rested by the door. In the middle of the floor, a pair of what looked like crude wooden stocks had been arranged. A length of bamboo cane glinted in the lamp-light as it rested on the striped zebra skin rug. The prostitute, Gretchen frowned as she gazed down in puzzle-ment, was still fully masked and cloaked, making no move to disrobe.

Her heart thumped excitedly and her dry throat constric-ted. Gretchen suddenly felt slightly dizzy – and ill. She could not bear to silently witness another example of brutal humiliation and submission. No. She could not stay to witness the cruel Austrian army captain force the nude into the subjugation of the wooden yokes and lash her bared buttocks with the whippy cane.

Back in her bed, Gretchen pressed her fingers into her ears to stop the sounds of punishment from the room below. But her arms began to ache – and her curiosity became intense. Easing her elbows down on to the mattress, she shuddered as she heard the eerie sound: the thin, terrifying whistle of the lashing cane. *Swish, swipe*. Then, a heartstopping pause. Another *swish, swipe*. A prolonged pause. *Swish, swipe*. It was a measured punish-ment. Unhurried, signalling the total dominance of the caner over the caned.

Gretchen strained eagerly as she listened. No sound, no cry of anguish or grunt of satisfaction, accompanied the strokes of cruel wood across naked flesh. A warm bubble silvered at Gretchen's sticky labia. She clamped her thighs together, denying this treacherous betrayal of her body over her purer spirit. The action merely caused the bubble to burst silently. The warm scald dripped down, soaking her cleft. Gretchen, appalled at her own powerlessness over her Judas flesh, whimpered. No. She would not crawl back to the spy hole and peer down upon the scene of domination and discipline. No. Memories of her beloved Bohemia ravaged by Austrian sword and flame forbade it. No, Gretchen thought, pressing her fingers back into her ears.

But the images behind her eyes burned deeply into her brain. As if in a trance, she unstopped her ears once more and listened. Eagerly. Anxiously. There it was again. The haunting swish and slice of the punishing cane. Out of bed, as if drawn by the mesmeric rhythm of the unseen – but understood – strokes being administered below, Gretchen crawled on all fours to the spy hole. *Swish, slice.* Her nipples grazed the rough wood as she bent down to the gleam in the darkness before her. *Swish, slice.* Her breasts bulged as, crouching intently, she crushed them beneath her.

Gretchen's cry of joy almost betrayed her presence to those she spied upon. Down below, straining in his yoked bondage, the Austrian army captain writhed as the prostitute, dressed only in his black boots and her concealing mask, viciously plied the stinging bamboo. Treading dominantly down with her booted left foot, the masked nude pinned her helpless victim into utter submission. From time to time, between the searing strokes across his severely caned buttocks, the whipper brought the toe of her polished boot to the lips – and then up between his thighs to the dangling balls – of the whipped.

Gretchen came immediately, without having to use her fingers at her seething heat. Grinding her breasts and pubis into the rough floorboards savagely, she hammered her hips as her first orgasm ebbed then exploded into the climax of its successor.

The prostitute was bending down now. Gretchen blinked away the crimson blur from her drunken eyes. She watched the masked nude carefully threading the oiled lash of a dog whip around the thick cock and sac of her yoked victim. Gretchen moaned and held her breath, fearing that it would take only the slightest of sighs to trigger off yet another savage paroxysm of sweet ecstasy. The army captain, commissioned to proudly bear the Austrian black eagle, fluttered like a ragged crow in his subjugation. The prostitute rose up, gripping the ivory shaft of the dog whip in her left hand. She jerked it. Her naked victim groaned – Gretchen thrilled to the sight of his hands, protruding from the wooden stocks, splay in agony. She knew that under the controlling tether of the dog whip at his cock, he could not release his hot seed. Gretchen blushed but savoured his anguish – just as she savoured the justice of the red weals across his cheeks and the oiled lash tied tightly around his churning balls.

The yellow cane glinted as it rose. *Swish*. Another thin red line blazed across his whipped buttocks. The masked nude lashed the cane three more times then, kneeling, probed the tip of her bamboo rod into the cleft of her victim. The army captain yelled; his protest was silenced by the polished boot at his lips. He kissed the boot then licked it, like a whipped cur licks its wounds. Back at his buttocks, the kneeling prostitute inserted two, then four, inches of the cane between the whipped cheeks.

Gretchen came again, threshing and gasping aloud as her naked body writhed in ecstasy on the hard wooden floor. On the hard wooden floor – above the spectacle of surrender, submission and savage suffering below.

Gretchen slept heavily, awaking to the clear chime of the nearby clock tower striking seven. She was late. Without washing, she dressed and ran, slipping twice in the snow, all the way to the Hildburghausenplatz bakery and coffee shop.

In the kitchen, she diced cherries and peeled vanilla pods, her fingers clumsy with both tiredness and the cold. Otto Kitzler returned from the bank and toured his kitchens, inspecting every worker. At Gretchen's wooden table, he gazed down at the shining red cherries piled up in their white porcelain bowl. He nodded his approval. In the blue Dresden dish, stripped and diced vanilla pods met with his satisfaction. Gretchen was washing apricots, one by one, before thumbing their soft flesh open to extract the dark stones.

The master patissier paused, sniffing inquisitively. The air was richly perfumed with the cloying aromas of *sachertorte* ingredients, but through the sweet miasma his nostrils caught the feral tang of Gretchen's unwashed pussy.

133

Standing directly behind her, his hot breath on the nape of her neck, he clutched at her hips with his fat hands. Drawing her dominantly back into his rough embrace, he raked her buttocks with his engorged prick. Her soft cheeks squirmed, enflaming the twitching shaft at her cleft. Imprisoning her firmly, his cruel fingers digging into her shoulders, he once more forced her soft bottom on to his bulging white apron.

The apricot fell from her trembling fingers, rolled from the wooden table and dropped silently on to the tiled floor.

'Gretchen,' Frau Kitzler cried, scurrying towards them through the noise and steam of the busy kitchen. Her laced boot stamped on the escaped apricot viciously, splitting it wide apart. 'Wicked girl. Get a fresh apron on and come and wait on your Austrian masters.'

Gretchen, her dark Magyar eyes clouding with shame, ran out of the kitchen, head bowed.

'Table forty. The private booth. Here, take their order and no mistakes, slut. You've earned one whipping already. Do not give me reason to double your stripes, understand?'

Gretchen approached the private booth. Her heart sank. In the seclusion of high, velvet-padded screens, two notorious female pianists from the Vienna Conservatoire smoked small cheroots in languid silence. Gretchen had overheard the girls in the kitchen speak of these two mannishly attired young musicians – and of the scandal their intimate friendship had created. They lived together, Gretchen understood the rumours to say, as man and wife.

'What is your pleasure?' Gretchen murmured shyly, pencil poised.

The severely dressed woman, wearing a man's tie and waistcoat, ordered Turkish coffee and strudels for two. Gretchen's nervous pencil scribbled the order down hurriedly.

'Pretty little piece, just as Frau Kitzler promised us,' the second musician remarked, scrutinising Gretchen as if she were a cake on a tray.

Gretchen curtsied, flinching under the sparkle of the woman's monocled eye.

'Little village wench,' her partner murmured, fingering her tie. 'Fresh as a newly stringed violin.'

'Unplucked,' whispered the other, raking Gretchen's bosom and thighs with her monocle.

Frau Kitzler approached, rubbing her hands. 'Everything to your satisfaction?' she purred.

'Quite delicious,' the mannish musician replied, palming several schillings across the white linen towards the patissier's wife.

'Thank you.' Frau Kitzler pocketed the coins, then rested her thumbtips inside the tight stretch of her leather belt. 'She is yours, from now on. She will serve you with whatever you wish.'

Gretchen, burning with shame at the cool hands stroking her buttocks and thighs, departed, returning to serve the Turkish coffee and strudels faultlessly, despite her hammering heart.

'No. Don't scuttle off, girl. Sit,' the waistcoated woman commanded, patting the upholstered banquette firmly. 'Sit here, next to me.'

'No, girl. Come and sit next to me,' her partner snarled, grasping Gretchen's wrist and tugging her. 'I want you.'

Gretchen struggled, whimpering softly as she tried to escape the pawing hands at her breasts and waist. Lurching and toppling, she lost her balance briefly, her hip bumping the table. The coffee pot wobbled and crashed down, its dark stain rapidly covering the spotless linen; the burning liquid trickling down on to the monocled woman's unprotected lap. She screeched, drawing Frau Kitzler to the private booth almost immediately.

'The stupid girl,' the scalded woman spluttered. 'I'm soaked, and my clothes quite ruined –'

'Please, madam, come with me at once,' Frau Kitzler soothed, dabbing at the woman's pubic mound with a napkin. 'I will see to it personally that you have complete satisfaction.'

'Satisfaction?'

'First, your clothes. To save them, we must retire and apply cold water to them at once. There is a private room where you can undress.'

'Complete satisfaction?' the monocled woman prompted.

'I will send Gretchen to you for punishment. You may have this,' the master patissier's wife purred, unbuckling her leather belt, 'to whip her bare bottom.'

At nine, Gretchen stole away into the darkness of the night. Her whipped cheeks still burned, and the tight calico cami-knickers stretched across her punished flesh rekindled the fierce heat of the leather belt's merciless lash.

At the Prater, a uniformed military band was playing a spirited 'Trennugswaltz'. The crowd paused, their breath smoking the lamplit air, and swayed gently to the music. Gretchen hated the helmeted bandsman and the martial music they blared. She blundered on through the Prater, tears stinging her large, dark eyes. Then she heard the faint sounds from her childhood. A Magyar tune. She followed the thin, reedy notes to their source – an accordion player beside a carousel. The roundabout was painted red and yellow. On it, large black cockerels waited patiently for the next ride, their shining black wooden forms gleaming under the bright naptha flares. The accordionist played another Magyar tune. Its sweet pathos brought tears of pleasurable remembrance to Gretchen's frost-pinched cheeks.

She would have one ride. Fishing out five groschen from her frayed pocket, she held them out to the gypsy. Seeing her dark, tear-brimmed Magyar eyes, he smiled, waved away the proffered money and bodily hoisted Gretchen aloft, planting her astride a handsome black cock. A hiss of steam warned that the ride was about to commence. Chains groaned and pulleys whirred as organ music bellowed out – and the turning carousel gathered speed.

Gretchen closed her eyes tightly and gripped on to the red-and-yellow striped pole. Faster. The organ music grew more frantic. Faster. The cold night air stung her upturned face. Clinging on to the pole, and gasping as she took in painful lungfuls of the freezing night air, Gretchen squeezed her thighs together as she rode the huge cock between them.

The ride slowed and came to a graceful stop. Gretchen, panting and exhilarated, allowed the courteous gypsy to help her alight. He squeezed her playfully; she kissed him shyly and scampered away into the throng.

There were other rides, other attractions, but she was very tired after her long day drudging for the Kitzlers. A pang of hunger stabbed her empty belly. She pondered the wisdom of buying a baked potato, or a blue twist of paper overflowing with roasted chestnuts.

A single trumpet note rose above the tumult. Gretchen followed the surging crowd and found herself at the roped-off perimeter of a sawdust-strewn arena. In it, naked to the waist and sporting tight red-and-yellow breeches, a handsome Bohemian was conducting two magnificent Leipzig whites through their curvetting paces. Under his command, the horses pranced, pirouetted and reared up, pawing the air with their gold-painted hooves. Austrian horses, obedient to the snapping whip and curt command of her fellow countryman.

Peering into the arena from the outer gloom, Gretchen watched admiringly as the horseman coached his spirited pair into absolute submission. She glowed with fierce pride as the Leipzig whites rolled over on to their backs, scattering sawdust everywhere.

Gretchen felt quite exhausted. She closed her eyes, swaying gently as her knees trembled. She suddenly had the violent fancy that she was inside the arena, ankle-deep in the soft sawdust. Whip in hand, she was in control of the Kitzlers. Pale, shivering and naked, she made them prance obediently under her flickering lash.

Gretchen grinned, amazed at the enormity of her rebellious impulse – but emboldened by her overwhelming contempt. Frau Kitzler would drop her hands down from her breasts to shield her pubis. *Snap*. The whip would curl and kiss her knuckles with its stinging lash. The seared hands would fly up to crush the breasts above, exposing the pattissier's wife to shame and disgrace. Gretchen giggled. Yes. Another flick of the whip would stripe the naked woman's buttocks. Screaming softly and driven by the lash, the tamed Frau would stumble round the arena, puffs of sawdust rising from her stamping feet.

Then it would be the turn of the naked, flabby cake-maker. Gretchen sighed softly, wondering if it would hurt – enough – to be whipped up between the thighs. Yes. That was how she would make him prance to her stern command. Behind closed eyes, Gretchen pictured the fat Otto Kitzler loping around the arena, cradling his cock and balls, his buttocks criss-crossed with the searing slice of her controlling whip.

Gretchen opened her eyes and sighed once more. It was time to leave the Prater and get back to her attic in Kapellstrasse. She turned her back on the noise and lights – and froze. There, over by the booth selling slices of fried knackwurst, was her master. Gretchen blinked her disbelief. Moments ago, she had imagined herself conducting him around the arena, naked beneath the threat of her stinging whip. Now, there he was, parleying and haggling with a masked prostitute. Showing her a fistful of schillings. Gretchen hid herself in the shadows and watched. The schillings were refused, as were his advances. The prostitute had scorned him. Otto Kitzler cursed her loudly as she stalked away back towards the bandstand. Gretchen, shivering, kept to the shadows as she scuttled back to her lodgings.

Outside her house, a fiacre stood, a steaming mare stamping impatiently in her jingling harness. The cabman was loading the small, four-wheeled carriage with a large trunk and two leather valises. Stepping out from the front door, after pressing a gold coin into the upturned palm of the hovering concierge, was the prostitute from the room below Gretchen's attic.

'I will be back in twelve days. Be sure not to let my apartment out in my absence.'

The concierge nodded, spat on her sovereign and shuffled back inside. The pieces of luggage safely aboard, the cabman assisted the prostitute into her seat. The whip cracked and the mare responded, the clatter of her hooves echoing along the cobbles of Kapellstrasse.

* * *

Gretchen listened to Otto Kitzler as he conducted a group of admiring Viennese worthies around his establishment.

'Planning and timing, my friends, are the most important ingredients in the creation of a medal-winning *sachertorte*. Bringing the necessary parts all together in the right sequence and at the appropriate time. That is the secret of my –'

'Success,' they chorused, raising their schnapps.

Otto Kitzler made no modest protest, but bowed smugly as he accepted their salute.

Planning and timing. Gretchen took note of her master's words, as every good apprentice should.

She needed *kümmel* and a whole *sachertorte*. To steal a mere slice of the delicious cake would be too dangerous. She would be suspected, closely questioned by the bullying Kitzlers and soundly thrashed. To steal an entire cake would be too monstrous a crime for them to credit her with – she trusted in their contempt for the abilities of mere Magyars. Carefully choosing her moment, Gretchen stole both the *kümmel* and the cake and smuggled them back to her lodgings.

She needed the prostitute's mask and dark cloak. She needed a willing young messenger boy in attendance. And, to be successful, Gretchen needed to plan and prepare – arranging all these parts to her plan in the correct sequence.

The Prater. Not too early. That would attract the attention of the other prostitutes. Sisters in sin, they would grow inquisitive – resentful of her intrusion, perhaps. But not too late, either. She must time everything carefully. Giving the stolen *kümmel* to the concierge would only ensure a couple of hours to complete her task.

The next night, she saw Herr Kitzler at the bandstand. Despite the protection of her mask and cloak, she trembled as he approached. A whispered exchange, a brief glimpse of her breasts. Minutes later, Gretchen was leading him by the hand through the crowded amusement park. They left the Prater by the west gate, taking a short cut through the ghostly white stones of the Hundstrum graveyard. She became playful, blindfolding him with a black velvet band before taking his cock in her hand and leading him back to her lodgings. Otto Kitzler followed, his lust and vanity blinding him more thoroughly than the velvet at his eyes.

Halfway through her *kümmel*, the concierge surrendered the prostitute's key once more without objection. Up in the room beneath her attic, Gretchen remained silent, masked and cloaked. The master patissier raised his fat fingers up to his blindfold. Gretchen moved quickly, undressing him and tantalising him until his erection strained. She pushed her blindfolded captive gently down on to the sensual zebra skin rug, then straddled his nakedness, rubbing her buttocks at his groin.

'Smell,' she whispered, disguising her voice as she brought a slice of *sachertorte* to his nostrils.

Otto's cock twitched excitedly, raking her cleft with its fierce heat. He sniffed greedily then, exposing his yellow teeth in a wide grin, bit into the dark chocolate confection.

'But this is excellent,' he cried, spitting moist crumbs. 'Where did you buy it?'

Gretchen could not resist tormenting the patissier, now utterly in her thrall. She whispered the name of Kitzler's deadly rival, grinning as she watched his face purple and contort in jealous fury. She fed him another slice, but he refused – until she clutched and squeezed his balls. Kitzler promptly opened wide, choking on the *sachertorte*. He struggled, but Gretchen became dominant.

Naked and blindfolded, he knelt down in obedience to her sternly whispered command. She took a thick slice of the chocolate cake and pressed it into his groin, impaling it upon his engorged erection. He grunted inquisitively, trying to make sense of the strange sensation. Kneeling down before him, Gretchen, now naked except for her mask, deftly twisted the wedge of *sachertorte* between her controlling hands, then slowly dragged it gently back and forth.

Otto Kitzler's pale face prickled with sweat. His knuckles whitened as he clenched his fists. Nodding his approval at this unusual pleasuring, he knelt before her helplessly as she pumped him with increasing vigour. He slumped and groaned; she caught the spurt of his hot seed moments later in the rich, soft cake.

She fed him again, open-mouthed with silent glee as he frowned at – but obediently swallowed – his own creation. 'Nice?' she mocked.

'Not bad,' he conceded, 'but I knew it was his,' he added, managing to name his deadly rival without swearing. 'It was a little sour. The cream was off.'

Getting him into the stocks was a piece of cake. He bellowed, once the wooden yokes had snapped into place, but gagging the helpless, blindfolded man was even easier. The apprentice had listened well to her master. She was bringing all the elements together, in the correct sequence and with perfect timing.

Otto Kitzler tensed at the sound of the cane. Its eerie, spine-tingling swish filled the ornate room as Gretchen executed several practice strokes. She watched with satisfaction as he cowered in the stocks, his hands writhing as the veins at his temples throbbed. She thrummed the bamboo once more, slicing the whippy wood down with a note of pure venom. The master patissier jerked in his bondage, his fear now a palpable frenzy.

Bending down over her captive, the pretty young apprentice positioned the yellow cane between the pale buttocks of her quivering master. Retreating to where she had tossed his discarded clothing down, she plucked up his black frock coat and returned to the stocks.

She extracted his wallet and poured out all his gold. He rattled the wooden stocks in renewed rage, his fierce curses muffled by the tight gag at his lips. Despite being blindfolded by the velvet, he knew what was happening. He was being robbed. Gretchen took a silver schilling from the heap of gold and, removing the cane from his cleft, planted the cold coin between his cheeks. He squeezed them tightly, denying her. Three crisp strokes of the cane later, he parted his buttocks for the humiliation, shuddering as the schilling rasped his anal whorl.

That is what I think of your Austrian schillings, pig, she laughed silently to herself. The gold I will keep. Gold knows no frontiers. It will be of equal value back in Bohemia.

Then she searched for his secret recipe book. It was no bigger than a cigarette case, bound in green leather and securely locked. A search of all his clothing for the minute key proved fruitless. Gretchen returned to the stocks. There, around his creased neck, she saw the fine silver chain. On it, dangling down at his chest, was the small silver key. She snatched it free and unlocked the recipe book.

The master patissier threshed wildly as Gretchen pretended to tear out each page and destroy his livelihood – secretly adding the famous recipes for *sachertorte* and strudels to her stolen gold coins. Carefully setting each page down for later safe-keeping – and use back in her native village – she continued to deliberately rip and shred a page of newspaper she had prepared for the purpose of fooling him. Otto Kitzler almost broke free from his bondage, such was his wrath and fury.

All was going sweetly to plan. Having humiliated him, robbed him and then maddened him into a rage, Gretchen reached the next stage of her carefully planned enterprise exactly on time. Punishment. Rising, she plucked out the silver schilling from his cleft and threw it away. Gathering up the bamboo cane, and stroking the cool length of wood affectionately, she tapped his cheeks twice before raising her supple wood aloft.

Whipping him was a delicious sensation. Gretchen quickly found that, just as *sachertorte* made her mouth water, the pleasure of lashing him juiced her prickling pussy. Each slicing stroke left painful reddening lines that quickly turned to a purplish blue across his jerking buttocks. After administering thirteen cuts – the traditional baker's dozen – Gretchen could contain her intense excitement no longer. Kneeling astride, then behind, his whipped cheeks, she kissed them with her wet pussy-lips twice then savagely raked her wet heat against the punished flesh. He writhed beneath her total domination but the stocks held him securely, allowing Gretchen to ride Kitzler mercilessly. She hammered herself with supreme contempt as she started coming violently, smearing his reddened, striped buttocks with her wet sheen – just as he would glaze a framboise tart.

Another thirteen strokes followed in crisp succession. Gretchen's arm ached heavily as she dutifully honoured the baker's dozen once more. The bamboo began to sing its cruel song more slowly after the seventh cut. The next three were slowly delivered: slow, searching measured strokes – just as the prostitute had flayed the Austrian army captain. Gretchen paused, suddenly remembering. What had the prostitute done? Her eyes sparkled as she sliced the whippy wood down for the concluding stripes, eager for the final humiliation.

The thirteenth lash. Gretchen shivered as she heard the wooden stocks creak and strain as her victim writhed in agony. Kneeling once more at his blazing cheeks, she nuzzled the tip of the cane between the ravished buttocks. Slowly twisting the thin bamboo, she guided the quivering tip to the dark circle of his sphincter – and probed.

Up in her attic, her gold coins and stolen recipes tucked away, Gretchen nestled down at her spy hole. She knew that she was going to the Hildburghausenplatz kitchens tomorrow, and for another week or so. She would quietly depart one night, at nine, for ever. To leave Vienna too soon would arouse suspicion.

Gretchen peered down through the spy hole at the naked patissier in his yoked bondage. She counted the red and purple cane strokes across his punished buttocks. Had she really given him such a terrible thrashing?

Timing. Gretchen giggled softly. The empty wallet and gutted recipe book were waiting – waiting for Frau Kitzler to discover on her arrival. Gretchen had given the messenger boy two notes and the remaining half of the *sachertorte*. One note to Frau Kitzler, summoning her immediately to her sick husband in Kapellstrasse. Another note to be handed to the police, an hour later. The boy had taken both notes and the *sachertorte*, solemnly promising to deliver the notes on time.

Timing, and careful preparation. Gretchen pressed her dark eye to the spy hole, glimpsing the dog whip she had left at her master's feet for the convenience of her mistress. Frau Kitzler, finding her foolish husband cheated and robbed, would no doubt seek vengeance.

Timing. The nearby clock struck sweetly in the chill night air. The rattle of an approaching cab. Gretchen tensed excitedly. Footsteps thumping up the stairs. The door would burst open. Soon, Gretchen grinned, she would be witnessing Frau Kitzler lashing the dog whip. Then, more footsteps on the stairs. The black uniformed police would tumble into the prostitute's lair. The sweet-toothed Kitzlers would taste the humiliation of public ridicule and shame – adding the cherry to Gretchen's perfectly baked cake.

7

A Penalty to Pay

The student hall of residence echoed to slamming doors and running footsteps as unshaven, unbreakfasted young men dashed out to catch their early morning lectures or to secure a computer terminal in the IT block ten minutes away across the park.

Luke opened a bleary eye, yawned and rolled over in his bed. He had a five-thirty deadline to meet that evening – the completion of his musicology assignment. An essay on the French pianist Satie. It would be his first tutorial. He needed to make a good impression. And he hadn't written a word.

He groaned, resolved to get up at once and take a brisk shower and some black coffee – then promptly fell asleep.

An hour later, the drone of a hoover woke him. Face down in his pillow, he tensed expectantly, spreading his thighs wide so that his cleft began to ache. As the hoover whined, he wriggled, crushing his fat cock into the mattress below. The domestic who came to clean his block each morning was a mature brunette. Luke was eighteen. The cleaner was twice his age. She was a strong-thighed Spaniard with glossy dark hair, full red lips which were always wet and parted. Luke adored her large bottom as it strained at the stretch of her pale green nylon overalls. He had been watching her furtively for some time, often shuddering with pleasure as she bent down to unravel the hoover's trailing flex. Yesterday, he had found and kept her yellow rubber glove.

The whine of the hoover became a shrill snarl. Luke strained up on his elbows, listening intently. The Spanish domestic was almost outside his room. His fingers stole under the pillow at his hot face, scrabbled blindly then emerged, clutching his secret trophy. He drew the yellow rubber glove up to his nose and inhaled deeply. His cock thickened. His mouth was dry and swallowing became difficult. He bowed his head down in reverence and slowly kissed the yellow rubber. As he tasted the haunting tang, his trapped cock pulsed against the firm mattress.

The throb of his shaft synchronised with his thumping pulse. He closed his eyes. In his fantasy, he willed the mature brunette through his door and into his room. He imagined her standing, dark-nyloned legs astride, by his bed. Her ripe breasts bounced as she tossed her glossy black hair in a contemptuous flounce. Chiding his laziness, her full red lips twisted in scorn.

Luke trembled with pleasure as his furtive fantasy unfolded. He tried to slow his thoughts down, tried to imagine every dark, delicious detail perfectly. But the pulse in his cock quickened. The firm-thighed, swollen-buttocked Spaniard was becoming angry with him now. He squirmed. She was shouting at him in her husky voice, the vowels blurred. A pigsty. Why was his room such a pigsty? Why was he so lazy? Why was he still in bed when the rest of the world had gone to work? In his fantasy, Luke burned with shame, acknowledging all of which he was accused.

His room was a pigsty, with clothing, books, unwashed coffee mugs and cassettes strewn everywhere. He was in bed when he should be up and busy.

In his fantasy, Luke quivered as he imagined the mature brunette bending down, her strong fingers snatching away his duvet – exposing his nakedness to the stern gaze of her fierce Iberian eyes. He clenched his pale buttocks, squeezing his cheeks in delicious dread. Stretching down her yellow-gloved index finger, he imagined her tapping his bottom dominantly, dimpling the taut flesh.

Lazy. His room a pigsty. She repeated the charges, her red lips glistening as she spat out her angry contempt. Her

146

dark eyes narrowed into fierce slits. Then he willed her gloved hand slowly down to clutch and talon his hair, forcing him face down into the pillow. He grunted as he imagined the weight of her nylon-stockinged knee descend to pin him ruthlessly – and groaned as he sensed her gather up the loop of hoover flex in her firm, gloved grip.

Outside his door, the hoover whined loudly. Luke knelt up in bed rapidly, his thick erection raking the white sheet then slapping his belly as he sank his buttocks down on to his heels. He drew the stolen yellow rubber glove up to his mouth and exhaled deeply into it. The fingers inflated and stretched, quivering, like the teats on a swollen udder.

Behind closed eyes, he drowned in the gathering vortex of his overpowering fantasy, letting himself be sucked deeper and deeper down into the swirling images exploding in his brain. The dominant Spanish domestic, pinning him face down into his bed. Snarling her contempt for him then announcing her proposal to punish him. Plucking at the plastic buttons of her pale green nylon coat, revealing her braless, heavy breasts, the nipples peaking darkly against the sallow, shining flesh. Dangling the looped flex across the curves of his upturned cheeks while tightening the grip on his neck.

Luke blinked. Outside his door, the hoover was moaning as it was patiently dragged back and forth. Luke sucked hard – the yellow glove collapsed, smothering him until he panted for air. He inhaled the sour tang of the warm rubber mingled with the trace of her cheap scent. His erection bulged and strained, aching sweetly. The veined cock now twitched impatiently. Shuffling on his knees, he parted them wide and thrust his hips forwards. He brought the glove down to the shining snout of his erection and, gripping his hot cock with his left hand, forced its length into the forefinger of the empty glove. Tightly sheathed by the clinging rubber, his shaft strained painfully for release.

He closed his eyes. She was whipping his bottom now. Luke could almost hear the cruel swish of every imagined, craved-for stroke. He was getting the harsh punishment he deeply desired. *Swish, swipe.* Each fierce stroke bit mercilessly into the flesh of his clenched cheeks, kiss-lashing them with a pinkish weal that he knew would deepen to a shade of red exactly matching his punisher's wet lips. Again, and again, the thin black flex whipped down.

Open-eyed, he stared down at his yellow-gloved shaft. He moaned softly as he tugged and stretched the restricting rubber, dragging it down savagely into his coiled pubic nest. His unblemished buttocks spasmed as he imagined them seething under her strokes.

Behind closed eyes, he luxuriated in the dark-eyed Spaniard's vicious domination, screaming softly as she dropped the electric flex down on to his thighs and firmly finger-stroked the sticky cleft between his freshly whipped cheeks.

Luke gasped aloud as he tossed his head back, gripped the rubber glove and pumped. He silently whispered his frenzied litany aloud. Stern domestic. Nyloned legs. Dark, cruel eyes. Whip me. Punish me. Lash my bare bottom and ignore my squeals for mercy. He pumped himself ruthlessly – seconds later, he buckled as the loud liquid squirt of his agonised release flooded the taut finger of the yellow rubber glove.

During – and immediately after – the exquisite agony of his spurting seed, Luke yoked fantasy and reality violently together. He saw her bending over his naked, punished buttocks, her bared breasts glistening with the sweat of her exertion. As she brought her face down to inspect his striped cheeks, her bosom bulged as it bunched against his thigh.

The soft rake of her stubby nipples was almost real, so vivid were his feverish longings. Luke slowly peeled away the rubber glove and stretched face down into his bed. Twisting his arm up behind him, he dangled the glove above his bottom – his outstretched arm aching as the yellow rubber danced. His warm semen dripped, smearing his buttocks which, in his fantasy, the Spaniard had just cruelly lashed.

* * *

148

Luke opened his eyes and yawned. His small white clock told him what he already knew. It was getting late. Half the morning had gone. He listened. The hoover was busy upstairs, buzzing softly down along the second-floor corridor, its distant drone like an angry wasp at a window pane. Guiltily, he buried the wet rubber glove under his mattress, blushing hotly with both confused delight and a sudden stab of shame. Up out of bed, he rinsed himself at the small sink and then shaved. In the mirror, he asked himself how the hell he was going to get that essay on Satie finished before five. The anxious face in the steamed glass could give no helpful answer. It was a course assessment requirement. No essay, no grade. Failure to submit on time would incur a penalty that could jeopardise the classification of his degree. Suddenly stung by this realisation, Luke resolved solemnly to get dressed and go straight to the library. He would skip breakfast and get down to work.

In the college canteen, halfway between his room and the library, Luke sat alone with his buttered teacake and glass of milk. There were plenty of pretty young girls in the canteen. Some sat alone, pretending to read and waiting to be approached. Others sat in pairs and small groups. Laughing, talking, flicking their hair. Smoking and eating toast, eyes ever alert on the door for the next young man to walk in.

Luke chose to sit alone. He felt shy in the company of younger women. Shy and awkward. When he flicked through his magazines to masturbate, he preferred not to look at the smiling faces of pretty young girls. For him, mature women held all the allure and excitement. Women whose breasts had ripened to a majestic fullness that strained their bulging bras. Women whose buttocks had swollen from their former girlish softness to stretch the panties that hugged them fiercely. Luke longed for the imperious, not the impish. He yearned to be in the thrall of stern experience, not the soft simper of innocence. As a growing boy, around at his auntie's for Saturday dinner, he would reluctantly but obediently accept the moist, pale flesh of breast meat she would carve with her jewelled fingers – secretly, Luke had lusted for the taste of darker thigh meat. Once, arriving early, with the chicken browning in the oven, Luke had tiptoed upstairs and glimpsed his auntie naked in her bedroom after a bath. She had caught him kneeling, cock in hand, on the landing. Over her knee, bare-bottomed, he had howled as her spanking hand reddened his squirming buttocks. The chicken had burned to a crisp before she had finished the delicious discipline. She had made a cheese salad for them both, later, after towelling dry his semen-splash from her thighs.

Luke ate his toasted teacake in blissful contentedness. The butter glistened on his fingertips and chin. He had deliberately paid for the small breakfast with a tenner, emptying the change from the cashier's till and leaving her very annoyed.

'Nothing smaller?' she had demanded.

'Sorry,' he had lied, hoping the pound coins in his pocket remained silent.

Flashing her eyes angrily at him, she had been forced to count out his change from the last of her float. Luke had relished her suppressed fury, squirming with delight as she snapped out a sarcastic thank you.

Nibbling at the last of his teacake, he wished that the canteen was empty. Just himself, the cashier and the two women working behind the servery. Capable, competent women in their early forties, probably chaffing at the heat of the kitchen in their crisp red-and-pink striped uniforms.

Alone, the door locked, with the three women. The cashier would summon him curtly to her till. Perched on the leather-topped stool, her glossy nyloned legs crossed, her curved buttocks taut in her uniform, she would call out to the two servers. At the till, they would stand and stare, nodding ominously. The three women would surround him in silence – a loud, menacing silence – while he submitted to their will, bending belly down across the leather surface of the stool still warm from the weight of the cashier's plump buttocks.

150

Cool hands would loosen his trousers and drag them down to his ankles. Polished fingernails would rake his cheeks as his pants were roughly peeled away from their bunched flesh. Bare-bottomed and bending, he would cringe beneath their cruel gaze. Then the spanking would commence, the angry cashier claiming the lion's share of his humiliation, suffering and shame. Red-bottomed, he would squirm under the harsh onslaught as their hot, firm palms savagely caressed his helpless cheeks. Writhing, he would shrink from the splayed fingers of the cashier as she dominantly inspected his hot, punished flesh. Moaning softly, he would endure their laughter and tormenting hands as they spread his buttocks painfully apart and thumbed his exposed cleft.

In the kitchen, the radio played a jingle for the half-hour headlines. Luke, who had finished his buttered teacake and milk twelve minutes ago, sat at his table, pretending to read. He could not get up just now. No. Not yet. His cock was engorged, straining urgently at his bulging trousers. He was so stiffly erect, he could not walk out of the canteen. Satie would have to wait. By the time the radio gave out the weather, leading up to the news on the hour, Luke rose up from his corner table and departed.

He walked through the streets of South Wimbledon, enjoying the late autumn sunshine. He knew he should have taken a bus to the library but he was feeling disturbingly aroused and needed to clear his head.

The reference library had been built in 1938. Squat and quite ugly, the red-brick building was imprisoned in a ring of shining black iron railings. Inside, Luke approached the polished wooden counter. It was an intimate library, specialising in musicology and providing an archive service of original scores. Knowledge of its existence was what had brought Luke to this sleepy part of London.

He waited to be served. He had three books to return, all overdue. He fingered the coins in his pocket, mentally amassing the fine, as he read the tariff neatly typed under the notice above. In large red lettering, it advised borrowers with overdue returns that there would be a penalty to pay.

From an adjacent office, the sound of a softly tapping typewriter filled the silence. Luke coughed – a soft, apologetic sound. The tapping ceased. A chair scraped. High heels clicked on the polished wooden floor. The glass-panelled oak door, already ajar, squeaked as it opened wide. Luke's knees trembled involuntarily as the librarian stepped out of her office and approached the counter.

She was in her late thirties. Ash-blonde hair, cut chic and severe, framing her oval face. She had the eyes of a cat. Grey, wide and unblinking. Luke's cock unfurled from its sleepy repose, surging up against his pants as it lengthened. Her nostrils, he noticed, were small and dark. Her broad mouth, curved impatiently, bore the faintest trace of pale pink lipstick. No make-up concealed the gleam of her faultless skin. Luke, pressing his erection in against the wooden counter he now leaned upon, thrilled to the tiny lines at the corners of her eyes and pursed lips. She bent her head down. Her hair remained unruffled as she inspected his books.

'Late,' she pronounced, her fingertip tapping the stamped date on the gummed issue page. She stared at him steadily as her straightened finger rose slowly to the tariff of fines.

Luke mumbled his apology, swallowing as her colourless nail varnish glinted beneath the neon light above.

'There's a penalty to pay.'

At his desk, four biographies of Satie opened out before him, Luke sat in a waking dream. The librarian – new, Luke had never seen her before – had just stepped out for a brief, tantalising moment from behind her wooden counter. Peeping at her furtively, Luke had glimpsed her small, firm breasts, slender hips and pert bottom. Svelte rather than thin, and not yet overly ripe and matronly, she had an athletic suppleness and grace beneath her beige cardigan and black pencil skirt. The hem of her skirt fell just above her knee. Turning on her shiny high-heeled shoes, she allowed Luke the merest glimpse of her deliciously nylon-stockinged legs. Slender, shapely legs, with a gently muscled hint of strength. Luke imagined being pinned and trapped across one leg – for a bare-bottomed spanking – as the other pressed in against his thighs. He noted the seams running primly from her ankles up to the slender swell of her tightly skirted buttocks above.

She had returned to her office, almost but not fully closing the door. Luke heard the soft tapping of the typewriter. Satie remained neglected as Luke drifted into an enchanted daydream. In it, the beautiful librarian slowly stripped herself naked before flexing her bare arm at the elbow to test the whippiness of the bamboo she gripped – gripped in readiness to administer a crisp caning to his bare bottom. As the thin wood whistled down, her small, rubbery breasts bounced.

Satie, Erik, b. Honfleur, 17 May 1866, d. Paris, 1 July 1925, remained neglected. The clock on the library wall reminded Luke that he really should try and concentrate. He picked up his pen and started to scribble. Dates of publications. Dates of performances. Twenty minutes later, he found himself doodling, sketching out a scene from his early-morning fantasy. His pen scratched frantically as he depicted the dark-eyed Spanish domestic sternly punishing his upturned buttocks with the looped hoover flex.

The office door opened and the ash-blonde librarian approached the counter. As she swept by, a date stamp toppled down on to the grey carpet in front. Luke saw her snatch at it, frowning as she missed. Still frowning, she stepped out and squatted down, knees becomingly squeezed together, her buttocks perched above her high heels. Luke peeped furtively. His cock tensed as he saw the glistening sheen of her nylons at her gently squashed calves. She scooped up the date stamp, returned it to the counter by the ink pad and entered her office, closing the door. Luke returned to his doodles – richly embellishing his earlier fantasies with fresh etchings now featuring the lovely librarian in dominant mode.

* * *

No. He couldn't dare. Not here. In the music library. At five past three in the afternoon. In broad daylight. But he did. Alone, except for the soft, persistent tap-tapping of the typewriter, Luke deftly fingered his cock out and slowly masturbated. Squeezing his eyes shut, he thumbed his glans – imagining the strict librarian being very severe with him – and came in silent violence just as he conjured up the mental picture of his suffering beneath her lash. By the time the library clock joined its hands together for quarter past, Luke's head was lolling down on his neglected Satie notes. A minute later he was fast asleep.

She pursued him in his dreams. He was about to be caned. Luke saw the librarian not as a mistress of the belt or strap but of the bamboo. Touching his toes – did anyone actually touch their toes for their stripes? Luke asked himself in the tangled logic of his dream. Yes, Luke happily told himself. Yes, they did. Red-faced as the blood rushed down, those bending for their punishment did scrabble their fingers at their toes – encouraged to do so by the admonishing tap of a quivering cane at their upturned cheeks. The punished, bare-bottomed and bending, had to suffer the delicious agony of waiting for the striping strokes to commence. In his dream, Luke waited. The librarian, studying the tip of her yellow cane, stood behind him. Dominant and supreme over his submissive nakedness. She stretched down a controlling hand and touched his shoulder. Bend down. No. Further. Right down. I want your bottom up, young man. Give me your bottom. Luke moaned. The controlling hand gripped his shoulder tightly, shaking him. Luke squirmed.
  'The library is closing in five minutes,' he heard, waking up with a start. 'Five minutes to closing,' she rasped, shaking his shoulder once more.
  Blinking under the neon light, Luke pocketed his pen, sleepily gathered up most of his unfinished notes on Satie – and slunk out into the pale evening sunshine.

The librarian gazed down at the curious scribblings and doodles as she closed the four biographies of Satie and

154

heaped them up in her arms, cradling them against her bosom. Students, she fumed. Lazy little sods. Too lazy to return the books to the shelves. She paused. She suddenly realised that she was looking at the doodles the wrong way up, rendering them quite meaningless. Arrowing down her finger, she rotated the page. The doodles swam into focus, making their meaning clear. The librarian's grey eyes widened as she saw a scribbled image of herself, cane aquiver, punishing the bare-bottomed young man. She hugged the books she was carrying tightly to her breasts. Her nostrils flared. Surely not? Spilling the four books back down on to the desk where Luke had sat, and slept, she bent down. This time, her thighs were splayed as wide as the tight pencil skirt would permit. Her nylons sparkled beneath the neon light above. Straining, she peered down under the table. The rank whiff of semen haunted her nostrils. A tiny dark puddle caught her eye. She stretched her finger down to the grey carpet and dabbed into Luke's small, sticky semen-splash. Raising her moistened fingertip up to her mouth, her grey eyes darkened as her pale pink lips slowly sucked.

Five past five. Luke ransacked his room, found the number, palmed a fifty-pence piece – you could never find ten pence when you wanted it – and dashed down the impeccably hoovered corridor to the pay phone.

Four minutes later, he came back into his room and sighed his relief aloud. He'd done it. Phoned in and told the department secretary that he'd have to cancel his tutorial. A sudden migraine. He'd put the essay in the post and arrange another time.

Telemann. Tallis. Tartini. Luke had over two hundred tapes, all carefully labelled and indexed. Malipiero. Mascagni. Messiaen. Luke had them all at his fingertips. He turned out the light and stretched out on his bed as Lennon blasted out 'Imagine'. Luke liked Lennon's haunting song – because that's what Luke did. All the time. Imagine.

When the chicken had charred in his auntie's oven, Luke had experienced – just the once, across her lap – his very own glimpse of heaven. Ever since, he had had to imagine the pleasure he pined for: domination and discipline. He had had to conjure up in his mind the delights he craved: surrender and submission. In the darkness, Lennon's curdling piano tinkled. Imagine there's no –

Three sharp taps at his door. Luke groaned, ignoring the threat of intrusion. Some silly sod out of coffee, he supposed. Three more sharp taps. Luke stretched out and pressed the pause button, then got up and switched on the light. Slipping on a pale blue pair of boxer shorts, he padded barefoot across to the door.

'Yep?'

The grey eyes of the music librarian gazed unblinkingly into his startled face.

'Migraine?' she drawled. 'I didn't know Lennon was a recommended cure for migraine.'

Luke blushed, acutely conscious of his boxer shorts and her searching gaze. Grey, penetrating eyes. 'It's better now –'

'Perhaps you imagined it.'

'But how did you –?'

Sweeping him aside – Luke flinched as her firm hand brushed against his chest – she strode into his room. 'My first love is my work at the music library, young man. Sadly, the philistines at the town hall will only fund a part-time post. So I make up my salary by teaching. I am your tutor. You cancelled. I cannot afford to do so; that is why I tracked you down here. I want to see that Satie essay you claimed was completed and ready to be put into the post.'

Luke blinked, slowly comprehending his awkward position. He stooped, hastily snatching up his pullover and jeans.

'There is no need to get dressed, young man. I had occasion to look under the desk you occupied in my library this afternoon. I am perfectly aware of what you did. I discovered the nasty mess you left behind. I will require you naked for your punishment.'

156

Luke gasped, letting the clothing he was clutching drop limply to his feet. 'I – I –' he stammered, blushing furiously.

'After I have punished you, bare-bottomed, we shall take a look at your Satie. Heaven help your bottom, young man, if it isn't up to scratch –'

'I haven't – It isn't –' Luke mumbled, boxer shorts twitching and beginning to bulge slightly as he retreated backwards to his bed.

'Not completed? Now, I can't say that I am entirely surprised. I found your notes. Remarkable,' she purred, extracting from her pocket and slowly unfolding the page of graphic doodling depicting discipline being dispensed. 'Satie would cover entire sheets with scribbling and not a single note. Remarkable coincidence. Shorts off, young man.'

Luke slumped down on the bed, head bowed, his fingers plucking at the duvet.

'Let's see what we can find in here,' she said, her voice grim but bright, as she strode across to his wardrobe. Opening it, she rummaged briskly.

Luke looked up.

'Belt? Or do you have a preference?'

Luke's eyes betrayed his incomprehension.

'I'm looking for something to whip your naughty bottom with, young man. Just as you depicted in your sketch. Belt? Or do you have a nice, supple slipper, hum?'

'No, please,' he protested hotly. 'That was not me, under the desk. That picture was not mine. I didn't –'

'Bend over across the bed at once,' she instructed, her tone firm but disturbingly pleasant. 'Bare-bottomed, like I told you.'

Luke remained sitting sullenly on the bed. 'Nothing to do with me –'

'At once,' she barked into the wardrobe, her hands groping in the dark.

Luke closed his eyes and shuddered. Suddenly, the heaven he had imagined was becoming a glimpse from hell.

'Ah, this will do,' she pronounced, clicking the wardrobe door shut and turning to face him, brandishing a wire coat hanger. 'Do you really think, young man, that you can come into my library, draw lewd and indecent pictures of me and then masturbate on my carpet? Well? Do you?'

Her crisp clinical voice, her cool use of the words 'lewd' and 'masturbate', brought home the enormity of his offence. Luke squirmed and covered his face with his hands. Anything to avoid her penetrating eyes.

'Look at me, young man. Hands down on the bed. Look at me.'

Slowly, burning with shame, he obeyed. He flinched as her grey stare searched out his misery.

'Well? I asked you a perfectly simple question.'

'No –' he whispered, his voice drying.

'No,' she echoed tartly. 'Very well. Across the bed. Arms stretched out. At once. Bare-bottomed and bending.'

Twisting around, Luke obeyed her command, dragging down his boxer shorts and spearing the duvet's softness with his hard shaft.

'Bottom up.' She pressed her stockinged thigh against his as she arranged his kneeling nakedness to her complete satisfaction for the impending punishment. He whimpered as she forced him to inch his thighs apart – and moaned aloud as she tapped his balls dominantly with the curved end of the coat hanger.

'And I have not heard an apology yet.'

'Sorry,' he mumbled into the duvet, clenching his buttocks.

'Sorry? Sorry for what?'

'I'm sorry for –' he faltered. Shame choked his words into silence.

'I'm waiting,' she murmured, stroking the curve of his straining cheeks with the blunt tip of the wire coat hanger.

'Please, don't. Just punish me. I deserve it. But don't make me say –'

She guided the thin wire down between his cheeks, rasping the shadowed cleft until it began to burn. 'Sorry for what, young man?'

His buttocks jerked and spasmed, trapping the tormenting wire. 'I'm sorry for drawing pictures –'

'Vile, wicked pictures.'

'Vile, wicked pictures,' he confessed. 'And for – for –'

'Masturbating,' she prompted, primly.

'Masturbating,' he whispered softly.

'In a hallowed place dedicated to the enlightenment of the mind, not the sordid pleasures of the sullied flesh.'

Broken, he merely nodded, choking on his shame.

She raised the whippy coat hanger up, took a pace and a half back, bent down swiftly to smooth out the page of obscene doodling on the bed before him, and then slashed the coat hanger down. Luke hissed his pleasurable pain as the eight strokes were briskly administered. He raised his left foot up, pawing the air in an ecstasy of agony. She tapped it down imperiously and swiped the cruel wire down across his reddening buttocks five more times. They were slow, deliberate strokes. He smothered his soft screams in the duvet and drew his thighs together sharply as his striped buttocks spasmed.

Another searing lash. He grunted. Then another, biting viciously up into the lower curves of his defenceless flesh. His moaning melted into a soft sigh. The final stroke: *swish, swipe.* He slumped into the bed, hips jerking and whipped cheeks writhing, coming massively. She stood dominantly over him as he emptied his long liquid spurt over the crinkled page of erotic doodles.

The grey-eyed librarian raked the wire coat hanger down his spine as the semen splashed noisily. Taloning the hair of her victim, she dominantly forced his face down into the soaking page, rubbing it into the shimmering smear.

After forcing Luke to wash his sticky cock and belly at the sink, watching him intently as he obeyed, she motioned him over to the bed upon which she sat, her thighs and knees tightly together.

'I know there is no Satie essay. I am paid to tutor you and, now that I have punished you, that is exactly what I propose to do. Across my knee.' She patted her lap, the tender gesture full of potent malice.

Luke stumbled to her feet, knelt down before her and kissed the edge of her black high-heeled shoe.

'Brought to heel so soon, my boy?' she purred.

Raising his face up to hers, he nodded, then lowered it submissively. He hugged her legs below her knees, burying his hot face in her softly nyloned flesh. Moaning happily, he nuzzled her, kissing then licking her glossy legs devotedly.

'Up,' she whispered. 'No more of that now. Later, perhaps. We have all term, all year. And I have so much to teach you.'

Shivering with delight, he stretched his naked body, belly down, across her skirt. She gripped the nape of his neck. He squirmed, submitting and surrendering his red-striped buttocks up to her. She planted her other hand, palm down, across his seething cheeks. He wriggled at the dominant touch, rasping the wet glans of his thickening cock into her taut skirt.

'Erik Satie, as you should already know, was a dreadful student. Lazy, indolent and much given to day-dreaming. He wasted his student years. Strict discipline saved him. Oh, yes, young man. Only the strict discipline he was made to endure saved him from ignomy and failure.'

Smack. She smoothed the cheeks that she had just sharply spanked. *Smack*. Again, her slightly curved palm savagely caressed his hot cheeks.

'Satie came under the stern spell of a very strict tutor. If it worked for him, I see no reason why strict discipline will not rescue you from failure. As your tutor, it is my duty to take you in hand. Severely.'

The spanking was fierce. Afterwards, he strained, twisting down from her lap, to kiss her. She forced him to kneel against his bed. Soaking the duvet as he orgasmed violently, Luke froze in his jerking contortions – the grey-eyed librarian had promised him a kiss. Hitching up her skirt and dragging down her wet panties, she prised her sticky labia apart and pressed them against his hot buttocks. With flesh whispering against flesh, she kissed him farewell – until their next appointment.

8

Night School

Adam returned to the caretaker's office at the rear of the Institute and carefully filed away the evening registers. The car park was quiet – both gates locked against thieves and vandals – so he had the next hour to himself until the classes finished at nine.

He sat down and pulled the desk lamp closer. He opened and closed the desk drawers, enjoying being temporarily in charge. George, the regular caretaker, had gone to be with his sister for a week or so. Her heart. Adam, assistant caretaker, had assumed control.

He slid a trembling hand into his overall pocket and extracted the small glass bottle of nail varnish. He had found it in the downstairs ladies. He gazed down at his trophy, gently thumbing the cold glass, then grasping it tightly in a tightened fist of triumph. With delicate strength, he twisted the white plastic cap and bent down to sniff the pungent polish. Twelve minutes later, he splayed his fingers out under the yellow glare of the desk lamp, inspecting his shiny pink nails. How long would they take to dry? He'd furtively watched women applying varnish. They often waved their drying nails in the air afterwards – just as if their fingertips had touched something hot. Adam waved his fingers. The varnish glinted as it dried.

As an assistant caretaker, Adam's duties did not require him to enter the ladies. But with George away, he had entered the white-tiled room for the very first time. The drip of a cistern had sounded hauntingly loud as he trod the hallowed ground, thrilling to be trespassing in this place of female secrets. Stretching out a hesitant fingertip, he had rubbed then stroked the plastic toilet seats, seats that were kissed by warm women's bottoms. Without raising the lid, he had unzipped and had a long pee, but his cock was so stiff with arousal he missed and soaked the floor. Down on his knees, he dried the tiles. Down on his knees, before the white porcelain that was dedicated for female use only.

Adam worshipped women. Adored them. Kneeling down at the toilet, he felt a delicious thrill in the delicious intimacy of being there, being so close to their secrets. Being where all males were excluded and forbidden. His nipples had grown tight and sore and his balls ached as he lingered in the cool, white-tiled room. Then he had spotted the forgotten bottle of nail varnish.

No need to panic. George was away. Adam was in charge. It was official. He could go into the toilets, into the changing rooms. But Adam felt his face grow hot as he pocketed the bottle of nail varnish. If anyone came in now, they would be angry. He trembled, almost swooning at the image of two severe matrons challenging him, then punishing him severely for his trespass – leaving his bottom pink and shining. As pink and shining as the nail polish in his overall pocket.

A car horn sounded impatiently at the locked gates. Adam rose, guiltily, spilling the nail varnish across the wooden desk. The sudden pink splash spread instantly, then dripped thickly down in a sticky spindle into the waste paper basket below. The car horn sounded again. Two sharp blasts. Spreading the evening newspaper hurriedly over the spillage, Adam trotted out of the office, crossed the square of asphalt and reached the gate. Unlocking it, he admitted the latecomer, watched her park then locked the gate. Pocketing the key, he tugged at the gate to check. With over sixty young women to guard, he was extra careful, protecting those placed in his precious care.

At five to nine, the first salvo of high heels skittling down the stone steps announced the end of the secretarial class.

162

Word processing. Adam liked to peep at them as they sat, heads bowed, gazing into their blue screens. Lovely little secretaries, chattering noisily. Always first away, in their second-hand VW Golfs and Ford Fiestas, to the pub. The language classes – French and Spanish – went next. Then the local history group, maturer women who walked and never ran down the corridor. Serious, stern women in beige cardigans and polished brogues. The practical classes were always the last out. Especially the cookery class. Always late away, cookery. Waiting for cakes to cool before being tucked away in tins and carried off in triumph. Adam liked the cookery class. The teacher often called him in, offering him something on a wooden spoon to sample. He always nodded his approval, even when it was chutney which he hated. Once, she had wiped his chin with a napkin. Adam had swallowed the mouthful as his cock had hardened.

He often lingered outside the cookery classroom, peering in through the glass-panelled door, watching the women clap their busy hands, dusting the air with flour. He adored the crisp white aprons tied tightly above the swell of their plump buttocks. He wanted to untie those apron strings, kneeling down, his face buried in the soft bottoms.

He hovered, as usual, at the door. Ten past nine. George knew how to clear the room. He would rattle his keys, bringing the lesson to an abrupt end. All Adam could manage was a timid cough. He coughed again, apologetically. Quarter past. The flushed women bustling at their sinks and ovens ignored him.

Finally, when the main block was cleared, across the car park in the crisp November night air, he approached the gym. Tuesday and Thursday evenings were Dancercise. George usually locked up the gym. It was Adam's first time.

The neon lights were blazing. Music thumped out deafeningly. At the window, Adam peeped in cautiously. He swallowed with difficulty as the tongue in his dry mouth thickened. In front of a leaping instructress, nine beautifully svelte, trim-buttocked lovelies stretched and strained. Their thighs shivered as they stomped to the rhythm, their tightly leotarded bottoms joggled as they pranced.

Adam pressed his hot face against the cold glass, clouding it with his breath. Inside, the ripely breasted instructress twirled, clapping her hands sharply as she span, then stamping her feet on the polished wooden floor. Adam held his breath as the nine students obeyed instantly, their multicoloured legwarmers becoming a blur as they pirouetted and did the flamenco stamp.

Loose and lovely, with only the tight lycra to tame and control their warm weight, bosoms bounced deliciously. Straining within their satin sheaths, firm young buttocks bulged. Adam, raking his groin against the breeze block wall, gently crushed his thickening cock into its hard surface. He ached to be closer to them, to be in there with them. To be one of their number. To be one of them.

A car door slammed and the headlights of a Maestro punched the darkness with a blaze of white. As the car turned, Adam flinched. The white light swept along the wall towards him. He ducked, crouching. If he was caught spying they would be ruthless with him, those stern matrons from the local history class. They would drag his overalls down and whip his bottom with leather belts. The squealing girls from Dancercise would emerge, angry and shouting, urging the matrons' stinging belts on. Adam's cock unfurled to its fullest stretch as he shivered in both fear and delight. The Maestro drove off.

Face pressed against the window once more, he gazed longingly at the Dancercise class. He whimpered, yearning to feel the tight lycra biting up into his own cleft, to feel the multicoloured leg-warmers prickling at his thighs – to have his naked body strictly bound by the taut stretchy leotard. He wanted to be elegantly graceful, like them. To be sensuous, tantalising and deliciously feminine. Not to be Adam, but Eve.

All the lights were out, and the Institute was deserted. Out in the empty car park, the night frost slowly glazed the black asphalt with a silver sparkle. Adam had to set the alarm system just before leaving. George had shown him how. But first, a final walk down along the glazed tiled corridor to check each classroom.

In the hairdressing salon, where white sinks gleamed in the gloom, Adam gently fingered the array of wigs left on their blocks. In the torchlight, he saw the cascade of golden curls tumbling down and the tight, auburn curls glistening. A shorter wig, the brunette hair razor-cut pertly, caught his eye. He played the beam of his torch upon it for several seconds, before stretching out his hand and plucking it up from its stand. It fitted him perfectly, bestowing on him a gentle, feminine appearance. Patting the wig repeatedly, he gazed into a mirror. It was perfect.

Keeping the wig on, he entered the beauty and cosmetic skills room next door but one. There, under a single spotlight, he dipped his fingertips inquisitively into various pots of cream and sniffed the delicious scents of oils and lotions. A pink lipstick, unearthed from a white leather cosmetic case, weighed lightly in his open palm.

Twisting the golden barrel slowly, he felt his cock stiffen as the shiny pink wax emerged, lengthening from its golden sheath. Adam grunted as the soft lipstick's snout pressed into his upper lip – and as his stiffness strained into his bulging overalls. Applying the lipstick carefully, he mimicked what he had often seen, and always adored, women do a thousand times. On the bus. In the street. Into their rear view mirrors when waiting at traffic lights. He closed his eyes and remembered. A woman applying lipstick distorted her lips, pressing them together then rolling them inwards to spread the sticky shine. Adam opened his eyes and gazed into the mirror. Slowly, he worked his mouth, shivering with delight as a perfect pair of pink lips smiled back at him.

The door creaked. Adam dropped the lipstick in a panic. If he had been caught in here. He flushed, but the sweat on his face was cold. Returning from checking the deserted corridor outside, he stooped and picked up the pink lipstick, returning it to the white leather vanity case. If he had been caught . . . Adam shivered with delicious dread at the image of being punished, the cane strokes striping his bare bottom with stinging pink weals – just as if a pink lipstick had been firmly applied across his upturned cheeks.

Before he crept out of the beauty and cosmetic skills room, Adam had sampled the eye-liner, concealent and blusher. He dabbed the powder on to his nose and chin gently, thrilling to the image in the glass as Eve slowly emerged, smiling up at him bewitchingly.

At the end of the long corridor, the assistant caretaker, his appearance now transformed by the wig and skilful make-up, roamed the dark stillness of the dressmaking room. He pressed a red button on a sewing machine. The needle chattered for five loud seconds, setting his heart racing. Pulling open a drawer, he fingered the seductive fabrics, then held the felt, crisp linen and fluffy wool firmly between a pincered finger and thumbtip. Back in the darkness of the open drawer, a ripple of sheer silk arrested his fingertips. He drew it up, playing it out over his knuckles then, twisting his wrist, grasped it fiercely in his fist. As he scrunched the silk repeatedly, the ache in his balls became intolerable. Silk against soft skin. Panties and stockings. His cock throbbed, almost bursting for release.

Adam stood before a full-length looking glass. Eve smiled back at him – her chic hair, pale face and pink lips teasing and tormenting. He unzipped and, painfully, dragged out his engorged erection, binding it tightly with the sinuous silk. Gripping his silk-sheathed shaft, he stared into his transformed reflection and moaned softly as he pumped. Pumped, slowly and firmly at first, then with an increasing frenzy as, in the glass, dark-eyed Eve parted her pink lips and mocked him.

As Adam approached his furious climax, he stared directly into the eyes of Eve. Shuffling closer to the silvered glass, he strained to plant his lips into their pink reflection. As his lipsticked mouth smeared the cold glass, he came, soaking the silk with a prolonged squirt of molten seed. He stumbled and collapsed on to his knees as he came, his sticky semen dribbling down the looking-glass, his head lolling into its cold surface. Shuddering as his knuckles shone with hot seed, Adam struggled to kiss the lips of Eve. But in the glass, his smudged eyes could only make out the disturbing image of an assistant caretaker recovering from a shattering orgasm. Where he had sought to find the beautiful female trapped behind the silver wall, he had found the contorted features of his own twisted longing.

Hot and confused, Adam wiped his face and mouth clean with a handful of snatched tissues before rinsing his semen-soaked fingers. He rolled up the spoiled silk and binned it carefully before replacing the chic little wig on its stand. His head still felt dizzy as his fingers fumbled with the alarm system. He wanted to get out, into the cold, clear night air. He began to panic when the alarm system failed to kick in. George had showed him. Two green lights and a red one.

Then Adam remembered. The gym across the car park. He must have forgotten to set the switch. Scrabbling in the darkness for the correct key, he unlocked the double doors and entered the gym. It was dark. Dark, and oppressively silent. But the air was heavy with delicious traces of female warmth, female perfume and female sweat. He stood still, sniffing at the heady mixture of talc and punishing exercise.

His footsteps took him to the showers. A silver head fizzled softly in the darkness, dribbling luke warm water. Adam flashed his torch around, spotted the tap and tightened it. The fizzling ceased abruptly. He raked the torch beam down. In the silver drain, something golden gleamed. He bent down and plucked at it with his fingertips. A tuft of golden pubic hair. Squeezing it dry, he raised it up to his cheek. Crisp, golden pubic hair. The torch clattered down on to the wet tiles as Adam moaned.

Stripped, trembling with excitement, Adam stood naked beneath the stream of hot water. He soaped and rinsed himself twice, reluctant to leave the place where women – naked and shining as they had offered their wet breasts up to the drumming sluice – had stood only an hour before. To be here, naked, where they had stood, naked. The sheer thrill electrified him. He pinched his nipples and ravished them brutally – as he thought women would when naked and alone, or indeed together, in the shower. His erection grew thick and hard. His hands cupped his buttocks and stretched them painfully apart. His balls churned. Moments later, still standing in the shower cubicle, glistening under the swirling cloud of steam, he trapped his erection between his palms. Rolling and rubbing his hands together, he rose up on skidding tiptoe – almost slipping on the wet surface. He gasped, pretending it was the statuesque, tightly leotarded Dancercise instructress thumbing his tingling glans. Yes. The severely beautiful, dominant, ponytailed instructress. Her thumbs, not his, punishing his hot snout. He cried out aloud, shooting off the thick silver squirt against the perspiring plastic shower curtain.

It had been a sweet orgasm. His most intense ever. Fiercer and more furious than when he paraded up and down his bedsit in bra and panties, spanking himself with a hairbrush. Almost as intense, Adam thought, as he watched his smear of semen slither down the plastic shower curtain, as intense as Eve would have. Almost, but not quite. A sadness stole over him as he sensed that he could never achieve the vicious delights that Eve, soft buttocks clenched together, would sweetly suffer.

As he shivered in the darkness – he'd forgotten about a towel, in his excitement – he felt the deep ache, the empty longing. What he had and what he had done was not enough. There must be more. He yearned to get closer, much closer, to the soft warmth, the breasts, the velvety buttocks and the slender thighs of elusive Eve.

The following Thursday, at 8.45 p.m., Adam weaved between the neatly parked cars and tiptoed into the entrance to the gym where the Dancercise class was pounding out into the night. Since coming in the shower on Tuesday night, he had been possessed by the overwhelming desire to be there, in the changing rooms, among the young women. Driven by his powerful compulsion, he had made his plans carefully. When the class was dismissed, he would be there, waiting.

Stealthily, in the dark, he pinned the out-of-order notice on to the outside of the shower curtain, then wedged a brush diagonally across the entrance. Ducking low, he slipped into the cubicle, carefully arranging the plastic curtain behind him. With mounting excitement, he stripped naked, tossing his overalls down on to the tiles, then silently unzipped the brown hold-all. From it, he took out the stolen wig, lipstick and cosmetics and small mirror.

Just as the doors burst open from the gym a little after nine, Adam was prepared. Transformed – into Eve. The dark wig sat pertly in place. His eyes were large and smudgy, his face pale beneath the light application of powder, his mouth a luscious pink beneath the wet-look lipstick.

He stood, naked and shivering, listening to the sounds of the Dancercise class getting undressed to shower. He thrilled to their laughter and giggling – and the occasional curse as protesting limbs stiffened and ached. He relished their girlish confidences and sweet whisperings. He squirmed as he heard elastic snap and soft stretchy lycra rustle as they stripped for the shower. He quivered, knowing that, inches beyond the opaque plastic curtain that shielded him, semi-naked young lovelies were bending as they struggled out of body stockings and peeled off their thigh-hugging leg-warmers. He closed his eyes tightly, imagining the bare breasts bulging and the soft buttocks parting to reveal their yawning clefts. Spilling breasts, absently crushed up by indifferent palms. Wobbling cheeks, softly dimpled as idle fingers scratched their swollen flesh. Glowing young naked female bodies, bumping and colliding softly as they lined up impatiently for the showers.

Nine students and the stern, ponytailed instructress. Six showers, one out of order. They would share, Adam suddenly realised, hugging himself in delight. Colliding softly under the steam and stinging hot rain, breasts would bump and buttocks would crush together. Sinuous, shining hands would force the soap to cream, covering the naked flesh of the girl in front with curds and frothy suds. They

169

would soap each other, he realised, straining to listen to their soft squeals, then hold each other's buttocks as they stood, breast to breast, nipples peaked, to be rinsed pink and shining.

To complete his illusion, Adam had sellotaped his cock between his legs and carefully combed his pubic hair down. Pleased with the transformation, he felt like one of the girls – one of the laughing, naked girls. But the excitement coursed through his veins, surging down like spilled quicksilver to engorge his hidden cock. To his dismay, it thickened and strained, tugging at the tape that bound it. Suddenly, with a soft, tearing sound – Adam clenched his teeth as the tape tore at his tender thigh-flesh – his prick flickered up, nodding ponderously. He would use a stronger type of tape next time. Next time? Of course, the small voice inside his head reasoned. Next time. Next Tuesday, when he would come to the Dancercise class in a wig and leotard – and really be one of the girls.

The shower in the next cubicle burst into life. Adam held his breath and listened. He heard the rasp of the plastic shower curtain opening and then being dragged across. He heard the soft humming of a naked woman, singing her wordless song as she squirted scented gel on to her palm then rubbed it across her soft bosom. He fingernailed his own nipples as he imagined hers, pink and alert beneath the drumming sluice. Now she would be turning, offering her glistening buttocks up to the hot rain. Turning, Adam parted his thighs and shuddered as the hot water raked down his spine, scalding his cleft below.

Out in the changing rooms, the naked young women were scampering to and fro, squealing as they collided in their eagerness to shower and go. In the adjacent cubicle, Adam caught the sharp gasp of pleasure as the nude squeezed and cupped her breasts, offering them up submissively once more to the punishing, stinging waters. He imagined the stubby, pink nipples peaking in their sweet ache. He savaged his own nipples once more, teasing them up into pinched points of pain. This is what Eve suffered. This, he moaned softly, was what Eve endured. A pleasurable pain.

The soft grunt from the nearby shower warned him that the wet nude was now soaping herself between her thighs. Now she would be creaming her buttocks. He pictured the gleaming bar of white soap biting deeply into her dark cleft. Smothering his groan of arousal, he collapsed against the cold tiles. The thrill of their forbidden proximity ravished him. The exquisite torment of their intimacy engorged his straining shaft. He battled to ignore the urgency of his pulsing erection but was overwhelmed by the need, the desire, to masturbate. His fingers failed him – too wet and slippery. He was too agitated. Snarling softly, he snatched off his chic wig and smothered his cock with it. Pumping and squeezing, pumping and squeezing, he almost fainted as he suddenly spurted long and hard, soaking the shining black hair with his silvery semen. Slumping silently down on to his knees, his eyes prickling with scalding sweat, Adam gulped for air – shivering as he tasted the pink lipstick in his mouth. The taste of Eve.

The days – and nights – dragged by slowly for him. His anticipation of joining the Dancercise class disguised as a young woman became an exquisite agony. Each evening, in his bedsit, Adam would undergo a careful dress rehearsal.

On Friday afternoon, he had applied wax stripes to his legs, thighs and arms. Painfully, he had removed all his body hair from his limbs. Later, smoothing baby oil over his stinging flesh, he had glimpsed at the effect in the mirror.

On Saturday, he plucked his eyebrows. They remained red and swollen until Sunday night. Chest and armpit hair went on Monday morning, and he carefully varnished his nails with a clear, colourless tint later that night. On Tuesday afternoon, he stood before the mirror for a final appraisal. A final appraisal before setting off for the Institute.

The new wig – soft, brown curls – was a perfect fit, as was his black leotard. He loved the way it held his buttocks in a firm hold. Each cheek taut and rounded in its lycra bondage. Industrial strength tape kept his cock and balls in check, rendering them unobtrusively discreet. Pale blue-and-silver sweat bands concealed his bony wrists. The one around his forehead gave him extra confidence with the wig. Soft tissues, scrunched up firmly, moulded a small, unprovocative bosom for him. More tape gave the breasts stability. The coloured leg-warmers smoothed his legs down into the required svelte shape. He was ready.

After collecting the registers and locking the car park gates, Adam returned to the caretaker's office. He changed there, folding his overalls neatly. In the mirror, his hands trembling with excitement, he made a few last-minute adjustments. He had filled out an enrolment form earlier, managing to stamp the receipt in the secretary's office when she had been busy on the phone. Then, as if in a dream, he walked across the car park and through the entrance to the gym.

The thump-thump of the music almost hypnotised him as he walked through the changing rooms, pausing to gaze in rapture at the rolled-up tights, scattered bras and abandoned panties. Secret, intimate wisps of delicious femininity. Clutching his membership credentials, he took a deep breath and sidled into the gym.

The instructress, lithe and supple in her gold, stretchy leotard, was bending down repeatedly, touching her toes in time to the relentless beat. Nine superb bottoms rose up to greet him as the class stretched down in obedient imitation. Then the instructress rose up, hands stretched high, raised her left knee up and turned to one side. The left buttocks of the nine young women bulged deliciously as they copied their leader. Adam froze, petrified. He suddenly found it difficult to breathe. Already, his taped cock twitched painfully.

The instructress paused briefly, head on one side, frowning slightly as she gazed down across the gym. She was an ash-blonde, with firm hips and big bouncing breasts that almost burst out of her golden lycra. Adam, recovering his nerve, was edging gingerly towards the back of the class. He smiled timidly and held up his enrolment form. She nodded, smiled, and launched into a bout of pelvic thrusts, her fingertips splayed around the smooth curve of her hips. The nine class members, intent on the vigorous Dancercise, ignored him. He positioned himself at the back. Looking around and focusing for the first time, Adam almost fainted with delight.

For the next half hour, Adam experienced a bliss he had never thought possible. The beautiful bodies before him offered themselves up willingly, candidly and submissively, surrendering their forbidden secrets to his hungry eyes. He was Adam, among all these unselfconscious Eves, furtively eating the forbidden fruit.

He drank in every detail avidly, carefully storing up each image for his private pleasure in the winter months ahead. The long, dark winter nights in his bedsit, where he would sit, cock in hand, remembering.

A blonde in a blue-and-white leotard paused in her prancing to finger the band of shrivelled lycra out of her hot cleft. Adam felt his face burn as he watched her knuckles dimple the curve of her heavy cheeks. Keeping in time to the blaring music, he followed the Dancercise routine faithfully, but his mind wandered as his eyes feasted.

The girl over to his left, in the red lycra, bending down to smooth her wrinkled leg-warmers up her thighs. Adam's cock rebelled against the industrial strength tape binding it fiercely as he saw the shining red lycra mould and define her labial lips. Then he saw her pluck a dark pubic hair from her bikini line. He shuddered, his exposed glans rubbed painfully against the sticky tape that trapped it. To his mounting alarm, the ooze of pre-come smeared his inner thighs.

Over there, by the breeze block wall, a girl in green dropped out for a breather, squatting down on the floor, legs splayed; her swollen buttocks crushed down deliciously into the polished wood, and her cleft was deep and darkly inviting. The gold-sheathed instructuress, still with the beat, raised her hand up to adjust the left strap of her leotard, then cupped and bunched her breasts unashamedly as she eased them within the taut lycra's stretch.

That did it. Adam started to come. Before he realised it, the sudden urge overwhelmed him. As he jumped, clapping his hands above his head, his burning shaft pulsed – then squirted massively, soaking his upper thighs and lower buttocks. Stumbling, panting and awkward on shivering legs, he managed to steady himself. The hot semen was silvering the backs of his thighs. He had to get out. Now.

He wobbled and slipped. Several girls turned, their pretty faces showing sudden concern. Adam managed a weak smile, shrugged an apology and scuttled out of the gym. He heard the instructress call out after him just as the double doors closed shut behind him. Out in the car park, crouching down and shivering behind the safety of a Metro, he watched the entrance to the gym. Nothing. Inside, the music and the feet of the Dancercisers pounded on. He exhaled, his hot breath billowing in the cold night air. He had done it. He had entered the Garden of Eden – and had tasted forbidden fruit.

In the caretaker's office, it was a struggle. Panicking, he tore off the wig, peeled away the sweaty leotard and scrabbled out of the leg-warmers. A handful of tissues restored his pale, lipsticked face to normal then dried his soaking groin. Back in his overalls, and breathing normally, Adam snatched up the huge bunch of keys and checked the time. Five past nine. Time to lock up.

He patrolled the empty corridor, switching off lights and securing doors. Crossing the car park, he approached the gym. One single light shone in the changing area. His heart started hammering, his hands felt hot and clammy.

Inside, he found the instructress briskly combing her ponytail. Adam turned the keys over gently in his hand. She tightened the laces in her trainers and stood up, shouldering her bag as she prepared to leave.

'Just coming,' she said. 'I see you've fixed that shower. Thanks. Bit of a squeeze, as you can imagine.'

Adam imagined. He nodded shyly.

'New pupil tonight. Came late, left early,' the instructress remarked. 'I've put her enrolment slip inside the register.'

Again, Adam merely nodded.

'See you Thursday, then.' She smiled, handing Adam the register.

Pocketing his keys, he stretched out his hand to accept it. Her eyes narrowed as she saw the glint of nail polish, then widened suspiciously at the blue-and-white sweat band on his wrist.

George had phoned. Another week should do it, either way. Hearts were tricky. Adam felt a great sense of relief. He didn't want to go through that again – transforming himself into Eve and trespassing into the Dancercise class. Not too soon. He would do it again. The week after next, perhaps. Or maybe after half-term, when George usually had a week's leave.

He had been unable to sleep all Tuesday night. One thought blazed in his brain, burning away any delicious memories. What would have happened if he had been caught? The tiniest mistake. The simplest slip-up. It had been madness. He couldn't believe that he had done it. The shame. The local newspaper. Magistrate's court, even. Then months behind drawn curtains throughout the summer's sunshine.

Towards dawn on Wednesday morning, he had slowly conjured up the images and delicious sensations he had enjoyed, thrilled to, come to. Yes, he resolved, lapsing into a fitful doze. He would do it all again. Become Eve. But not too soon. Not just yet.

'Go on. Just have a little taste,' the buxom teacher cajoled, guiding the brimming spoonful up to Adam's mouth.

The cookery class watched, waiting for his judgement. He sniffed cautiously. Something savoury and spicy. He closed his eyes and opened his mouth, accepting the spoon. It was fiery. Strong and fiery. Blinking, then swallowing, he pronounced it delicious.

'Hungarian goulash,' she smiled. 'Paprika, garlic and beef. Nice bit of topside. That'll put hairs on your chest.'

Adam, conscious of his egg-smooth torso, blushed.

'There,' the cookery teacher purred, applying a napkin to his chin. 'You've got gravy. All gone now.'

Five to nine. The secretarial class clattered down the stairs, first away. Quiz night in the pub. Adam rose from his desk and fished down the keys from the brass hook. His mouth was still sore from the paprika.

'But my dear, there is simply no evidence of a Saxon fort on Captain Turner's land. The man is deluded. Nothing from last year's dig indicates –' The local history ladies carried their folders and firm convictions out into the cold, dark night.

Adam felt suddenly tired. He strode down the long corridor. To his relief, all the classrooms were silent and deserted. Even the cookery class had cleared up and gone, leaving the room heavy with the rich aroma of their warming winter stew.

In the car park, Adam was surprised to see four cars remaining. He skirted them as he walked across to the gym entrance. It was in darkness. Still preoccupied by the remaining cars, he hesitated at the door. He knocked. No reply. He entered. All was still and silent. He shrugged, flicked the security alarm and, locking the door after him, walked back to his office.

'Sorry to trouble you, Adam. It is Adam, isn't it? I think I've left my purse in my locker. Would you mind?' It was the ponytailed instructress. She was sitting at his desk.

He nodded, signalling that it was no trouble. No trouble at all. They crossed the car park in silence. Still four cars parked there in the moonlight. He wondered. Unlocking the gym door, Adam switched off the security alarm and flicked the single entrance light on.

'There's a broken tile in one of the showers,' she said casually. 'You wouldn't take a quick look?'

As he walked through the changing room towards the shower cubicles at the far end, the neon lights suddenly

176

blazed. Adam turned, dazzled, to see the stern instructress and three of her Dancercise class standing between him and the door.

'Forget about the broken tile. What is the meaning of this?' She held up the wig savagely in her raised fist – as if she had just scalped a slain foe. 'And this?' Scrunched up in her other fist, the leotard he had worn on Tuesday night. She waited in ominous silence.

Adam opened his mouth to speak. But remained speechless. He thought frantically. Of course, she must have found them hidden away in the bottom drawer of the desk in the caretaker's office. The tiniest mistake. The smallest slip-up. He had made them both.

She broke the tense silence, her voice was soft but stern. 'We all thought it was a bit strange. Coming late and going early. Running out like that. And that run. All wrong. Set me thinking. Then I saw your blue-and-white wrist-band. So I sniffed around and found these.' She threw the items down on to the ground. 'Into the gym with you,' she snapped.

Adam, pale and trembling, was too frightened to stir.

She clapped her hands sharply. 'At once.'

'But –' he stammered, searching for the words of denial.

'Silence. Now get yourself into that gym. We have decided to deal with you right here and now.'

Her three silent companions nodded.

'I didn't mean any –' Adam whined softly. His voice failed him. He swallowed and tried again. 'I just wanted to see –'

'See?' she barked. 'You'll have plenty to see in the mirror tonight, by the time we've finished with you.'

He bleated a loud protest as they grappled with him and marched him into the gym and ordered him to undress. He resisted, but outnumbered and overpowered, he succumbed to their firm hands. Firm, eager hands – which soon had him stripped naked and shivering under the harsh neon lights.

'Kneel.'

He knelt. They examined him intimately, noting the lack of any body hair except the dark coils at the base of his

177

belly. They splayed his fingers and scrutinised the glinting nail varnish. He blushed furiously as a hand weighed his balls, pushing them to one side to reveal the red marks where the sticky tape had trapped his cock out of sight.

'Better gag him. He's going to squeal,' a pert blonde suggested.

The instructress nodded. Adam writhed. In seconds, Adam was tightly gagged with a pair of white panties. His eyes bulged, pleading mutely for mercy.

'And tie his hands tightly. Behind his back,' the instructress ordered.

Willing hands accomplished the task. Adam squirmed as, bound and gagged, he knelt before them, utterly helpless and totally in their thrall.

The instructress held out her flattened palm. 'Razor.'

The pert blonde placed a slender, black electric shaver in her colleague's outstretched palm. The instructress thumbed it, turning it on. It buzzed, the eerie sound echoing throughout the gym.

'We don't know quite what you hoped to achieve by your little escapade, young man. Perhaps we never will. But we can certainly guess. Get a good stiffy on, hmm? Get it up nice and hard, Tuesday night, did you? After watching us from the back of the class. Bet you did, naughty boy.'

He averted his gaze, blushing furiously. She caught his chin and tilted his head back, forcing him to endure her angry glare.

'Wanted to be one of the girls. Was that it?' she purred.

He tried to shake his head free but she held him dominantly in her controlling grip.

'First thing, then, a shave. A really close shave.' She thumbed his chin. He relaxed, fearing nothing more than the loss of his five o'clock shadow. She clicked the razor off and gently placed it down on the polished wooden floor of the gym. 'But first, we'd better make ourselves more comfortable. OK, girls?'

Her companions nodded. They stripped off quickly down to their bras and panties. One, a shapely, firmly

178

thighed brunette, wore dark tights. Adam's cock thickened in response.

'Look,' squealed the blonde. 'He's getting big.'

'Oh, he's male, all right. Just curious about girls.' The instructress smiled, fingering the elastic at her waist then smoothing her fingertips down across the swell of her pubic mound. 'Hold him down.'

Giggling, her pupils seized him, splaying his legs and pinning him down on to his back. Adam writhed as they each knelt, their knees pressing him into the hard floor. As they jiggled above him, Adam glimpsed their breasts bulging. His cock stiffened fiercely and rose up in salute.

'Don't let him wriggle about,' the instructress warned, picking up the electric razor and switching it on. 'I'm going to give him that shave now.'

Adam closed his eyes and grunted through his tight gag as the sharp burn of the skimming blades rasped – not at his chin but through his thick coils of matted pubic hair. He froze, rigid and terrified, as the razor peeled away the crisp curls at the base of his erection.

'Hold him still,' she ordered, deftly straddling him and planting her buttocks down on to his face. He lay trapped beneath her soft, warm cheeks, his nose pressed firmly into her feral cleft. She enclosed her curled fingers around his shaft and shaved him until every wisp had disappeared.

'Turn him over.'

With his cock crushed into the hard floor, Adam lay helpless, face down, as they spread his legs apart. The razor was still buzzing fiercely. He shrank as it swept up along his cleft, nipping out the odd little hair. He sensed the other girls craning to see. Twisting his head to one side, he saw their bosoms bouncing as they knelt over him, thigh to thigh.

The instructress switched off the razor and blew sharply into the blades. 'Now let's give him a real taste of femininity. He's seen plenty, but not tasted the real thing, I'll bet.'

They forced him up into a kneeling position, guiding his face into the glistening tights stretched at the upper thighs of the brunette. The dark tan sheen grazed his face. The others held him firmly as she peeled her tights down slowly, squirming her hips and buttocks sensually. She, like him, was clean-shaven. His nostrils caught her strong odour. Her labia were parted in a wet pout.

'Lick,' he was instructed as his gag was roughly removed.

He inched his face closer. Closer still. Then he tasted her wet warmth as his lips pressed against hers.

'Lick, don't kiss,' the instructress snapped, taloning his hair.

Adam obeyed, crying gently in his shame and humiliation. He licked, then sucked, the dark fleshfolds of her pussy, flickering his tongue between their slippery velvet.

'Deeper,' urged the brunette, tossing her head back. 'Harder.'

'We'll show you what a girl really likes,' the blonde added.

Adam pulled away, despite the controlling hand of the instructress taloning his hair. The blonde bent down, her hand hovering just above his bare bottom.

'I said deeper,' she hissed, spanking him harshly. She swept her hand down five more times in savage succession.

Adam's tightly bound hands writhed above his reddening buttocks. He buried his face obediently into the brunette. But she moaned her lack of satisfaction and grunted her cruel frustration.

'Get the belt,' the Dancercise instructress ordered. 'He needs some persuasion.'

Quivering and jerking at every stroke, he yelled into the brunette's wet pussy as the belt whistled down to lash his defenceless cheeks. Three more vicious swipes of the supple leather across his blazing cheeks. Adam mouthed his agony into the creaming crease. Another blistering swipe. The hide licked his bottom, adding a fresh crimson weal. He buried his open mouth into her to smother his scream. She rose up on her toes, shrieked her loud ecstasy – then raked her splayed labia down over his upturned face. The taloning grip made escape impossible. She rode him wantonly, ruthlessly and mercilessly. The final lash of leather drove his tongue into her deeply. The brunette came violently, hammering her hips and burying his face completely.

Adam, whipped, dominated and humiliated, lay curled up at their feet. They had used him ruthlessly for their unbridled pleasure for just under two hours. Sharing with him dark, feminine secrets. He had tasted the salt of their tiny love-thorns and the sour of their tight little sphincters as, panties dragged down, they made his mouth their obedient plaything. They had breastfed him, nipples peeping out between fingers of cupping hands that squeezed their swollen bosoms. He had been spanked afresh, yelling as their hard palms cracked down, each loud swipe echoing around the breeze block walls. He had come three times, but in shame and tears, not in pleasure. His face and chest shone wetly with their spilled juices. His buttocks burned red with their wrath.

'Finished? It's almost eleven. We'd better go,' the blonde murmured, reluctant to leave.

'I'm done,' the brunette grinned, drying her pussy with her rolled-up tights.

'Just one more thing, I think,' the instructress replied softly. Her cleavage shone with the perspiration of exertion. 'Pass me my purse.'

The blonde obliged. The instructress swished her ponytail as she rummaged in her purse and extracted a seven-inch dildo. She twisted the base. It purred menacingly. Adam opened his eyes – then tried to wriggle frantically away as quickly as his bound hands behind his back would allow him.

Taking three short paces, the instructress trod him dominantly face down into the floor. 'You two, get his legs. You, hold his cheeks open. Wide open.'

Giggling with glee, the four girls obeyed. Two gripped his legs just below the knee, the other two dragged his buttocks painfully apart. His pink sphincter puckered and shone beneath the neon above. The tip of the dildo dimpled his reddened left buttock. Adam cried out. The instructress raked it down his cleft, briefly kissing his anal whorl with the shining tip. Adam screamed.

'I wouldn't make too much noise, young man. Might attract attention. Awkward questions would be asked. Awkward answers required. Better keep quiet, eh?'

He didn't, so they gagged him for his final humiliation.

'Get ready for the ultimate female experience, my boy. Hold his balls,' she snarled. 'That'll keep him still.'

The blonde's soft hand held him, squeezing hard till he lay passive and quivering.

'There, there,' the instructress murmured, cradling Adam's sobbing face after driving the dildo slowly but firmly in between his buttocks. 'That's what it feels like to be a woman. Nice, isn't it? Not quite what you expected, hmm, the first time you put that pink lipstick up to your mouth, I'm sure.'

9

Party Line

'So which do you want? The laboratory or the wine cellar?'

'I don't know. I'm not sure. You decide. You're in charge.'

'That's right. I'm in charge. And don't you dare forget it, or you'll pay. Painfully. I'm in charge. What am I?'

'In total control.'

'Of what?'

'Of me. Of all of me, naked and kneeling before you. Of –'

'Slowly. You know the rules. Speak more distinctly. I must be able to hear every miserable word or I'll make you say it all over again. Understand?'

'Yes. Sorry.'

'That's better. Continue.'

'You control me. All of me. I am yours to do with what you will. You own my bottom. My bare, helpless bottom. It is yours. I give it to you absolutely –'

'It is not yours to give, wretch. It is mine to take and punish as I please.'

'Yes –'

'Silence when I am talking.'

'I'm so sorry.'

'That's better. So we know who is in charge?'

'Yes. You.'

'Totally?'

'Oh, yes, mistress. Totally.'

'Good. Then I think we'll go into the laboratory tonight. You shall be Graham. I shall be Doctor Jane. Understand?'

'I understand, yes.'

'Yes, what?'

'Yes, Doctor.'

'We are in the laboratory. You are wearing a pullover, shirt, dark tie and jeans. It is hot in the laboratory. You want to loosen your tie, don't you?'

'Yes, Doctor.'

'And take off your pullover, mm?'

'Oh, please, Doctor.'

'You may not. I will not tolerate scruffiness or a slack, casual attitude. I have already voiced my displeasure at your wearing jeans.'

'Sorry, Doctor.'

'I am wearing a crisp, white coat. Unbuttoned, but closed together by my hands in my side pockets. You want to peep, don't you, Graham?'

'Yes. No. I'm sorry.'

'You do, don't you? You want to peep at Doctor Jane's breasts.'

'No. Yes –'

'Because you know that Doctor Jane only wears a black leather thong underneath her white lab coat, don't you, Graham?'

Silence.

'Don't you?'

He confessed.

'Yes. I am naked underneath my crisp, white coat. My nipples chafe against the freshly starched cotton –'

'Yes. Please. Tell me –'

'Silence. How dare you interrupt your mistress while she is speaking?'

Frantic whimpering, sprinkled with 'sorries'.

'That's better. You're learning. Slowly. But you're learning.'

'Thank you, mistress.'

'My black leather thong. So sleek. So shiny. It is slippery at my pussy and burns where it bites deep into my dark cleft.'

Silence. The soft sound of rasping breath.

'Graham. Are you touching your cock?'

184

'No, Doctor –'

'Are you masturbating?'

'No, I promise –'

'You know the rules perfectly well. You must not do that until I give you permission. Understand?'

Silence.

'Do you understand?'

'Yes, Doctor.'

'That's better. But what's this? You've left the fridge door open, Graham. You stupid idiot. Can't I trust you to do anything right? The specimens will spoil. All of yesterday's hard work ruined. Why are you trembling, Graham?'

'Because I have made a mistake, Doctor.'

'Precisely. You are trembling in my stern presence because you have made a very foolish mistake. And what happens to men like you who are stupid, Graham?'

'I will be punished. You must –'

'Must?'

'Sorry, I didn't mean –'

'Never, ever tell me, your mistress, what I must or must not do.'

'Sorry.'

A pause. A long pause.

'I'm sorry, mistress. Do you forgive me?'

'Perhaps. We'll see. You really are a stupid idiot, Graham. What am I going to do with you, hmm?'

Silence.

'I asked you a question and expect an answer.'

'P-punish me?'

'That is the correct answer, Graham. Punish you I shall. We are alone, together, in the laboratory, aren't we?'

'Yes, Doctor.'

'And the door is locked, isn't it?'

'Yes, Doctor.'

'Bend over that wooden stool. At once.'

'Shall I take my jeans –'

'Silence. Face down across the stool. I will bare your bottom for your stripes when and only when I deem it fitting to do so.'

'Yes, Doctor.'

Silence, broken by the sound of excited breathing.

'Are you playing with your cock?'

'No, honestly –'

'I've warned you. For disobeying me, I'm putting you on hold. I'll be back.'

'No, please, mistress, don't go –'

Annette put her phone down on the desk and took a sip of ice-cold lemonade. It was so cold it burned. Let him sweat. It was important to increase the tension slowly. Important to pace the mounting excitement and build towards a satisfactory climax.

She worked from home now. After two months at the busy exchange, she had won her sharp spurs as a tele-dominatrix. It was much better here in the spare room of the flat. She told Tom, her partner, that she was busy selling advertising space. She must have a couple of hours every evening alone. Completely undisturbed. Tom found it easy to oblige. After eight months together, all the sparkle seemed to have fizzled out of their affair. He didn't even follow her into the shower any more. Tom found it easy to leave Annette alone. Undisturbed. While she went to 'work' on the phone, he was next door, in their bedroom, busy surfing the net.

'Graham.'

'Yes, Doctor Jane.'

'It was extremely stupid of you to leave the lab fridge door open like that. I'm going to have to teach you to be more attentive to important details. It is, I'm afraid, going to be a very painful lesson.'

'Yes. I deserve to suffer. Please –'

'Now that I have you at my mercy, bending bare-bottomed across the wooden stool, I am going to whip you. And can you tell me what I am going to use to whip you with, Graham?'

'No, Doctor. Tell me, please. Tell me, I beg you –'

'Oh, come now, Graham. I think you do know, don't you?'

186

'The riding crop?'

'Did you say riding crop, Graham?'

'Yes, the one you keep hidden behind the red fire extinguisher.'

'Oh, so you have found that, have you? That was my little secret. I'm not sure I like the idea of you snooping around, Graham –'

'I'm sorry. I didn't mean to –'

'I won't be spied on, Graham. Do you understand?'

'Yes, Doctor. I won't do it again.'

'Of course you won't. And you know all the painful reasons why you won't, don't you, Graham?'

'Yes, Doctor.'

'No, it is not to be the riding crop for your bottom. Not this time, although I am sure there will be other occasions for its use. I was rather thinking of the flexible rubber hose attached to the bunsen burner –'

'Oh, yes, please, Doctor.'

'So rubbery, so satisfyingly whippy. Shall we say a dozen strokes?'

'Yes, a dozen strokes.'

'But then you are forgetting, Graham, aren't you, that it is in fact not for you to say what punishment I dispense? It is for me and me alone to prescribe your suffering. Two dozen.'

Silence.

'I have the tubing in my hand, Graham. So firm, so pliant, and yet surprisingly soft. It is as thick as your cock.'

A soft grunt.

'I am squeezing it. Mmm. It is helpless in my clenched fist.'

A moan.

'Now I'm tugging it, stretching it. How obedient it is to my firm touch. I like obedience, Graham. In fact, I insist upon it.'

A gasp. Excited breathing.

'Now keep your hands up where they can be seen, as I've taught you. Now dip your tummy, Graham, so that your bare bottom is big and round.'

'Yes, Doctor.'

'I'm raising the rubber hose up. It is hovering above your naked cheeks. Close your eyes, Graham.'

'Yes, Doctor, yes.'

'Close your eyes tight and picture me. Doctor Jane. My rubber lash is raised above your squirming bottom. My thigh grazes yours as I position myself at your proffered cheeks. Oh, look. My white coat has fallen open. My breasts are spilling freely. See how their soft flesh bulges, how the ripe curves shine, how the cleavage is deep and warm –'

'Yes. Yes.'

'After the seventh stroke, I will pause to palm your hot buttocks, then finger every red stripe –'

'Oh, God, yes –'

'After the eleventh stroke, I will drag your tear-stained face up and gaze down pitilessly as you slavishly lick, twice and twice only, my slippery leather thong –'

'Please. Please –'

'After the sixteenth stroke, I will bring my naked bosom to your suffering flesh, crushing them against your whipped buttocks. You will cry out as my hard nipples pierce your crimson –'

'Oh, Doctor, I adore you. I want to kneel and serve you always. I beg you –'

'I'm afraid that is all for tonight. You have not been the perfect slave, have you? Think, when I am gone from you, what it might have been that you did to displease me, wretch.'

'No, wait, don't go –'

'Your mistress is going now, slave.'

'Please stay, don't –'

'Try this number again. But not for at least forty-eight hours. Not until then. I'll see if I can squeeze you in.'

Treat 'em mean and keep 'em keen. It had been written in large red letters above her desk at the exchange during her training. And it worked.

Annette knew as she hung up that her tele-slave would be masturbating furiously. It thrilled her to think that out

188

there, in the anonymous city, a man was grunting in ecstasy because of what she had just said to him down the line.

Her words haunted her. A natural dominant, she found it both easy and pleasurable to come up with delicious scenarios of humiliation and punishment for her select clients. Tom, her partner, had never shown or spoken of any desire to enter into the dark delights of erotic mistress-slave games. Frustrated and denied her longings, Annette had discovered sweet release in her role as dominant tele-bitch.

Doctor Jane. She always gave herself a superior rank or title. It automatically created the necessary fixed gulf between mistress and slave. Between the penitent and the stern punisher. Doctor Jane. Cool, severe and totally in control. Annette wriggled as if the leather thong she had described really was biting into the wet heat of her slit. After the call, she was prickling and juiced with arousal. She closed her eyes. Graham. She pictured his bare buttocks waiting with impatient patience for their pain. Her mouth grew dry. Opening her eyes, Annette blinked the image away and finished off her lemonade.

Time for bed.

Next door, she found Tom already naked under the duvet. He seemed a little feverish tonight. More so than usual. He'd probably found some obscure new website and cyber-chatted with other sad geeks. Annette pouted as she released her swollen breasts from her bra. Nothing under the duvet to put out her fire. She tossed the lacy half-cupped confection aside. Stepping out of her panties, she thought she heard Tom grunt. Indigestion. He would raid the fridge when her back was turned.

In bed, they lay face to face. No kissing. He was, to her surprise, extremely hard already. He guided her hands down, holding her wrists gently, to his erection. She dealt with it competently. He came almost at once, spurting her belly and nipples as he moaned, then rolled over and promptly fell asleep.

Annette lay awake staring at the ceiling as the semen dried to a crisp second skin on her flesh. Had she imagined it? Had Tom murmured something when he orgasmed – splashing her with his wet warmth? Something that had sounded startlingly like Doctor Jane? Impossible. She dismissed it out of hand. But as she drifted towards sleep, the vague suspicion returned, taking shape like a shadow in a corner of the darkened room of her mind.

Forty-seven hours and thirteen minutes since speaking to his mistress, the slave dialled her number. Annette picked up. The brief business preliminaries were dealt with quickly – she liked to get into role almost immediately.

Following her half-formed plan, she did not offer a variation to the previous scenario. She continued where she had left off as Doctor Jane.

Graham was thrilled.

'I am not wearing my thong. It got very sticky when I whipped you. I had to take it off.'

Silence.

'You took your whipping well, Graham. The doctor is pleased with the way her slave took his medicine. Quite pleased.'

'I was foolish to leave the lab fridge door ajar. I deserved my punishment.'

'And afterwards. Remember how I made you examine your red bottom in the mirror?'

'Yes, Doctor.'

'How you moaned softly as I placed my cool hand, fingers splayed, across your striped cheeks –'

'Yes. Yes.'

'And how you almost buckled at the knees when I squeezed your punished buttocks?'

'Yes.'

'Well, Graham, as a reward for being a tolerably good slave I have decided to grant you a small treat. Just this once, mind. Do not think for one moment that I make a habit of indulging those who serve me. I am a harsh mistress. Do not mistake my kindness for weakness.'

'No. No, I shan't.'

'Can you guess what your little treat might be, Graham? What has Doctor Jane got for you, hmm?'

'I don't know. Tell me, please, I beg you –'

'Can't you guess?'

'Please tell me.'

'My thong. It is soiled and sticky.'

'Let me wash it for you, Doctor. Allow me to –'

'No, Graham, I do not want you to wash it. Not exactly. But clean it, you certainly must. Yes. I certainly want it cleaned.'

Silence.

'You will kneel down. Kneel down before me and open your mouth.'

An excited voice promised to obey.

'Are your eyes closed?'

'Yes, Doctor.'

'Open wide.'

Silence.

'I'm putting my soiled, sticky thong in your mouth, Graham. No, don't speak. Close your eyes. You can feel my fingers forcing the soft leather into you, can't you? I want you to chew gently. I am using your mouth like a miniature washing machine –'

'Mmm.'

'That's right. Mmm. Make it nice and clean. Nice and clean and worthy of my slit –'

A grunt.

'No, don't spit it out, Graham. Swallow. Swallow your juices.'

Silence.

'I'm watching you. If Graham dares to spit it out, Doctor Jane will have to use that riding crop behind the fire extinguisher after all. And it won't necessarily be used on your bottom. Just imagine that cruel little leather loop being flicked up repeatedly against your balls –'

An anxious whimper.

'That's right. Just swallow like a good, obedient slave. It is a privilege for you to taste the stickiness of your mistress, after all. And now, before I put my nice, clean thong back on, I require you to clean me –'

191

'Yes, Doctor. Anything you demand, Doctor.'

'I will wipe my wet slit dry with a tissue. Your tongue is not worthy enough to lick me there.'

'Not worthy. No, mistress.'

'You, Graham, will be permitted to kneel behind me, gazing up in adoration at my heavy buttocks –'

'Yes, yes, please –'

'And then tongue my cleft until it is fresh and clean.'

A choking whimper of delight.

'You'd like that, wouldn't you, Graham? Hmm? Doctor Jane is right, isn't she?'

'Yes, Doctor. Permit me to kneel down before your bottom and worship you devotedly with my tongue between your buttocks.'

'Good little slave. And what do good little slaves deserve. Occasionally?'

'A reward?'

'The ultimate reward, Graham. Pleasurable pain.'

'Yes. Oh, God, yes.'

'You may masturbate while you lick between my cheeks, Graham.'

'Thank you, Doctor, thank you.'

'But be very careful not to splash my legs or thighs when you come –'

A sweet groan.

'A good slave never, ever soils his stern mistress with his hot seed –'

'No, never.'

'Unless, of course, she is deliberately and dominantly milking him with her leather-gloved hand –'

A harsh grunt of arousal.

'There is one more thing I wish to mention, Graham, before I permit you to commence masturbating as I prescribed.'

'Yes, Doctor. Anything you say.'

'When you come, I give you my permission, just this once, to whisper my name.'

Annette listened intently, the phone hot against her ear. Down the line, she heard the frenzied breathing as her

192

tele-slave gripped his cock and pumped savagely. She broke into the silence briefly, to remind him of the soft weight of her heavy peach-cheeks burying his upturned face. She described the feral tang of her acrid cleft as he tongued it devotedly – and warned him severely not to succumb to the temptation of probing her anal whorl with his tongue-tip.

As he approached his gathering climax, Annette spoke briefly. Her tone was crisp and cruel. 'Whisper my name, Graham, as you come.'

She held her breath. He gasped, took a lungful of air and then groaned long and loud. Annette could picture the squirting jet of his sweet agony. Then, straining, she heard the two words – whispered in a smothered frenzy – she had calculated for.

'Doctor Jane.'

Annette let the phone slip from her trembling fingers. The whispered words had sounded exactly as they had the other night. The other night, in bed. In bed with Tom. When he had come.

'Anything?' Annette smeared blackcurrant jam on her unbuttered toast. She hoped her voice sounded natural. Natural and calm. She took refuge in her toast, biting into it.

'Just the usual. Nothing much,' Tom replied, tossing down the post by the coffee pot.

'No bills?' Annette countered, managing a forced laugh.

'Nope,' Tom shrugged, pouring himself another coffee.

'Thought the phone bill was due. Need it to make out my expenses. Selling ad space on cold calls doesn't come cheap.'

'Mm? Paid it Monday,' Tom murmured, burying himself in a software catalogue.

Bastard, Annette thought. Still, she could always request a copy. Later, when he'd gone out. Then, when it arrived, she'd secretly check through the itemised billing. She had to know, had to be sure. Had to snuff out that tiny little spark of doubt glowing deep down in her brain.

The copy of the phone bill came three days later. Nothing. Her tele-bitch line number did not appear in the printout.

He's got a bloody mobile. The bastard rings out on a mobile. And he gets so excited he doesn't know it's me on the other end.

She hunted around the flat and found the mobile in a shoe box at the bottom of his wardrobe. But when she thumbed the small green button, the memory display did not feature her dial-a-dominatrix number. Still no proof positive. Nothing else in the shoe box or buried deeper down in the darkness of the wardrobe. No magazines, depicting bound, naked men kneeling to kiss the crop that had just whipped their defenceless buttocks. No men, wrists tightly handcuffed at their belly, scrabbling to protect their erections as cruel, leather-clad vixens tormented their balls with bulldog clips.

Nothing at all to betray his desire for dominance and discipline. Was she imagining it all? She had to know.

Four days later, her slave was once more hooked on the end of her line. Speaking crisply into the phone, Annette was being deliberately stern.

'No. My decision is final. Graham and Doctor Jane are over. I will dictate the new game. The rules, the place and the players. I will be the Right Honourable Pamela Cashcallan. You are my gardener's boy. Not head gardener. Merely the gardener's boy. Understand?'

'Yes, Lady Pamela.'

'You will address me as milady.'

'Yes, milady.'

'And your name is –'

Annette paused. Dare she?

'Yes, mistress?'

'Address me as milady.'

'Sorry.'

'It is very important that you address me correctly, Tom.'

She heard the short gasp.

'We are in the summerhouse. The climbing tea roses have not been pruned. Why have they not been pruned, Tom?'

'Sorry, milady. I must have forgot to –'

'Then I must give you a sharp reminder, mustn't I, Tom?'

'Yes, milady.'

'I will make a note of your omission in my pocket book. I write down the offence, Tom, and the punishment I propose to administer. We walk towards the greenhouse. You keep four respectful paces behind, cap in hand.'

'Yes, milady.'

'In the greenhouse, I inspect my peaches. You say that you sprayed them for blight on Saint David's day. It is now June. A hot summer's day in June. I can detect signs of blight spotting the budding fruit. See how I cup the small, swollen flesh in the palm of my gloved hand. Well, Tom?'

'Milady?'

'Did you or did you not spray my peaches as I instructed?'

Silence.

'Do not try to attempt to shroud your errors by concealing them in lies, Tom. Speak up. Did you or did you not spray my peaches?'

'I – I think so, milady.'

'I am not the least interested in what you think, Tom. I am only prepared to entertain certainties. And now I am going to punish you.'

An excited intake of breath.

'There are to be two punishments. Never let it be said that the Cashcallans are mean-spirited or anything less than generous in all we undertake.'

'Most generous, milady.'

'Firstly, Tom, as you failed me most miserably with my peaches, I propose to use the syringe on you. It will be an experience I trust you will never forget. Especially next Saint David's day, when I hope you will do your duty.'

'I promise to remember, milady.'

'After the painful syringe, you must of course be thrashed –'

'Oh, yes, milady. Yes, please.'

Annette took a deep breath. She had to be very careful in her attempt to land her catch. Jerk the rod too harshly and she would fail to net him. She had to play her line with consummate skill, she knew, if she hoped to reel him in.

'Are you bending over, Tom? Touching your toes?'

'Yes, milady.'

'And your moleskin trousers. They are unbuckled and around your boots?'

'As you instructed, milady.'

'It is so hot in here, isn't it? The sun is high in a cloudless sky. Here in the greenhouse, insects buzz. The moist heat is almost overwhelming. See the silver water sparkling from the tap, Tom?'

'Yes, milady. My mouth is parched.'

'But I sternly forbid you to drink, understand. Can you feel the heat, Tom?'

'Yes, milady. My shirt is wet and sticks to me.'

'Keep touching your toes, Tom, even though the sweat trickling into your eyes scalds them. Understand?'

'I will obey.'

'You will remain in that position, bare-bottomed and bending, while I prepare the syringe. I am going to fill it with ice-cold water from the tap. Remain exactly as you are, Tom. I will return.'

Annette put the phone down softly, stole to her door, opened it and silently trod the carpet across to their bedroom door. The door was closed. Damn. She could not risk opening it, just a fraction even, to see if her partner was bending over as instructed by his tele-dominatrix. She returned to her room, picked up the phone.

'I want to hear you whimpering, Tom. Whimpering with fearful dread at the thought of my gloved hands guiding the brass nozzle of the syringe in between your buttocks. Understand?'

'Yes, milady.'

'Do not disappoint me, Tom. I want to hear your fear.'

Back at the bedroom door, she knelt and listened. Tom was whining like a whipped cur. She plucked at her pussy, the labia opening its sticky lips in response. She listened as her partner whined to order – just as she had made him come on command. Rising, and sweetly dizzy as she relished the dark delights of true domination, Annette paused, her fingers at her hot pussy. No. Not now. She had to return to the phone. There, as the Right Honourable Pamela Cashcallan, she would be able to indulge her every whim. Including the urgent heat at her weeping quim.

'No, keep still. Don't flinch. First you will feel the cold brass spout between your hot cheeks. Do not be alarmed. It is dribbling water, that is all, Tom. There. It is now inside your bottom.'

A soft grunt.

'Now, as I plunge the syringe, the icy water surges deep inside you, swelling you painfully. But it is no more than you deserve, is it, Tom?'

'It is a fitting punishment, milady. Hurt me, please, humiliate me –'

'Stop that. I can see what you are doing with your hands. Keep them stretched down at the toes of your boots.'

'Sorry, milady.'

'What fine buttocks you have, Tom. I am quite familiar with them, of course, having had occasion to redden them frequently. Haven't I?'

His answer came in an excited whisper.

'I thought I told you to keep your hands away from your thickening manhood, Tom. You are a disobedient, wicked wretch. My cane is eager to stripe your disobedient bottom.'

A smothered moan of sweet sorrow.

'There. I've emptied the syringe into you. Squeeze your cheeks together, Tom, and don't you dare spill a single drop. I am going out into the garden, now. We will not be disturbed. We are quite alone. All the servants and stablemen are taking tea up at the castle. I have you all to myself.'

'Don't go, please, milady.'

'I shall return, of that you may be certain. You will hear the crunch of my boots upon the cinder path as I return from the raspberry bushes, gripping a bamboo cane freshly plucked from the dark, warm loam. The cane is for your bottom, Tom. A dozen strokes. Perhaps two dozen. But remember this. During your punishment, if you relax your cheeks the merest fraction, the water will spill. And for every drop you spill, my cane will extract hot tears from your sorrowful eyes. Understand?'

'Yes, milady.'

'And when my cane is quiet, I will prise your cheeks apart and watch the silver water gush from your dark hole –'

'Yes, please, oh, please –'

'Then, Tom, I will take you in hand. In my softly gloved hand.'

She cooked risotto, substituting squid ink for the chicken stock, and added stir-fried chunks of monkfish. They had enjoyed it together in Naples, where she had first met Tom. She chilled a dryish, mellow Soave and spooned extra strawberry ice cream on top of his sticky chocolate pudding. Over coffee, they talked, soft-voiced and unhurried.

He rose, gathering up the dishes. 'I'll do these if you have to go and sell your ads.'

'No. Not tonight. I'm for bed. Sod them,' Annette smiled.

Tom piled everything into the sink and followed her into their bedroom.

'Would you mind undressing me?' Annette murmured. 'I'm a little tired.'

He was willing to oblige. His fingers fumbled with the tiny buttons on her blouse.

'Be careful,' she rasped, a waspish sting in her sharp rebuke.

'Sorry,' he mumbled.

He removed her bra and bent down to kiss her gently bobbing breasts, his mouth eager for her nipples. She held up her firm palm.

'No. You may not kiss me yet. Not until I give you permission.'

He was delighted. 'When will I earn that?' he whispered.

'Not until you have undressed me properly. And I mean properly. To my complete and utter satisfaction.'

He dropped down to his knees. She felt his hot, excited breath on her belly. She sensed the yearning of his impatient lips and tongue as they burned to pay homage to her bosom.

'I'm waiting.'

Tom's eager fingers unzipped her skirt. Feverish, trembling hands palmed it down over her thighs. Naked now, except for lacy black panties that stretched provocatively across her cheeks and pubic swell, she planted her thighs dominantly apart, drawing her hands to her hips. He tried to steal a kiss, his lips brushing the pubic nest trapped beneath the taut black lace. She checked him, taloning his hair – gently, teasingly and then with a controlling dominance. Twisting around, she presented her pantied bottom to his adoring gaze. She released the fierce grip on his hair.

'Take my panties down. Using your teeth only. Then, you may dress me.'

'Dress you?' he whispered thickly, the lace panties muffling his words.

'Are you always this stupid, repeating everything I say?' Tom shivered with pleasure as she scolded him.

'Just get those panties down.'

Slave. She almost said it. It remained hovering in the air between the almost-naked woman, standing in triumph over the kneeling man. Unspoken, but understood. Tom bowed down briefly, elbows angled sharply, and fleetingly kissed both of her small feet. Back at her soft buttocks, he buried his upturned face into their warmth, silently mouthing his adoration, then obediently tugged the lace panties down, using his clenched teeth as instructed.

He waited as she stepped out of them, his face pressed into the carpet. He sighed deeply as she planted her left foot down on to his head, crushing him dominantly.

'I do not recall giving you permission to kiss or tenderly bite my bottom.'

'I – I'm sorry,' he gasped, thrilling to her cruel voice.

'If you wish to pleasure me, obey me.'

'Yes –'

'If you wish to serve –'

'Yes, yes. That's it. I wish to serve my –'

'Mistress. How very well matched we are, after all, for I desire to be served. And every dominant must have her slave. Mustn't she?'

'Yes.'

She kept her knowledge of his wants and needs a secret. Keeping it a secret added to the power she enjoyed over him. She decided never to reveal to Tom that it had been her he had been worshipping over the phone. Let him live with that little delusion, she reasoned. After all, as they slowly explored their newly discovered world of mistress and slave, she would tighten the net of domination around him until she had him utterly in her thrall.

'Now you may dress me. Go to the second drawer. No,' she barked harshly, 'stay down on your knees as you serve me. Take out the bundle of white tissue paper and bring it back, placing it down at my feet.'

Shuffling uncomfortably, burning his knees on the carpet, he obeyed the command. Gently fingering the folds of soft tissue apart, he gasped aloud.

'Before you put it on, I will allow you a brief glimpse of that which you desire.'

Annette presented her pussy to Tom, thumbing her outer labia apart to reveal the glistening pink within.

'Look. You may not touch or taste. Not until I say so.'

He gazed longingly.

'I know you want to kiss me there, don't you, Tom?'

He nodded frantically.

'And suck and serve me with your tongue.'

He whimpered frantically.

'Put the apron on. Tie it gently.'

His fingers scrabbled and plucked up the red leather apron. Crushing his face down into it, he sniffed the delicious hide.

Annette snapped her fingers. 'Put it on at once.'

Tom, still dressed, groaned as his erection raked his bulging trousers. He brought the soft leather apron up to her waist, and tied the supple tapes carefully.

Annette slid her fingertips beneath the soft leather scantily covering her pussy. The red hide rippled as she strummed herself firmly. Tom fisted the carpet at her feet in a paroxysm of frustration.

'When I have come, and juiced the red leather, making you watch as I alone drown in the sweet agony of orgasm, I am going to take your trousers down, Tom –'

'Yes, yes –'

'And slowly whip your bottom –'

'Oh, please –'

'Until it is as red as my little leather apron.'

He prostrated himself before her, moaning.

'If you are a very good slave, and take your whipping well, I will drape my apron across your hot, punished bottom, sticky side kissing your skin.'

Tom grunted, squirming on the carpet at her feet. She gazed down, her eyes narrowing, as his hips jerked. He was coming, right there before her.

'How dare you come before your mistress gives you permission?' she snarled, rolling him over with her foot. She prodded the spreading stain at his bulging crotch with five contemptuously curled toes. 'Now you're really going to feel my wrath.'

Unfastening her red leather apron, she smothered his face, slit-sticky hide inwards, tying it tightly. Dragging him to, and then across, their bed, she bared his bottom and raised her flattened palm aloft.

'Suffer the displeasure of your mistress, slave.'

Her domination of him was complete. She spanked him repeatedly with her punishing palm for almost a quarter of an hour. For the very first time since being together, they came together.

His computer screen slowly clouded with the dust of disuse. Software catalogues found their way to the kitchen swing-bin unread. Annette worked days, selling insurance. She didn't use the spare room after supper for her 'work' any more. But she often went in there, just before bedtime. Tom, sitting on their bed next door, would grip the mobile in his hot hand as they played the erotic games Annette allowed him to think he had introduced her to. That he had invented.

'But I didn't mean to –'

'Silence. You have sorely displeased your mistress, slave. Stupid, snivelling slave.'

'I'm sorry, mistress –'

'You will be. I am going to put the phone down in a moment. Then I am going to come into that room and teach you. Teach you a painful lesson. A very painful lesson. A lesson you will never forget.'

A whimper of arousal, of delicious dread.

'Tonight, in my shiny black basque, I am going to put you into harness. Bound and helpless in my thrall –'

'Bound and helpless,' he whispered softly.

'Unable to move an inch in the tight restraints. Gagged, to silence you as you plead for mercy –'

'Gagged,' he echoed, shuddering with pleasure.

'Then, at my mercy, your bottom will taste leather and suffer the sweetness of my lash –'

'Yes, oh, yes –'

'And then, whipped and sobbing gently, your cock will feel the severity of my leather gauntlet. The silver-studded leather gauntlet. The leather gauntlet you bought secretly and hid as a surprise for me. But I found it, didn't I?'

Silence.

'Didn't I?'

'Yes,' he whispered softly.

'Because you cannot hide anything from me. I am the perfect mistress, and the perfect mistress knows every little secret thought of her miserable little slave. Doesn't she, hmm?'

'Yes. You own me. Control me, absolutely.'

'That's right.'

A groan.

'I will use the gauntlet on your cock, and slowly, very slowly, milk the liquid obedience out of you –'

He cried out, almost choking on his delight.

Annette tossed her phone down. Aroused into a pulsing frenzy by her own stern words, she slid down to her knees, fingering her wet slit furiously.

Shivering on their bed next door, Tom pleaded into the mobile. 'Mistress, mistress, where are you? Please, I beg you, please come.'

10

Low Fidelity

Lady Carstairs settled into the comfortable arm chair before a blazing fire. Her pearls sparkled in the dancing light cast by the flickering flames.

'Coffee, your ladyship,' Adèle, the maid, murmured, entering the drawing room of Carstairs Towers.

'Thank you, Adèle.'

Everything was so different now. Coffee served after dinner by a maid, not a butler. Scrimping on the pruning of the ancient yew alley. Non-vintage port at table. Damp in the east wing. With Carstairs gone and capital funds depleted alarmingly, pinching economies simply had to be made. And Lady Carstairs had a daughter on her hands.

'Patience or the wireless, your ladyship?'

Lady Carstairs had a vile French novelette stuffed behind her cushion which she was burning to take up. Sighing, she resigned herself to more sober entertainment.

'The wireless, Adèle. Music, I think. Please spare me the Third Network with their interminable Norwegian dramatists.'

Adèle tuned in the Light programme. Bobby Kensington, the popular crooner, filled the large drawing room with his seductive charm.

Lady Carstairs brightened, her eyes as sparkling as her pearl choker. Bobby Kensington. Not in Debretts, admittedly, but very handsome and reputedly extremely wealthy. Lady Carstairs had made judicious inquiries before inviting the celebrity songster up to Carstairs Towers a fortnight since. He had arrived in a pale lemon Bentley and had tipped the servants generously. Julia, her daughter, had succumbed instantly. Lady Carstairs had found the vital evidence – soiled cami-knickers, a teeth-torn bustier – in the laundry basket in her daughter's dressing room.

Lady Carstairs closed her eyes. Her plans had come to fruition. Her hopes were buoyant. Adèle had faithfully reported everything back to her mistress. Bobby Kensington had deflowered Julia twice in the rose garden, once in the library and again, just before departing, behind the stables.

Lady Carstairs sipped her coffee. There had been seventeen letters, two telegrams and umpteen trunk calls since. Most satisfactory. Lady Carstairs anticipated an announcement in *The Times* imminently.

Upstairs in her bedroom, Julia Carstairs sighed as her fingers trembled on the bakelite tuning dial. Moments later, she was whirling around her bedroom, naked, clutching a pillow fiercely to her bosom, as she danced to the crooner's smooth song.

Kneeling, thighs astride her plump pillow, her soft buttocks buried firmly into its warmth, she drew her fingertips up to her nipples.

A clarinet pierced the air. Julia pinched her nipples, tweaking them up into savage peaks of pain. A trombone growled. Easing up a fraction on her whitening toes, Julia raked her sticky pussy along the pillow between her thighs. The pussy parted, tingling as the crisp cotton pillow case sliced into her pink moistness. The snare drum rattled. Julia's fingers dropped down from her bosom, dabbling rhythmically at her wet heat.

From her small wireless, Bobby Kensington's voice floated back. Julia squealed and squirmed into the pillow. She remembered his lips at her throat, then more urgently at her breasts. Sucking hard. Her thumbs peeled back her slippery labial folds. She remembered Bobby Kensington's tongue down there, stoking not quenching the fire.

* * *

Lady Carstairs frowned. Her maid, Adèle, had supplied graphic intelligence of the alliance. But summer love, like summer lightning, often died as quickly as it erupted. Rising, she strode across to the wireless in its gleaming walnut cabinet. Reaching down, she switched the set off.

Treading the carpeted landing outside her daughter's bedroom minutes later, Lady Carstairs paused. Bobby Kensington's mellifluous tones filled the bedroom beyond the stout oak door. Kneeling, the concerned mother peeped through the keyhole into her daughter's boudoir.

Down on the carpet, her supple thighs splayed wide, Julia cupped and squeezed her naked breasts viciously. Lady Carstairs narrowed her peering eye. It glistened as it watched the nude's right hand shoot down to the dark pubic nest below. It watched as two straightened fingers were driven ruthlessly into the pouting pussy. It watched as the buttocks spasmed. Julia cried out softly, her squeal of ecstasy drowned out at once by Bobby Kensington's faultless tenor.

Lady Carstairs opened both her eyes wide. A grim smile of satisfaction stretched her aristocratic lips wider. Already she was reading the impeccable small print beneath the Court Circular announcing forthcoming marriages. It would be an alliance of old rank and new money. Strawberry leaves and sterling. Lady Carstairs nodded vehemently. Yes. After a suitable period, she would approach her wealthy son-in-law to discuss the matter of restoring the office of butler to Carstairs Towers.

Mrs Bebbington-Booth patted her silver-fox stole complacently as she gazed around at the crowded tables in the smoke-filled, dimly lit room. The Dreadnought Club was crowded tonight. She would have preferred to be taking supper at the Ritz. Her wealth was equal to its prices, but she did not have quite the right connections or familiarity with the set who took its grandeur in their social stride. Mrs Bebbington-Booth (her late husband, plain Jimmy Booth, the liver pill magnate, had appended the name of his Pennine birthplace to match his increasing fortune) trembled on the outer edge of society, ever eager to buy her way one more step towards its inner circle.

Tonight, at the Dreadnought Club, Bobby Kensington was smoothly carolling the crowd. Trumpets squealed and two sudden spotlights pierced the smoke-laden darkness. One played directly down on to the white-tuxedoed tenor, the other bathed the naked shoulders and dazzled the green eyes of her only daughter, Sapphire.

Mrs Bebbington-Booth shivered with pleasure. It thrilled her to think that for the last five weeks Bobby Kensington had showered chocolates and orchids upon Sapphire. And there had been late-night spins in the lemon Bentley. Mrs Bebbington-Booth could almost smell the wet semen on the deep leather upholstery where, under a heavy rug, the singer had successfully prised open the nubile honeycomb and had tasted the sweetness from the oozing hive.

Mrs Bebbington-Booth, like her late husband, was a shrewd player, especially when the stakes were high. Staking all on one roll of the dice, she had thrown Sapphire at the celebrity, tactfully withdrawing the customary curfew allowing her daughter to be ruthlessly ridden on the tigerskin rug in Bobby Kensington's Mayfair lair.

The silken notes of the sultry song came to a husky close. Sapphire rose from the table and weaved sensually through the thunderous applause towards the powder room. Mrs Bebbington-Booth, already rehearsing dictating the announcement of her daughter's engagement down the telephone to *Variety* and *The Morning Post*, tightened her fur stole, rose and followed. What was this? Leaving before the stamps and whistles had elicited an encore? The widow of the late liver pill magnate felt a sharp pang of anxiety. Surely there had been no sudden cooling-off between them?

Tiptoeing into the quiet cool of the blue-tiled powder room and secreting herself in the cubicle next to the one Sapphire had entered, Mrs Bebbington-Booth held her breath and listened.

Next door, her silk panties dragged halfway down her nylon-stockinged legs, Sapphire's naked buttocks bulged as she squashed them against the cold wall. Scrabbling frantically in the blonde fringe at her pubis with scarlet fingernails, she sought and found her tiny clitoral bud. Bobby Kensington had found it for her – effortlessly, just as he found B sharp – and showed her how to apply a firm thumbtip to it to make the sweetest music.

Straining to listen in the adjacent cubicle, Mrs Bebbington-Booth frowned once more. Was that a muffled sob? Was that sob the sound of a broken heart? Then, to her immense relief and pleasure, she heard the sound of soft buttocks, of firmly fleshed peach-cheeks, pounding into hard tiles. She heard the low moan as fingers sought and found the prickling torments of a wet slit. The sound of flesh ravishing flesh. The unmistakable sound of female masturbation.

Sapphire jerked her head back and wailed her orgasm as thrillingly as any alto-sax. Flushed and delighted, Mrs Bebbington-Booth breathed out slowly – a deep sigh of relief. It would be a quiet affair. A Register Office do. Knightsbridge, of course. And then a month in St Tropez. She saw her future unfolding before her. Doors hitherto closed now ajar. And with Bobby Kensington warbling on the wireless every other evening, she'd be practically related to Lord Reith.

Monsieur Tuffant's Pond Street establishment was patronised by Town and Country alike. Monsieur Tuffant made no distinction between the aristocracy and the nouveaux riches as they flocked to the skilful corsetier to have their bosoms bound in silk and their bottoms sheathed in the sleek embrace of satin.

Lady Carstairs examined herself critically in the full-length looking glass in the privacy of her curtained cubicle. The bottle-green basque squeezed her tightly, giving a delicious balconette uplift and bulge to her swollen breasts. Disciplining her waist within its stern strictures, it defined the ripe contours of her hips within its cruel constraints. Lady Carstairs turned. Her bare buttocks joggled as she drew her thighs tightly together. She relaxed a trifle, planting her feet slightly apart. Peering over her right shoulder into the glass, she considered the effect of Monsieur Tuffant's superb corsetry skills upon her bottom. The cheeks loomed large in the silvered glass, the cleft was deep and dark.

'Oh, I do beg your pardon.' Mrs Bebbington-Booth, clutching a bustier to her bare bottom, hesitated at the velvet curtain she had just drawn apart.

'I am finished,' Lady Carstairs murmured imperturbably, still gazing down into the looking glass at the buttocks she lingeringly palmed.

Vanity is a splendid leveller of social rank. Within minutes, each was freely offering the other candid advice. Mrs Bebbington-Booth donned her lace-cupped bustier and requested an honest opinion. Lady Carstairs, perusing the effect, absently thumbed the dark nipples straining at the taut lace as she made minor adjustments to the positioning and the fit of the cups. Within half an hour, the two handsome widows had helped each other to choose – and don – silk stockings and suspender belts.

'I'm lunching at the Ritz,' Lady Carstairs remarked, settling her account with Monsieur Tuffant's cashier. 'Won't you join me?'

Mrs Bebbington-Booth quivered with delight at the precious invitation – just as she had quivered with delight when Lady Carstairs had inspected the seams of her stockings when the liver pill magnate's widow had stood, bare-bottomed, before the stern aristocratic gaze.

They ate angels on horseback then grilled sole, followed by a sound cheese, and drank a light Graves. Coffee and liqueurs were served with impeccable deference in the restful silence of the neighbouring lounge.

'But I think she has settled her heart at last,' Mrs Bebbington-Booth pronounced, gilding the brutality of the marriage market with a thin romantic veneer.

Lady Carstairs was becoming increasingly bored. Having secured a match for her own daughter, Julia, the hardships of another mother with an unmarried girl on her hands were of little interest.

209

'And I am so satisfied,' Mrs Bebbington-Booth confided in a sudden rush of candour. 'He has such a lovely voice.'

Lady Carstairs flickered her eye, lizard-like, at a hovering waiter. The waiter decoded the signal and discreetly prepared the bill. Mrs Bebbington-Booth was now in full flight.

'You possibly may have heard him. He was on the wireless the other night.'

Lady Carstairs waved the approaching waiter away as she would a wasp from a late summer plum. She leaned forwards, her sudden show of keen interest giving her luncheon partner acute pleasure.

'Playing the Dreadnought Club again tomorrow night. Sapphire –'

'Sapphire?' hazarded Lady Carstairs, bemused.

'My daughter –'

'But of course. Sapphire.' Really. You simply cannot trust people in trade to avoid the gross and the ostentatious, Lady Carstairs mused.

'And a lovely big Bentley,' the voice opposite droned on, carefully keeping her aitches under control.

Bentley. Lady Carstairs stiffened. No. It could not possibly be. Surely a coincidence.

'Yes, Bobby Kensington is certainly quite a catch,' Mrs Bebbington-Booth crowed.

Lady Carstairs paled.

Bobby Kensington was entertaining Julia in his late-Regency period Mayfair rooms. Adèle, instructed to do so by her mistress, having bribed the porter liberally, had secreted herself in the spacious service flat twenty minutes before their noisy arrival.

Julia wanted Bobby to play the piano.

'Tickle the ivories for me, sweetest,' she purred.

But Bobby Kensington had other ideas. The only ivory he wanted to tickle was her soft, inner thigh flesh. With his tongue.

He fixed the cocktails – Sidecars – and took them into the bedroom. There, to his delight, Julia was already stripped down to her bra, satin panties and seamed nylon stockings. The swell of her breasts bulged in their cups enticingly. She clapped her hands in glee as she spotted the cocktails. Her breasts wobbled. Bobby spilt his and swore. Wiping his chin, he glimpsed down and saw the dark shadow of her pubic nest behind the stretch of her satin panties. His cock thickened, raking up painfully against his bulging trousers as she giggled, twirled and proffered her buttocks to him, waggling them coquettishly.

Tossing off the dregs of his Sidecar, Bobby Kensington growled and sprang, dragging her down on to the bed. Julia squealed a token protest – but at her back her frantic fingers were busy with her bra. Unclasped, the silken bondage slithered from her bosom, allowing the pert breasts their brief freedom before his cruel hands enclosed them, brutal with their soft warmth.

From her hiding place, Adèle watched, wide-eyed and shivering pleasurably as she witnessed the expert seduction unfold. Watched the crooner slowly dragging down Julia's satin panties, leaving them in a tight restricting band at the brunette's knees. Watched the crooner drop his hands down from her breasts to her hips and draw the bared bottom roughly up for his intimate perusal and close inspection. Watched the daughter of her mistress wriggling in a half-hearted bid to escape. Watched as the masterful lover pinned his victim to the bed beneath her, his knee nuzzling the cleft between her splayed cheeks, as he used the abandoned bra to bind her wrists tightly to the brass bedstead.

Adèle's face grew hot. Her prickling pussy grew hotter. She slid her trembling fingertips inside her partially unbuttoned blouse and gently caressed her left nipple. As she continued spying, her fingers grew stern, tweaking the little flesh-bud up into a fierce peak. She pinched it as her eyes drank in the sight of Julia's bound hands, fingers splayed, writhing in their bondage. Adèle cupped her left breast at the sight of Bobby Kensington spanking the bare buttocks before him. Her hand squeezed, brutally punishing the soft flesh, as she gazed upon the naked singer straddling Julia's spanked, reddening bottom, then sliding back until his balls nestled into the satin panties binding her stockinged thighs.

Bobby Kensington lowered his face down. He kissed the crimson handprints on the left buttock twice, slowly, then brought his mouth to the punished right cheek. Julia murmured her delight into the pillow at her lips. The mouth at her chastised bottom became sharp, nipping teeth. Julia bucked and writhed as Bobby Kensington bit longingly and lingeringly. The teeth became a tongue. Thick and probing. Julia cried out as she felt the face bury itself deeply into her naked buttocks, then felt the wet tongue lapping hungrily and with increasing fervour.

From her vantage point, securely hidden, Adèle slipped off her shiny black patent leather court shoe. Guiding the tip of the kitten-heel up to her pubic mound, she tapped at it gently, drumming her delta as, on the bed, Bobby Kensington knelt behind his bare-bottomed captive, guiding the engorged snout of his huge cock into the parted lips of the smiling pussy awaiting him. Adèle jabbed the heel into her softening warmth more insistently as Bobby Kensington entered Julia, gripping her hips – each thumb dimpling the imprisoned soft cheeks deeply – then commencing to thrust. Inverting the heel of her court shoe upwards, and silently dragging her cami-knickers aside to expose her seething slit, Adèle used the tip of the kitten-heel to tease her outer labia apart.

On the bed, Adèle watched Julia's nakedness quiver in response to the furious thrusts. Bobby was riding her ruthlessly now. Julia's squashed breasts shuddered and her spanked cheeks clenched as he squeezed his thighs together and hammered his hips furiously.

The heel slid in between the slippery labia of the peeping maid. Adèle moaned softly as she pumped the shoe deeper into her wet heat. Her eyes narrowed and her vision became slightly blurred. She had to make herself concentrate – concentrate on the couple her mistress had instructed her to spy on.

On the bed, her hands splayed in surrender as she trembled on the brink of ecstasy, Julia bit into the white pillow at her lips. Her teeth tore it wide open. A snowcloud of tiny feathers swirled around her head. Grunting, Bobby Kensington arched his spine then froze. A final thrust of his straddling hips drove his hard sword into the warm sheath of the writhing nude. Julia screamed. The singer cursed aloud. Adèle slumped helplessly. All three collapsed into violent orgasm. The watcher, the rider and the ridden. Three separate beings blissful in the fury of the climax that united them.

Four nights later, Adèle, again acting under strict orders from Lady Carstairs, sat at her secluded table in a darkened corner of the Dreadnought Club. As the famous crooner finished his late spot, Adèle peered across the smoke-filled room and watched as Sapphire picked up her purse and rose from her table. At a discreet distance, Adèle followed Sapphire backstage. Outside the singer's dressing-room door, the maid knelt, listening. Listening and peeping.

Inside, Bobby Kensington was kneeling down before the green-eyed beauty, his taloning hands clutching her buttocks up and around which her evening gown had been dragged. His lips were kissing the pinioned girl's pubis fiercely. At the key hole, Adèle watched the girl's red lips widen into a silent scream as, below, the mouth at her pussy sucked hard.

Sapphire drew her hands to her breasts but Bobby Kensington intercepted them, snatching up at the thin wrists and, rising up from his knees, positioning the captive hands at a coat-peg affixed to the dressing-room wall. Sapphire wriggled but her lover was masterfully firm, soon using his silver and gold tie to bind the wrists to the coat-peg.

Adèle gazed at the helpless hands in their bondage. Hot quicksilver spilled from her pouting pussy. She pressed her

213

body against the dressing-room door, gasping softly as she saw the singer produce a small, glinting clasp knife. Thumbing out the blade, he brought the point between Sapphire's swollen breasts, probing the last inch of steel down into the dark warmth of her cleavage. A soft snarling, tearing sound followed. Sapphire's clothing fell away as the blade swept down her body – slicing through her evening gown, bra, suspender belt and oyster silk cami-knickers.

Bobby pocketed his knife and stood back to impudently peruse the result. Sapphire mewed aloud. The squirming nude, wide-eyed and helpless in her impromptu bondage, clamped her stockinged thighs together. Her bared breasts were proud in the unfettered freedom, each nipple pink and eagerly erect. Below, the white belly was tensed. The thighs trembled, causing the darker bands of her stocking tops to rasp together. Adèle saw the blonde fringe of Sapphire's pubic snatch, and the parted labia where the man's mouth had wakened the glistening lips.

Adèle watched intently. Bobby was brutal with his captive nude, taking his pleasures roughly then spinning Sapphire face towards the wall to which she was suspended in bondage. Her breasts squashed into the smooth plaster, her nipples crushed into its firmness as Bobby gripped her outer buttocks, spreading the softness of each cheek painfully apart with his controlling hands.

Adèle swallowed as she saw the tiny dark sphincter gleam. She shuddered as she watched him guide his thick cock's snout between the splayed cheeks – then plunge it deep into the warmth of the anal whorl.

The opulent cars which had brought the guests to Carstairs Towers had been garaged carefully by the gardener, Mrs Bebbington-Booth's Hispano joining Bobby Kensington's lemon Bentley in the converted stables.

Julia and Sapphire were taking tea together in the Japanese garden while, upstairs in her boudoir, Lady Carstairs and Mrs Bebbington-Booth listened attentively as Adèle gave evidence. No explicit detail was spared as the enormity of Bobby Kensington's duplicity was laid bare. Lady Carstairs sat grim-faced and silent. Her guest grew pale then purple as her shock succumbed to rage.

'And then he spanked her bare bottom –' Adèle was reporting conscientiously.

'The 'ound. The 'orrible little 'ound,' Mrs Bebbington-Booth cried, her careful diction finally collapsing under her wrath.

Adèle completed her report, then withdrew from the boudoir.

'The question is,' Lady Carstairs murmured softly, 'how do we tell our girls? We will have to be careful. Glamorising him could make him all the more attractive.'

Mrs Bebbington-Booth, partially recovering from her shock, nodded vehemently. 'Sapphire can be so mule-headed.'

'I am afraid Julia is the same. Our exposure of him may merely make him all the more desirable to one or both of our daughters. But there is a way –'

The other woman looked up sharply. 'There is?'

'What if the girls were to discover his infidelity for themselves?'

'I don't see 'ow –'

'I have spoken to my maid, Adèle. All is arranged. The minx is most competent and, fortunately, perfectly willing to oblige. Shall we join our daughters?'

Lady Carstairs was showing her guests the gallery in the east wing. Julia, bored, tagged along.

'And that,' the hostess announced, indicating a gaunt Victorian face executed in dark oils, 'was my late husband's Uncle Sebastian –' she broke off from the guided tour, frowning.

They were outside the billiards room. Muffled groans and smothered moans were just audible from beyond the closed door. Lady Carstairs raised her finger up to her lips for silence.

'Julia,' she whispered, 'open the door very gently, will you, and take a look.'

215

Julia obeyed – then shrank back from the open door and collapsed against the wall. She started to sob, softly. Sapphire, driven by curiosity, sprang to the door, peered briefly in, gasped and then joined Julia against the wall. Both wept openly.

'What the 'ell –?' Mrs Bebbington-Booth fumed. She strode into the billiards room. There, blindfolded and kneeling, was Bobby Kensington. Semi-naked, with her maid's uniform scattered on the billiard table, Adèle clutched the crooner's face and held it to her pussy. The wet-faced songster was lapping deeply, unaware of his audience.

Bobby Kensington was humming a couple of bars of his latest song as he sauntered into the drawing room for the rubber of bridge his hostess had suggested. The tune froze on his open lips as he saw Sapphire and Julia sitting together, leafing through an album. When he saw the two girls' mothers sitting together at the green baize-topped card table, he became flustered. Stammering something inaudible, he turned to go.

'Stay exactly where you are, Mr Kensington,' Lady Carstairs thundered. 'You were promised a game but I am very much afraid that there will be no bridge tonight. We shall,' she continued, her voice dropping to a velvet purr, 'be putting all our cards down on the table, however. Do take a seat. No,' she rasped, 'the sofa, I think.'

He sat down sullenly, obedient to her stern command. His face was pale, his eyes wary.

Adèle entered the drawing room, carrying an assortment of canes and cruel little riding crops and, closing the door behind her with a bump of her bottom, turned the key to lock it.

'Before we punish you –' Lady Carstairs announced.

Bobby Kensington half rose, his hands trembling as they pawed the velvet sofa for support. 'P-punish?' he echoed.

'Before we thrash you mercilessly, if you prefer to deal plainly, Mr Kensington, we will first hear evidence of your outrageous philandering from my maid, Adèle.'

216

'Now, your ladyship?' the pert minx murmured.

'Now, girl. Speak up and spare no detail, no matter how intimate it may be.'

'How do I begin, please, your ladyship?'

'Please give an exact account of what you saw taking place in Mr Kensington's rooms on the evening of the sixteenth –'

'No, mamma, please,' Julia yipped, blushing deeply, her cheeks as red as those Bobby Kensington had so soundly spanked that night.

'Very well. Adèle, kindly proceed to the dressing room of Mr Kensington. Tell us in detail exactly what took place backstage in the Dreadnought Club on the night of the twentieth –'

'Oh, please, Lady Carstairs,' Sapphire shrieked.

'I think I have made my point. Very well,' their hostess continued. 'Be good enough to disclose what took place this afternoon in the billiard room –'

Adèle briefly outlined how Bobby Kensington had, for the payment of a ten-shilling note (which Adèle produced disdainfully), purchased erotic excitation.

'He made me blindfold him then he knelt down, nice and submissive and obedient, milady, and begged for my pussy.'

'Knelt, did he? Begged, you say? Submissive and obedient. Well, I think we can provide Mr Kensington with a little diversion this evening which will meet his self-confessed needs.'

Julia and Sapphire, who had been standing together by the piano, exchanged significant glances and, hand in hand, approached the sofa. He lowered his gaze as they stood together before him, wagging their fingers in apparent mock-severity. Sensing, but misjudging, their mood to be one of stern playfulness, he brightened, patting the empty spaces on the sofa beside him with complacent palms.

They sat, snuggling into him gently – Sapphire ruffling his hair, Julia fingering his tie suggestively. He beamed, an oily smirk revealing carefully whitened teeth. His eyes sparkled with cocksure pride. This was all a charade. Parlour games played out by decadent aristocrats. Even the little maid was all part of the perverse sport. Bobby Kensington surveyed what he took to be his doting fans. If he played his hand carefully, he'd ride the two mothers as well.

Julia's fingers snaked around the knot of his tie, then tugged gently. Sapphire tousled his hair. He laughed. They giggled. Bobby Kensington tossed his head back and brayed aloud – forgetting in his sudden rush of relief the presence and the purpose of the assortment of crops and canes Adèle had carried into the drawing room minutes before. Loosening his tie, Julia took it between her lips, then bit into the silk. It fell down over his wrists. Her fingers followed its slithering descent, clutching it and insinuating it around his wrists – as Sapphire's grip on his taloned hair increased.

A flicker of fear clouded his sparkling eyes. He opened his mouth. Julia tightened the threaded tie. He struggled. Adèle skipped across to the sofa and pinned his shoulders down from behind. Too late: the knot was drawn tight, binding his hands into helplessness down at his belly.

The three younger women stripped him in seconds while the two maturer women looked on appreciatively, Mrs Bebbington-Booth's eyes widening as his cock sprung into view. Adèle fished out and used the clasp knife to cut away his sharply tailored suit, silk shirt and underwear. As they dragged his socks from his threshing feet, he pleaded aloud, raw fear curdling his rising shouts of protest.

Adèle scooped up the crops and canes and carried them across to the sofa, spreading them down on the carpet at the naked man's feet. His toes stubbed them. He glanced down. Bobby Kensington began to beg aloud for mercy.

'Gag him,' Lady Carstairs commanded, rising up from the green baize-topped card table.

Adèle supplied her starched maid's apron for the purpose. Julia wound the white tapes around his face four times before tying them tightly. Above the white gag, the silenced crooner's eyes bulged in terror.

'Across the sofa with him, please. That's right,' Lady Carstairs murmured approvingly as they positioned him face down, bare bottom up, for his impending punishment and pain.

'Now take a crop apiece, my dears. No, not you, Adèle. Come over here by me and watch. Julia, Sapphire, his bottom is entirely yours. You may do with him whatever you wish. But –' she paused, rubbing her hands together in a gesture of anticipatory pleasure '– be sure to punish him most severely.'

'Give it to 'im 'ot and 'ard,' Mrs Bebbington-Booth bellowed, throwing polite pronunciation to the winds. 'Make the bleeder 'owl.'

The two young girls were quite shy, at first. Neither of them had ever punished a naked bottom before. Betraying her breeding and exquisite manners, Julia offered the bare buttocks to Sapphire, tapping the rounded cheeks dominantly with the little loop at the tip of her quivering crop.

'After you, Sapphire, dear.'

Not to be outdone, and in keeping with the liver pill fortune lavished on her finishing school, Sapphire protested.

'Oh, no. You first. I insist.'

Julia accepted gracefully. Rolling the satin sleeve of her evening gown up to her elbow, she gripped her riding crop hard. Her knuckles showed white – as white as Bobby Kensington's toes straining as they dug into the carpet.

Julia admonished the naked man witheringly, teasing his clenched cheeks with her hovering crop and playing the little leather loop along the length of his tightly creased cleft. Her victim squirmed beneath the scalding sluice of her scornful contempt. The harsh rebuke concluded with some ripe epithets – then Julia, glowing becomingly after her chagrin, raised her crop up aloft.

In a final, desperate bid to escape, her naked victim rolled over, presenting his cock to her cruel gaze. She took one pace forwards towards the sofa and slowly guided the crop up between his trembling thighs. With the little loop of leather tap-tapping at his balls, she spoke briskly, her tone severe.

'If you want me to whip you there, Mr Kensington, I am perfectly prepared to do so. The choice, such as it is, is entirely yours.'

Whimpering through his gag, he rolled back, belly down, and slumped over the sofa.

'Bottom up, as it was a moment ago,' Julia prompted, flicking the cheeks with her crop.

He buried his toes into the carpet and strained obediently to present his bare buttocks up in the prescribed posture.

'Not good enough, Mr Kensington.' She flicked the crop against his proffered cheeks, the little leather loop leaving a second scarlet mark. 'More. I want your bottom right across the back of the sofa, Mr Kensington. Big and round and ready for my crop –'

'Thrash 'im –' Mrs Bebbington-Booth, for whom the tension proved too much, shouted.

'Mother,' Sapphire murmured reproachfully. 'Julia is perfectly right. Once Mr Kensington's bottom is positioned perfectly, then he will feel our displeasure.'

They all heard the bound, naked man moan. Adèle giggled, her thumbs stroking her little black skirt at the spot usually covered by her starched white apron.

Swish, crack. Adèle's thumbs became a blur as a thin pink line appeared instantly across the pale buttocks as Julia's crop lashed down.

'A capital stroke,' hissed Lady Carstairs. 'Well done, my girl. Again, if you will.'

Ever the dutiful daughter, Julia cracked the leather-sheathed crop down twice more in succession. Bobby Kensington's knees dug into the back of the sofa as he screamed silently into his tight gag. *Swish, crack.* The strokes were measured, the aim vehemently accurate. The whipped buttocks jerked and writhed as the crop bit into them, seething the helpless cheeks with blistering heat. Swishing the crop down again, and then again, Julia administered a blitz of vicious strokes that lashed down across his rounded cheeks with savage venom, each swipe of leathered cane bequeathing a reddening weal in its wake. Already, the opening strokes were changing colour, each

220

earlier stripe now deepening into a pale purple shade of pain.

Julia whipped him with controlled fury for a full six minutes; then, placing the crop down on the carpet before slowly rolling the sleeve of her evening gown back down to her wrist, she strode around the sofa to confront her whimpering victim. Kneeling down in front of him, she reached out and cupped his tear-stained face. Cradling him dominantly, she brought her lips to his tear-filled eyes and kissed them slowly.

'Goodbye, Mr Kensington. It was a pleasure whipping you,' she whispered.

Adèle grunted as she came, her stockinged legs aquiver. Lady Carstairs glanced at the maid, her aristocratic eyes sharp with impatient severity.

Sapphire, crop in hand, was more savage with the bare bottom before her. Her veneer of drawing-room decorum which had been expensively schooled into her was stripped away by her outrage. In a flurry of fury, she lashed his jerking buttocks fifteen times in blistering succession until the crop dropped from her grip. Her aching arm hung lifeless down by her side as she stood, panting, her breasts heaving with both anger and arousal.

'That it?' Mrs Bebbington-Booth demanded, clearly disappointed in her daughter's display of discipline. ''E's due more, darling. Much more.'

Biting her lip, Sapphire snatched up the crop, then suddenly burst into tears. Tossing it aside, she ran from the drawing-room, sobbing.

'Julia,' Lady Carstairs whispered. 'Go and see to her.'

Julia scurried after the weeping girl.

'Remember your daughter's tears as you select a cane, Mrs Bebbington-Booth,' Lady Carstairs remarked, scooping up her own choice of whippy yellow bamboo. 'There is unfinished business here for us to complete. Are you game, my dear?'

'Let me at 'im,' the liver pill magnate's widow cried, thrumming the air with a couple of practice strokes.

* * *

Bending down and capturing his sweat-wet hair in her taloned hand, Lady Carstairs addressed the singer's gagged lips with the tip of her quivering cane.

'Going to take the gag off, Mr Kensington. It will be instructive to hear you sing to a different tune.'

She ungagged him and was instantly rewarded with his broken sobs. The outraged, cheated mothers stood face to face above his crimson-striped buttocks, canes crossed in a guard-of-honour above as if a groom were passing through below.

'One moment,' Lady Carstairs hissed. 'My sofa.'

Palming his whipped cheeks dominantly, she rolled Bobby Kensington over, revealing his thickening cock. 'Look at that,' she remarked, prodding the engorged shaft with her cane-tip. 'Adèle.'

'Milady?' the minx responded.

'Interpose yourself between Mr Kensington and my Belgian sofa, girl. I will not have it ruined when he ejaculates, and,' she explained to Mrs Bebbington-Booth, 'I fear the antimaccassar will not take up the soak.'

Lowering their canes, the two women held him away from the sofa as Adèle hitched up her uniformed skirt above her bottom and yanked down her cami-knickers to her knees – then sidled in between the singer and the sofa.

'A little treat for the girl. She has been so obliging throughout this wretched affair.'

'Waste not, want not,' Mrs Bebbington-Booth agreed, voicing the maxim that had made her late husband a very rich man.

Adèle fingered the thick cock; it immediately squirted her bare bottom with a hot splash of milky semen. Bobby Kensington grunted thickly; the shuddering maid squealed.

Swish. Lady Carstairs sliced her bamboo down, searing the already punished cheeks with fresh torment.

'Wretched man. Nearly ruined my Belgian sofa.'

Adèle, sticky-fingered, dragged the spent cock to her buttocks as the canes whistled down. She rubbed the hot snout rhythmically against her wet cheeks, coaxing it back into stiffness. The canes whipped down. Bobby Kensington cried out in anguish. Adèle guided the slippery erection in between her parted buttocks and, contracting her anal muscles, absorbed almost half its length. Speared by the whipped crooner's shaft, and pinned into the sofa by his dead weight, she squirmed happily as the bamboo continued to bite.

'We'll have a song, I think,' Lady Carstairs opined, pausing for a breather. 'Any requests?'

'Red Sails In The Sunset,' Mrs Bebbington-Booth grunted, levelling her cane down dominantly across the punished buttocks.

They forced him to croon. He faltered. The bamboo rain fell heavily. He managed to perform, the ragged notes snatched from his trembling lips.

Adèle squealed again as, driven by the searing cane strokes, Bobby Kensington jerked then plunged deeply into her tight heat. *Swish, swipe. Swish, swipe.*

'Come along, Mr Kensington,' Lady Carstairs cried, plying her cane viciously yet again. 'Let's hear you hit the high notes.'

Both canes sliced down. Bobby Kensington screamed – but it was Adèle who hit high C first: crying out her shrill delight as the whistling bamboo drove the crooner ever deeper between her clenched cheeks.

11

Double Yellow

Jackie shivered as she stood in her white cotton panties before the full-length mirror. The door to the changing room opened. Jackie's arms flew across her bosom, squashing the full, round breasts as she swiftly sought to cover their swollen splendour. A woman's voice told her to relax.

'Blokes get changed next door, love. You one of the new lot?'

Jackie, grinning, dropped her hands down to her thighs and nodded.

'Look slippy. Better get into that uniform or else the Captain will be signing up another member for her Double Yellow club.'

Jackie frowned. That was the third time she had heard this club mentioned. Once, just after her interview at City Hall, once in training and again – in whispered giggles – in the staff canteen.

'Catch you later, love.' The other Car Cadet, pert in her trim uniform, shouldered her leather bag and, snatching up her black gloves, left the changing room.

Back in the full-length glass, Jackie studied her reflection. Weighing her breasts in her upturned palms, she slowly cupped their soft warmth and squeezed, pleased with their ripe curves, smooth satin sheen and deep, dark cleavage. Selecting a white cotton sports bra, she drew the cool cups to her swollen breasts and slipped it on, shuddering with pleasure as her bosom surrendered to the firm embrace. As she thumbed the straps at each shoulder, her breasts rose, bulging beautifully. Already, her nipples were thickening as they nuzzled the stretchy cotton cups.

Next, the pale blue blouse. She wriggled into it quickly but fastened it slowly, button by button, from her belly up to her throat. She relished the soft fabric kissing her flesh, and was proud of the pert thrust of her brassiered breasts now passive in their disciplined bondage.

The little dark blue bow-tie was a cheat. She only had to clip it on then finger the butterfly wings into place against her collar. She glanced into the mirror. The effect was thrilling. The crisp uniform flattered her soft curves, adding a hint of stern authority to her pretty face and girlish figure. Like a sixth-form prefect. One who patrolled the dorm after lights out, slipper gripped in her right hand, ready to punish the bare bottom of any naughty school girl caught breaking the strict rules.

Five weeks ago, Jackie was a meter maid, part of the traffic warden patrol. Then City Hall had called the consultants in, leading to out-sourcing. Privatisation, they said in the staff canteen. Jobs on the line. Jackie got an interview and a job. With it came new contracts and a new uniform. And new duties. No longer a meter maid, Jackie became a Car Cadet. City Hall's new strategy. Gone was her job-for-life with its dull blue serge trouser suit, stupid hat and sensible, ugly shoes. Now she enjoyed monthly targets to meet, renewable contract options – but a delicious uniform.

Jackie grinned. Even sixth-form prefects wore a skirt. She stared down at her naked thighs, and at the pantied pubic mound peeping out between the flaps of her blouse. Reaching out, she plucked her skirt down from its hanger. The pleated mini-skirt fell just below the swell of her thighs. Just like the sixth-form prefect ready for netball. Jackie fingered the narrow pleats. The mini-skirt flared when she twirled, revealing her tightly pantied bottom. Just like the pleated skirts on the school girls prancing at netball. She giggled. She'd have to be extra careful out there, when bending down to speak to drivers behind their wheel – or she'd cause more than a few shunts from excited drivers coming up behind.

And no stupid hat. Great. A blue beret. She tilted it then pulled it down on to her chic black curls. No lipstick or eye make-up. That was made plain in training. The captain had been very firm. Gloves. She had chosen the pale blue kid leather over the black. So soft, deliciously soft. She drove her fingers home into the tight warmth and then wriggled them, before clenching both hands into squeezed fists. A warm bubble silvered and burst at the white cotton stretched across her pussy. Leather always did something for Jackie. She used to go clubbing wearing black leather panties – scampering to the loo after a couple of hours to pluck their soiled warmth from her tingling labia and finger out the sleek hide from her aching cleft.

'Two minutes.' The door opened suddenly and a voice called out warningly. 'Hurry up.'

She did. Her first day as a Car Cadet. She mustn't be late for parade and inspection. Her training was complete; her uniform fitted perfectly, displaying her trim figure and lithe legs to their fullest effect. Legs. Jackie squealed. The hem of her pleated mini-skirt tickled the backs of her thighs as she raised each leg up in turn, wobbling unsteadily, for her socks and shoes. White ankle socks and neat little black shoes were donned in seconds. A final glance in the mirror. Yes. She was ready. But she'd have to remember how dangerously short her mini-skirt was. Wouldn't do to cause an accident on her first day.

The six new Car Cadets formed a ragged, slightly selfconscious line as they presented themselves on parade for inspection. Jackie mentally checked: note book; pens; leather shoulder bag and canvas holster. Gloves, beret and ID. All present and correct. She gasped softly as the captain, a stern, closely cropped blonde, fifteen years older than her own twenty, strode into the operations room. Instead of her customary track suit, the captain was wearing black, shiny biker's leathers.

'Attention.'

The line of uniformed young females smartened at once, buttocks tightened, thighs firmly clamped together.

'Come along, come along, heads up, arms straight, palms inwards against the thighs. You know how I want you, girls.'

The staccato of crisp commands brought the quivering girls into closer order. The captain, her leather creaking softly as she paced up and down before her squad, surveyed them intently.

'Not bad. At ease.'

Jackie breathed out. She kept her head still, but her eyes followed the black-leathered blonde as she prowled back down along the line. Sharp commands accompanied the blonde's progress. Breaking through the line, the captain inspected the girls from behind. Jackie flinched slightly as she felt the stern presence immediately behind her – and flinched again as strong fingers clutched at the hem of her pleated mini-skirt, tugging it firmly down.

'Too short, girl. Get measured for another when stores open again on Friday. Understand?'

Jackie nodded, blushing. 'Yes.'

'Yes, what?' the cropped blonde snapped.

'Yes, Captain.'

'That's better. You are all in my crew now. Under my authority. And I intend to run the best crew City Hall has ever seen. Understood?'

'Yes, Captain,' they chorused.

The stern blonde's breath was warm on the nape of Jackie's neck. The fingers at her hem released the pleated mini-skirt and fleetingly clenched into a firm fist. Jackie squirmed as she felt the knuckles dimple the swell of her left buttock, grazing the bare flesh just beneath the bite of her white cotton panties. The knuckles kissed her exposed cheek briefly, but the sensation set Jackie's pulse racing for several minutes. Her nostrils flared slightly as they caught the feral whiff of the shiny black leathers. Giddy, Jackie stumbled forwards slightly. Firm hands gripped her waist and drew her neatly back into line.

'I see I'm going to have to keep a close eye on you, my girl.'

For the second time in twelve minutes, Jackie's wet pussy glistened with a bubble of arousal, leaving her panties sticky at her pouting lips.

'I'll be ready for you Friday, girl. Get those thighs covered. Or else.' The concluding words were emphasised with a dominant tap of the captain's fingertip against her soft upper thigh-flesh. Jackie automatically clenched her buttocks together, squeezing her cheeks until her cleft became a thin, painfully tight crease.

'As the newly formed squad of Car Cadets,' the captain announced, 'you serve one purpose and one purpose only. Revenue. City Hall thinks that by setting up the squad, enough revenue can be made to finance a decent traffic scheme. Pedestrianisation. Park-and-ride. There is even talk of a metro-tram link. Who knows. But revenue is required. You're not out there to direct traffic or give directions. Just radio in the number plate of anyone double-parked, unloading or in a bus lane. Control here will do the rest. But they can't send out the ticket without the correct number plate. So no mistakes. Do not disappoint City Hall. Or me.'

Jackie's fingertips ached to pluck the damp panties from her slit. The hem of her pleated mini-skirt rippled as she brushed it. The movement caught the sharp eyes of the leathered blonde. The eyes narrowed dangerously. Jackie gulped and, head tossed back, drew herself smartly to attention.

'As your captain, I will be supervising you as you cover your beat. Forget the residential areas, moaning mothers on the school run. We're hitting the commercial zones. Targeting money. And we're going to hit them hard. What are we going to do?'

'Hit them hard, Captain.'

Out on patrol, on a beat stretching from the edge of the open-air market to the factories and small businesses adjoining the railway station, Jackie was surprised at the irksome weight of the radio in her canvas shoulder holster. In training, they had received operating instructions on how to use it, sharing one between the entire squad. Out on the beat, its weight was a drag. Jackie pulled it out and buried it in her shoulder bag. Much better. And her jacket fell smoothly down over the line of her proud bosom.

Turning into Archer Street, she saw that a line of traffic was being held up by a double-parked Sherpa van: back doors open, boxes busily being unloaded. Quickening her pace, Jackie approached. The driver spotted her, slapped the side of his van and jumped in behind the wheel. Jackie's fingers touched her empty holster. Damn. Struggling with gloved hands to unzip her shoulder bag, she swore softly as she heard the engine revving. The back doors were slammed shut and thumped just as she fished out her radio. She brought it up to her mouth, but only managed another soft curse. The Sherpa was now a white blur down at the junction with Station Road.

The congealed traffic loosened and crawled away. Jackie heard the snarl of an approaching motorbike.

'I saw that. Bloody little fool. Keep that radio where it's supposed to be.'

It was the stern blonde captain. Behind her tinted visor, her eyes flashed angrily. Jackie mumbled an apology. It was instantly spurned.

'That was a twenty-quid penalty in the bag and you let it go. Don't ever let me see that happen again, girl.'

Stamping down on the kick-start, the captain roared off, nosing her gleaming bike down Archer Street, her tightly sheathed buttocks bulging on the leather saddle.

Back in the canteen, word of Jackie's 'miss' had spread. Over beans on toast, they teased her.

'New recruit for the Double Yellow club.'

'She'll be a fully paid-up member soon. No danger.'

Jackie accepted their teasing and ate her lunch. Again, the mention of the Double Yellow club. Puzzled, she peppered her beans.

Two of the squad were peeling back the foil from their yoghurts.

'Captain about?' asked the raspberry yoghurt, dipping her spoon.

'Gone to City Hall,' replied the hazlenut and chocolate chip.

'Good,' came the response through a full, pink mouthful.

The two girls finished off their yoghurts and furtively showed each other their 'perks', one proudly revealing a box of peppermint creams and the other flashing two complimentary cinema tickets. A third Car Cadet, cottoning on, displayed a gleaming CD.

Jackie's puzzled look made them laugh.

'Not many "perks" on your lousy beat,' they commiserated.

Those Car Cadets who patrolled the smarter streets of the shopping sector were, Jackie discovered, rewarded with small presents for turning a blind eye to a bit of illegal delivery-parking. Just a couple of minutes, darling. Go on. A smile. The helpless shrug and the gesture of outstretched arms. Then a little sweetener for the obliging Car Cadet. That's how it was done.

Finishing her tea, Jackie thought about the grim streets she patrolled. Small, struggling workshops. Mean little outfits being squeezed hard enough by VAT and punitive rates. Not many opportunities for 'perks' there.

A fortnight later, her pleated mini-skirt an inch longer and her radio bulging beneath her jacket, Jackie was on patrol in Cooper Street. She paused outside two large green gates. No signs or name plates. Everything done over a mobile phone, Jackie presumed. No paperwork. Cash only. Jackie was learning fast. Beyond the green gates, in the shabby unit, cutting and sewing machines clattered loudly. A back-street sweatshop.

A Ford Transit squealed to a stop. A delivery. The gates opened and three youths emerged to manhandle the bolts of satin and raw silk inside to feed the machinists. The driver of the van winked at Jackie.

'Panties, or would you like a bra?'

She blushed, but withdrew her hand from inside her jacket, leaving the radio nestling in its canvas holder.

'Well, darling?' he grinned. 'Bra?'

Jackie nodded.

'Bra it is, then.' He gazed at her shrewdly, his large brown eyes feasting on her breasts.

Jackie squirmed.

'You'll be a 36.'

Jackie giggled and nodded. 'Cheeky bugger.'

He strode over to where she was standing by the green gates.

'Let's see,' he said, his voice warm and confident. He briefly placed his large hands on her breasts, squeezing them gently. Jackie noticed the missing thumb. She shrank back a pace.

'36C,' he laughed.

Her eyes widened with wonder. She was exactly that. 36C.

'Used to be a machinist,' he said over his shoulder as he walked back towards the cab of his van, 'before I lost this.' He jerked up his thumbless hand. 'Blue satin do you? Half cups, but you don't need any padding.'

That was how it had started. Emboldened, Jackie began to seek out and accept cash. The mini-cab drivers coughed up readily enough, happy to slip the Car Cadet a folded fiver in return for her blind eye. Jackie wasn't greedy – and whenever she heard the snarl of the approaching motorbike, she whipped her radio out and did her duty. Everyone was satisfied. Within a month, Jackie had her beat sorted.

The captain studied the projected figures against the actual returns. Almost thirty per cent down. City Hall had been on the phone, chasing her for an explanation. She checked the figures again and then studied the detail rota. Her fingers slid easily down the laminated chart, coming to rest – then tapping – Jackie's name. The captain frowned.

During the inspection parade the following morning, the captain ordered her squad to open their shoulder bags for examination.

'No purses, credit cards or cheque books allowed on patrol,' she instructed. 'I don't want to catch anyone shopping in my time, understood?'

Grumbling under their breath, the Car Cadets obediently put all their belongings back into their lockers.

'Can you break a twenty? Two tens or fivers will do,' the captain asked Jackie casually.

'Sorry.' Jackie shrugged, opening her purse and offering it up for inspection. 'No can do.'

The captain glanced down, counted the eight pounds, and smiled. 'Never mind. I just wondered if you could.'

That evening, Jackie undressed in the changing room and slipped into a cubicle, drawing the opaque plastic curtain across behind her. Her shower was lukewarm at first. She shivered, naked and impatient, waiting for the water to warm. She soaped her shoulders and breasts as the stinging sluice grew hot, filling her narrow cubicle with swirling steam. Soon the opaque plastic curtain was sweating. Crushing her breasts firmly beneath her flattened palms, she relished the shower, feeling the tiredness of her aching legs drain away with the suds at her feet.

Offering her throat and breasts up to the drumming cascade, she thrilled as it raked her nipples, bringing them up into stiff little peaks of delicious torment. Her left knee twisted inwards against her right leg as she squirmed pleasurably. Her fingers found her pussy and slowly, effortlessly prised the thick lips apart. Curds of foam slithered down her belly and spine as she tensed, planting her shining feet apart. Fingering herself rhythmically, she concentrated on the images darting behind her tightly shut eyes.

The smiling, confident Transit van driver who cupped her breasts to guestimate her bra size. He still did it, even though he had got it spot on the first time. And yesterday, when she had opted for a pair of briefs, fondling her bottom firmly for the silk panties. The mini-cab drivers, grinning as they popped folded fivers into her cleavage, the tightly rolled blue note probing down between her soft, warm breasts.

Jackie's fingers worked furiously as she remembered all her 'perks'. The owner of the take-away distracting her from the lorry on the pavement, his broad hand gently inching up beneath her pleated mini-skirt towards her cotton panties. The brief impudence of his swift thumb tip at her pubic mound. She had tried, half-heartedly, to slap his face. Laughing, he had gripped her wrists and kissed her fiercely, snatching her beret away like a schoolboy – returning it with a tenner tucked inside. And all the time the refrigerated lorry had been disgorging boxes of frozen chips on to the pavement in breach of at least three by-laws.

Strumming her labial lips, and palming them wider apart, Jackie squeezed her wet buttocks tightly together as she teased up her tiny hood of velvet and prised out her clitoral bud. Concentrating hard, she pressed her thumb-tips down.

She did not hear the changing room door open slightly, then yawn wide. She did not hear the soft creak of leather as the captain sidled in, closing the changing room door softly behind her. Under the drumming scald of her shower, the naked Car Cadet did not hear the faint chink of keys, or the squeak of the locker door being opened. Thighs trembling, thumbs busy as she masturbated luxuriously, Jackie did not see or hear the captain examining the contents of her purse, counting the thirty pounds in notes that had not been there during the snap inspection earlier that morning.

Jackie approached the windowless van. Out of town plates. Not a regular, new to her patch. 'Tortoise Couriers – we beat the hares' was splashed in red along the side. Jackie smiled.

The driver wound down his window, eyeing the hem of her pleated mini-skirt unashamedly. Jackie drew her thighs together primly. Better get him booked, she thought, fishing out her radio. Word in the canteen was that targets weren't being met.

'Have a heart, darling. It's my mobile. Signal keeps breaking up.'

'Can't let you stay here.'

'Four minutes. Five, tops. They're just sorting out my next pick-up. Only place I can hear them clearly. Go on.'

233

Jackie saw the fiver being thumbed out of his wallet.

'You deserve a quick break, love. Get yourself a coffee and a cake. No sugar, mind. You're sweet enough.' The blue fiver was promptly palmed through the window, as if they did it regularly.

'OK.' Jackie nodded, swiftly scanning the road up and down to check for prowling motorbikes. 'Make your call.'

'Thanks. You're a little cracker.'

Jackie turned, pocketing her bribe, and strode away. The driver stared hungrily at her mini-skirt swishing provocatively against her sensually swaying hips.

The driver turned to speak into the back of his van. A lorry thundered by, drowning out his words. He unsnapped his seat belt and twisted around into the darkness behind him.

'How was that? Got all you need?'

'Everything,' the captain whispered softly, her leathers creaking as she stretched to tackle a gripping cramp.

Jackie scampered out of her shower, clutching her white towel up to her bulging breasts. The captain, severe in her gleaming leathers, closed the changing room door and locked it firmly, pocketing the key in her leather jacket.

'Get back into that shower, you little bitch. I've got your number.'

Jackie froze in alarm. The towel dropped from her lifeless fingers, revealing her wet breasts, tightened belly and pubic snatch sparkling with undried droplets nestling in its matted coils.

'I don't –' she stammered, bending to retrieve her towel.

The cropped blonde glimpsed the bulging breasts and growled. 'Leave that alone. Back into the shower. At once.' She took two paces forwards.

The shivering nude squeaked her alarm and dashed back into the cubicle, dragging the wet plastic curtain across. It was torn back instantly, exposing Jackie to the stern, leather-clad captain's cruel gaze.

'I suspected, but wasn't sure.' The captain twisted the cold full on. Jackie, huddled and squirming, shrieked.

'Checked your purse. Full of fivers. Face the wall,' she snapped, propelling the naked Car Cadet around towards the white-tiled wall.

Jackie cried out aloud as the cold water streamed down, stinging her soft nakedness with its icy talons.

'Little cracker.' *Spank*. A hard hand smacked the bare bottom harshly.

Jackie twisted around, her mouth gaping in surprised pain.

'Yes, I was there this afternoon. In the back of that van.' *Spank*. *Spank*. Jackie shrieked.

'Set up a little sting? Tortoise and Hare, remember?' *Spank*. *Spank*. The creamy cheeks reddened and blushed deeply under the fierce onslaught. Again, then again, the hard hand slapped across the shuddering cheeks, punishing Jackie's naked, defenceless bottom until the wet buttocks were crimson. Jackie twisted in a desperate bid to escape. Slipping on the tiles, she steadied herself with outstretched arms, presenting her unprotected bottom to her tormentress.

'Stay exactly as you are. That's perfect,' the captain hissed.

The chastisement commenced in earnest, the sharp spanks – and Jackie's broken sobs – ringing out against the glistening white tiles. Her heavy buttocks shuddered and bounced beneath the harshly cracking palm of her cropped blonde punisher. With the cold water stinging her belly and breasts, and the hot spanking hand stinging her blazing bottom, Jackie begged for mercy.

The captain ceased, holding her hot hand out under the cold shower. 'Down,' she thundered. Still facing the white tiles, Jackie, snivelling loudly, knelt down uncertainly under the icy stream.

'No,' the captain barked, prodding Jackie's reddened bottom with the toe of her leather boot. 'Not like that. Get your arse under the shower. Cool it off. I want it ready for my strap.'

Jackie howled her protest but the captain taloned her victim's wet hair and forced the sobbing nude down, making Jackie squat on all fours.

'Turn around.'

Jackie scuttled on the wet tiles, turning awkwardly until her eyes met the polished toecaps of the captain's leather boots.

'Bottom up.'

Sobbing gently, Jackie strained to raise her spanked cheeks up to the icy deluge.

'Stay like that until I return. Move, and you'll really suffer.'

Out in the canteen, Jackie was missed.

'You want all of that tea-cake?'

'Go on, then. Where's Jackie?'

'The captain followed her into the changing room ten minutes ago.'

'Bloody 'ell. Jackie been on the take, do you think?'

'Something like that. They say the captain's been oiling her strap all afternoon. You know, linseed oil and cotton wool.'

'Poor Jackie. Up for the Double Yellow club.'

'Yeah. Poor cow.'

The leather-clad blonde relocked the changing room door and strode across to the shower cubicle. She grunted a grudging approval as she saw Jackie, naked, red-bottomed and shivering, still squatting obediently beneath the freezing shower.

'At least you are trainable. Dishonest, but there may be hope for you yet. Hope, discipline and punishment.'

Jackie, shivering, whimpered.

'Thought you'd get away with it, hmm? I was on to you at once. So were City Hall. Beat them to it, that's all. Now I'm going to beat you. No need to let City Hall know. Deal with it internally. Best way.'

Kneeling down, the captain – both hands gloved in black leather gauntlets – raked her straightened forefinger along the length of the dark cleft between the wet, reddened cheeks. Jackie moaned as the leathered finger skimmed the velvet of her sensitive flesh.

'OK,' the captain murmured, rising up to twist the cold off. 'We understand each other. Good. Now get out here and get dried.'

'I'm sorry,' Jackie mumbled. 'I only did it –'

'Don't lie,' thundered the cropped blonde, clenching the length of quivering leather in her tightly fisted gauntlet. She snapped the strap, viciously, twice.

Jackie, struggling with numbed fingers to dry her shivering nakedness, looked in horror at the evil strap.

'No, please. I'll never –'

'City Hall pay me to run an efficient squad. I'll get them their revenue – but I'll do it my way. You've forfeited your bottom, girl. It is mine from now on. Now hurry up and get dried. I'm running late. I've only got forty minutes to deal with you tonight.'

Tonight. The word exploded silently in Jackie's brain. Was there going to be more of this humiliation, suffering and pain? Tomorrow night? The night after that? Was her bare bottom really at the mercy of the cruel captain from now on?

'Most of you girls go on the take. Turn a blind eye. So do I, until someone gets greedy. I catch 'em all in time. Bring 'em to heel with my little pal here.'

Jackie crushed the towel to her breasts as the cropped blonde snapped her leather belt again. Twice.

'I run a sort of club. Exclusive, like. Except every Car Cadet on the squad seems to end up an unwilling member.'

Jackie looked up, her eyes dark and fearful.

'They call it the Double Yellow. You're just about to become a member. Bend over.'

Out in the canteen, the girls were impatient to go.

'No, wait. Just a few more minutes.'

They sat, nervously fiddling with KitKat wrappers and teaspoons. Nobody spoke, but each knew what the others were thinking. About bending over, bare-bottomed. About the leathered blonde standing directly behind the proffered buttocks. About the leather belt being raised aloft. About the *swish, swipe* as it lashed down.

'Ow.'

They looked at each other, nodding. The stroke down across the bare cheeks. They waited.

'Ow.'

They flinched as Jackie squealed a second time, almost immediately after her first shriek of pain.

Yes, that was it. The cruel strap snaking upwards to bite at the punished nude's exposed plum. The supple leather snapping up to kiss the tender pubis fiercely. Ow, ow, the punished yelled. The double 'ow' of all new members.

'Yep,' a Car Cadet nodded, gathering up her cigarettes and lighter. 'That's it. She's in the club all right.'

Leather always did something for Jackie. Whipped, her wet slit ablaze from the licking hide, she stretched across the captain's leathered thighs, her nipples raking the soft hide.

'Naughty girl,' the cropped blonde purred, already half an hour late for her almost forgotten appointment. 'Naughty girl. What am I going to do with you?'

Alone in the deserted, locked changing room, the captain palmed the punished buttocks of the wriggling nude across her knees. Jackie's trembling thighs inched apart and her wet fig glistened. The perfume of her arousal stabbed the cropped blonde's nostrils. Her gauntlet trapped and squeezed the captive cheeks firmly, dragging them apart to expose the sticky cleft within. Knuckling the whipped cheeks, the cropped blonde gazed down. Jackie mewed softly as she squirmed.

Leather always did something for Jackie. She nestled her nipples into the leathered thighs and rasped her splayed labia into its sleek warmth. The gauntlet released her soft buttocks from its cruel grasp – becoming one firm leathered finger at her wet plum.

'Not too sure you need much more discipline, my girl,' the captain purred, nuzzling Jackie's shining sphincter with her leathered fingertip. 'Perhaps I'll just fashion my strap into a leash and use it to curb you. A little touch of leather here –' she worried the tight little anal whorl vigorously '– and here –' she dragged the fingertip down between the sticky labial lips '– will suffice. Hmm?'

238

Leather always did something for Jackie.

The captain pinned her nude victim down, the gauntlet of her left hand firmly controlling Jackie's neck. Splaying two leathered fingers on her right hand, she guided them towards the naked flesh across her lap: the upper finger probing Jackie's sphincter, the lower, longer finger sliding into the writhing nude's slit.

Jackie came violently, creaming the leathered thighs across which she was arranged in her submissive helplessness.

NEW BOOKS

Coming up from Nexus, Sapphire and Black Lace

Surrender by Laura Bowen
August 2000   Price £5.99   ISBN 0 352 33524 6
When Melanie joins the staff of The Hotel she enters a world of new sexual experiences and frightening demands, in which there are three kinds of duty she must perform. In this place of luxury and beauty there are many pleasures, serving her deepest desires, but there is also perversity and pain. The Hotel is founded on a strict regime, but Melanie cannot help but break the rules. How can she survive the severe torments that follow?

An Education in the Private House by Esme Ombreux
August 2000   Price £5.99   ISBN 0 352 33525 4
Eloise Highfield is left in charge of the upbringing of Celia Bright's orphaned daughter, Anne. Disturbed and excited by the instructions left by Celia for Anne's education, Eloise invites Michael, a painter of erotic subjects, to assist her. As they read Celia's explicit account of servitude to her own master, they embark on ever more extreme experiments. But Anne is keeping her own diary of events . . . Celia, Eloise, Anne – three women discovering the pleasures of submission; three interwoven accounts of a shared journey into blissful depravity. By the author of the *Private House* series.

The Training Grounds by Sarah Veitch
August 2000   Price £5.99   ISBN 0 352 33526 2
Charlotte was looking forward to her holiday in the sun. Two months on a remote tropical island with her rich, handsome boyfriend: who could ask for more? She is more than a little surprised, then, when she arrives to find that the island is in fact a vast correction centre – the Training Grounds – presided over by a swarthy and handsome figure known only as the Master. But greater shocks are in store, not least Charlotte's discovery that she is there not as a guest, but as a slave . . .

Grooming Lucy by Yvonne Marshall
September 2000   Price £5.99   ISBN 0 352 33529 7
Lucy's known about her husband's kinks for a few years, but now she wants to accommodate them herself. She knows it won't be easy – she has heard how extreme his tastes are – and she's asked some special friends to arrange a unique training course for her. But her husband's not the only man with extreme tastes, and some of his friends have their own ideas about how to train Lucy.

The Torture Chamber by Lisette Ashton
September 2000   Price £5.99   ISBN 0 352 33530 0
Catering for every perverse taste imaginable, The Torture Chamber is an SM club with a legendary reputation. Inside its exclusive walls, no fetish is too extreme, and the patrons know how to make the most of every situation. When Sue visits in disguise, she realises that she cannot visit again – the intensity of her reactions frightens her. But others at the club will stop at nothing to share in her special education.

Different Strokes by Sarah Veitch
September 2000   Price £5.99   ISBN 0 352 33531 9
These stories celebrate all aspects of the pains and pleasures of corporal punishment. Disobedient secretaries, recalcitrant slimmers, cheeky maids – dozens of young women, and a few young men too, whose behaviour can be improved only by the strict application of a hand, a slipper or a cane. A Nexus Classic.

Wicked Words 3 various
August 2000 Price £5.99 ISBN 0 352 33522 X

Wild women. Wicked words. Guaranteed to turn you on! Black Lace short story collections are a showcase of erotic-writing talent. With contributions from the UK and the USA, and settings and stories that are deliciously daring, this is erotica at the cutting edge. Fresh, cheeky, dazzling and upbeat – only the most arousing fiction makes it into a Black Lace compilation.

A Scandalous Affair by Holly Graham
August 2000 Price £5.99 ISBN 0 352 33523 8

Young, well groomed and spoilt, Olivia Standish is the epitome of a trophy wife. Her husband is a successful politician, and Olivia is confident that she can look forward to a life of luxury and prestige. Then she finds a video of her husband cavorting with whores and engaging in some very bizarre behaviour, and suddenly her future looks uncertain. Realising that her marriage is one of convenience and not love, she vows to take her revenge. Her goal is to have her errant husband on his knees and begging for mercy.

Devils's Fire by Melissa MacNeal
September 2000 Price £5.99 ISBN 0 352 33527 0

Destitute but beautiful Mary visits handsome but lecherous mortician Hyde Fortune, in the hope he can help her out of her impoverished predicament. It isn't long before they're consummating their lust for each other and involving both Fortune's exotic housekeeper and his young assistant Sebastian. When Mary gets a live-in position at the local Abbey, she becomes an active participant in the curious erotic rites practiced by the not-so-very pious monks. This marvelously entertaining story is set in 19th-century America.

The Naked Flame by Crystalle Valentino

September 2000   Price £5.99   ISBN 0 352 33528 9

Venetia Halliday is a go-getting girl who is determined her trendy London restaurant is going to win the prestigious Blue Ribbon award. Her new chef is the cheeky, over-confident Mickey Quinn, who knows just what it takes to break down her cool exterior. He's hot, he's horny, and he's got his eyes on the prize – in her bed and her restaurant. Will Venetia pull herself together, or will her rough-trade lover ride roughshod over everything?

Crash Course by Juliet Hastings

September 2000   Price £5.99   ISBN 0 352 33018 X

Kate is a successful management consultant. When she's asked to run a training course at an exclusive hotel at short notice, she thinks the stress will be too much. But three of the participants are young, attractive, powerful men, and Kate cannot resist the temptation to get to know them sexually as well as professionally. Her problem is that one of the women on the course is feeling left out. Jealousy and passion simmer beneath the surface as Kate tries to get the best performance out of all her clients. A Black Lace special reprint.

NEXUS BACKLIST

All books are priced £5.99 unless another price is given. If a date is supplied, the book in question will not be available until that month in 2000.

CONTEMPORARY EROTICA

THE BLACK MASQUE	Lisette Ashton	
THE BLACK WIDOW	Lisette Ashton	
THE BOND	Lindsay Gordon	
BRAT	Penny Birch	
BROUGHT TO HEEL	Arabella Knight	July
DANCE OF SUBMISSION	Lisette Ashton	
DISCIPLES OF SHAME	Stephanie Calvin	
DISCIPLINE OF THE PRIVATE HOUSE	Esme Ombreux	
DISCIPLINED SKIN	Wendy Swanscombe	Nov
DISPLAYS OF EXPERIENCE	Lucy Golden	
AN EDUCATION IN THE PRIVATE HOUSE	Esme Ombreux	Aug
EMMA'S SECRET DOMINATION	Hilary James	
GISELLE	Jean Aveline	
GROOMING LUCY	Yvonne Marshall	Sept
HEART OF DESIRE	Maria del Rey	
HOUSE RULES	G.C. Scott	
IN FOR A PENNY	Penny Birch	
LESSONS OF OBEDIENCE	Lucy Golden	Dec
ONE WEEK IN THE PRIVATE HOUSE	Esme Ombreux	
THE ORDER	Nadine Somers	
THE PALACE OF EROS	Delver Maddingley	
PEEPING AT PAMELA	Yolanda Celbridge	Oct
PLAYTHING	Penny Birch	

THE PLEASURE CHAMBER	Brigitte Markham		
POLICE LADIES	Yolanda Celbridge		
THE RELUCTANT VIRGIN	Kendal Grahame		
SANDRA'S NEW SCHOOL	Yolanda Celbridge		
SKIN SLAVE	Yolanda Celbridge		June
THE SLAVE AUCTION	Lisette Ashton		
SLAVE EXODUS	Jennifer Jane Pope		Dec
SLAVE GENESIS	Jennifer Jane Pope		
SLAVE SENTENCE	Lisette Ashton		
THE SUBMISSION GALLERY	Lindsay Gordon		
SURRENDER	Laura Bowen		Aug
TAKING PAINS TO PLEASE	Arabella Knight		
TIGHT WHITE COTTON	Penny Birch		Oct
THE TORTURE CHAMBER	Lisette Ashton		Sept
THE TRAINING OF FALLEN ANGELS	Kendal Grahame		
THE YOUNG WIFE	Stephanie Calvin		May

ANCIENT & FANTASY SETTINGS

THE CASTLE OF MALDONA	Yolanda Celbridge		
NYMPHS OF DIONYSUS	Susan Tinoff	£4.99	
MAIDEN	Aishling Morgan		
TIGER, TIGER	Aishling Morgan		
THE WARRIOR QUEEN	Kendal Grahame		

EDWARDIAN, VICTORIAN & OLDER EROTICA

BEATRICE	Anonymous	
CONFESSION OF AN ENGLISH SLAVE	Yolanda Celbridge	
DEVON CREAM	Aishling Morgan	
THE GOVERNESS AT ST AGATHA'S	Yolanda Celbridge	
PURITY	Aishling Morgan	July
THE RAKE	Aishling Morgan	
THE TRAINING OF AN ENGLISH GENTLEMAN	Yolanda Celbridge	

SAMPLERS & COLLECTIONS

NEW EROTICA 3		
NEW EROTICA 5		Nov
A DOZEN STROKES	Various	

NEXUS CLASSICS
A new imprint dedicated to putting the finest works of erotic fiction back in print

AGONY AUNT	G. C. Scott	
THE HANDMAIDENS	Aran Ashe	
OBSESSION	Maria del Rey	
HIS MISTRESS'S VOICE	G.C. Scott	
CITADEL OF SERVITUDE	Aran Ashe	
BOUND TO SERVE	Amanda Ware	
SISTERHOOD OF THE INSTITUTE	Maria del Rey	
A MATTER OF POSSESSION	G.C. Scott	
THE PLEASURE PRINCIPLE	Maria del Rey	
CONDUCT UNBECOMING	Arabella Knight	
CANDY IN CAPTIVITY	Arabella Knight	
THE SLAVE OF LIDIR	Aran Ashe	
THE DUNGEONS OF LIDIR	Aran Ashe	
SERVING TIME	Sarah Veitch	July
THE TRAINING GROUNDS	Sarah Veitch	Aug
DIFFERENT STROKES	Sarah Veitch	Sept
LINGERING LESSONS	Sarah Veitch	Oct
EDEN UNVEILED	Maria del Rey	Nov
UNDERWORLD	Maria del Rey	Dec

Please send me the books I have ticked above.

Name ....

Address ....

....

....

.... Post code........................

Send to: **Cash Sales, Nexus Books, Thames Wharf Studios, Rainville Road, London W6 9HA**

US customers: for prices and details of how to order books for delivery by mail, call 1-800-805-1083.

Please enclose a cheque or postal order, made payable to **Nexus Books**, to the value of the books you have ordered plus postage and packing costs as follows:

UK and BFPO – £1.00 for the first book, 50p for the second book and 30p for each subsequent book to a maximum of £3.00;

Overseas (including Republic of Ireland) – £2.00 for the first book, £1.00 for the second book and 50p for each subsequent book.

We accept all major credit cards, including VISA, ACCESS/ MASTERCARD, AMEX, DINERS CLUB, SWITCH, SOLO, and DELTA. Please write your card number and expiry date here:

....

Please allow up to 28 days for delivery.

Signature ....